Forever, Again

Forever, Again

VICTORIA LAURIE

HYPERION

Los Angeles   New York

First Edition, December 2016
10 9 8 7 6 5 4 3 2 1
FAC-020093-16302
Printed in the United States of America

This book is set in Bembo
Designed by Tyler Nevins

Library of Congress Cataloging-in-Publication Data
Names: Laurie, Victoria, author.
Title: Forever, again / Victoria Laurie.
Description: First edition. | Los Angeles : Hyperion, 2016. | Summary: "Sixteen-year-old Lily Bennett becomes wrapped up in a murder mystery that she learns might be linked to her past . . . and future"—Provided by publisher.
Identifiers: LCCN 2015045683| ISBN 9781484700099 (hardback) | ISBN 1484700090 (hardcover)
Subjects: | CYAC: Mystery and detective stories. | Love—Fiction. | Reincarnation—Fiction. | BISAC: JUVENILE FICTION / Mysteries & Detective Stories. | JUVENILE FICTION / Love & Romance.
Classification: LCC PZ7.L372792 Fo 2016 | DDC [Fic]—dc23
LC record available at https://lccn.loc.gov/2015045683

Reinforced binding

Visit www.hyperionteens.com

SUSTAINABLE FORESTRY INITIATIVE — Certified Sourcing
www.sfiprogram.org
SFI-00993

THIS LABEL APPLIES TO TEXT STOCK

For Sandy and Steve
May your love for each other be
forever ... again ... and always

Amber

I FELT THIN AS PARCHMENT, DELICATE AS A HOUSE of cards, held up only by my own carefully poised architecture—so fragile I could come apart at the slightest breeze. Sitting on the edge of the bed, I held perfectly still . . . waiting.

It'd been three days since we found Spence, the memory of seeing him in the field seared itself into my mind like a hot brand. His face, so waxy and pale; his eyes—lifeless, staring up at a sky he could no longer see; his chest a wash of crimson, and his heart, permanently broken . . . just like mine. Slowly but surely that memory was waging battle against me, sucking out any will I had left.

I took a tiny breath, my only resistance against the onslaught. I closed my eyes and prayed for release. Soon, I thought. Let it come soon.

After setting things in motion, I didn't think I'd have long to wait.

Behind me I heard the bedroom door creak open. I took another small breath tinged with a tiny ray of hope. "Amber, honey?" Momma said.

I let out the breath. The hope went with it.

Momma came into the room and I stiffened as she sat down next to me. I curled my fingers around the note in my hand, hoping she wouldn't notice it poking out of my closed fist.

"Sweetheart, won't you come have something to eat?" she asked.

I opened my eyes and stared out the window, willing her not to touch me.

"We were thinking of taking you out," she continued. "Bill Metcalf came by this afternoon and said that the football team is heading to Bennigan's after they visit the funeral home for the viewing. I thought it might be good for you to be around Spence's friends."

Momma put a gentle hand on my shoulder, threatening the architecture. I trembled with the effort to hold myself upright. "Your dad says you went out earlier. Did you go for a walk, honey?"

I said nothing, all of my focus intent on holding up the house of cards. Around us the air was still and hot. Summer was about to come early to Fredericksburg.

Momma sat there, looking at me expectantly, and I waited. Finally, she got up and said, "We'll bring you back something to eat. Bailey's sleeping in our room. The poor pup is exhausted with worry over you, I think." Momma paused, and when I didn't acknowledge her or what she'd said, she sighed softly. "We'll be home by eight, but call us at the restaurant if you need us, okay, baby?"

I said nothing, and at last she left the room and I was alone. A few minutes later the house fell silent as my parents drove to dinner.

The sun began to set and with it, the searing memory of Spence lying in that field burned hotter. I'd found him at dusk. He'd died just as the last rays of the sun painted the sky pink, lavender, and deep indigo. It'd been a beautiful night. A perfect night. A night of hopes and dreams... until it wasn't. Until it'd become a nightmare I couldn't wake up from.

In my mind I replayed the moment I'd gone to look for Spence and heard something odd. A small pop. Nothing more than that. Just a small popping sound piercing the spring night. And then, a few moments later, a second pop. I'd thought little of it. A firecracker. A toy gun. A car backfiring. Nothing unusual, and yet, that had been the moment I'd lost him.

The house of cards quivered and I took a breath, reinforcing it for just a little longer.

The sun dipped lower, sending magenta rays streaking across the sky and in through the window to bathe me for one final time in soft light. I wondered if I could ride one of those rays and find my way to Spence. Would it be that easy?

Behind me, out in the hallway, I heard light footsteps on the floorboards. At the same time a cool breeze fluttered the curtains and caressed my skin. I closed my eyes and let out a sigh. Death had found me. At last.

Upstairs I heard Bailey bark once—a soft woof to alert me. A tear slid down my cheek for Bailey. For leaving her. For leaving them all.

I'd placed a letter on the desk, trying to explain, but I couldn't seem to get the words right, and it pained me greatly to think they'd always wonder why.

My door protested squeakily as it eased open, and I stiffened as the whisper of fabric and footfalls approached me from behind. A moment later the bed depressed slightly and a viselike hand gripped my shoulder. I made no move to fend off the attack, and had only a moment to wait for the sharp pierce of the knife as it drove into my flesh. The pain was excruciating, and I gritted my teeth against it. Fresh tears leaked out of my shuttered eyes. With my right hand I reached up to grip the knife, holding it to me as I sank backward onto the bed where I let my limbs fall. My last act of will opened my left palm to expose the note: payment for the deed.

A shadow hovered over me before the note was lifted away and then the shadow departed and the world above me blurred. I inhaled one final ragged breath, but I couldn't hold it in. I exhaled on a wave of release. And then, the house of cards crumbled completely and the soft rays of dusk carried me up and away, toward Spence.

Lily

IN THE CENTER OF MY CHEST THERE'S A BIRTHMARK that looks like a bloodstain. It's red, elliptical, but the bottom trickles away from the center, like blood leaking out of my heart.

It's one of those things that, when I look in the mirror, seems completely foreign to me, even though it's been there my entire life. It's not the imperfection of it, but the implication that bothers me. It feels sinister, like a terrible memory of a horrible event I try to recall but can't.

Sometimes I swear I even feel it burn.

And I've never been able to figure out why it always hurts the most the morning after a recurring dream I keep having. Recurring nightmare actually.

The dream has always been the same—it has never, ever varied. It begins with me running toward a field. It's dark out, but the field is lit by fire, and yet, there's no smoke. The flames are alive with movement, pulsing over the grass of the meadow, but there's no heat.

I'm fueled by panic, but I don't know why. I just know I need to run toward the middle of that field. And then I come to the center and there lies the most beautiful boy I've ever seen. He's staring up at me, a half smile on his lips, but his eyes are lifeless. I drop down beside him as the flames lick across our skin. I take him into my arms, willing for life to come back to him, but he's cold against me. He's already gone.

And always I feel as if I'm the one dying.

I've woken up crying every single time, shaken and so profoundly sad that I think it's a wonder I ever knew joy. In those moments, the birthmark burns, and I always touch it with my fingers and then check to see if there's actual blood.

There never is, but I can't shake the feeling that there should be.

I don't know who the boy is, and I don't know why I keep having that nightmare, but I do know that I've been having the exact same dream since I was four. I think it has importance. I think it means something. But what that could be I have no idea.

The dream had been intermittent, never coming more than a few times a year, but it's been waking me up every night for the past two weeks, ever since Mom and I moved into my grandmother's guesthouse.

I know most people would say that the dream is happening more often now because of the stress from the divorce. But what's weird is that I was so much more stressed-out when my parents were fighting under the same roof. It was bad. Every single day they just shouted accusations and obscenities at each other. My dad cheated on my mom, but really, I felt like he cheated on all of us; the us that'd been a family until he'd gone off and gotten himself a girlfriend.

And as if my life wasn't miserable enough, in the final week of my sophomore year I'd found out that Tanner—my boyfriend of two years—was cheating on me with Sophie— my best friend since first grade. At least their secret had come out at the very end of the school year and I was spared the humiliation of having to see them together in the hallways and hear the whispers about poor, pathetic me.

Soon after summer vacation started, Mom came to me to tell me that Grandmother Bennett had learned about my dad's affair and the divorce, and, disgusted by her son's behavior, she'd reached out to Mom to offer us a place to live on her estate. Grandmother had also used her influence on the board at the hospital in Fredericksburg to get Mom placed as a resident there.

She'd asked me what I'd thought about moving out of Richmond, and I'd told her I could be packed in a day. I wanted nothing more than to run away from all of the reminders of how messed-up my life had become.

So we'd packed our stuff and, toward the end of the summer, we'd moved.

Through all of that mess, I hadn't had the dream of the boy in the field even once, but ever since we'd settled into Grandmother's guesthouse, I'd woken up in a cold sweat every night, breathing hard, trembling, and crying.

The boy's death always had the same devastating effect on me, and I knew it was impossible to fight the tears, so I settled for allowing them to rinse the heartbreak from my muddled, sleep-deprived mind before chancing a look at the alarm clock next to my bed.

I groaned when I read the time: two thirty.

"Why?" I whispered, putting fists to the side of my head. "Why, why, why?"

I'd need to be up in three hours for my first day at my new school. I wanted so bad to figure out the dream. Or to make it stop. I'd prefer to figure it out and then make it stop, but neither choice seemed open to me at the moment.

With a sigh I pulled back the covers and sat up, rubbing my chest where the mark was burning. I took a few deep breaths and pushed myself out of bed. I knew from experience that I wouldn't be able to get back to sleep.

Padding out of the room, I made my way to the kitchen, careful to step around the few boxes that hadn't been unpacked yet, when I heard a noise behind me and jumped.

"Lily?" Mom said. "Honey, it's two thirty in the morning. What're you doing up?"

The light came on, and Mom was standing there. She looked like I felt—tired to the bone—but probably for very different reasons.

"Couldn't sleep," I told her.

She shuffled over to me and put a hand on my brow. "You're coated in sweat," she said. Then she cupped my face and peered down at me. "Do you feel sick?"

"No, Mom," I assured her. She had enough on her plate without worrying about me. "Just had a bad dream."

But Mom's brow lifted and she said, "The one with the boy in the field?"

"Yeah," I said, a little surprised. I'd been having the dream most of my life, but we hadn't talked about it in years. "How'd you know?"

Mom seemed surprised herself. "I didn't," she said. "But it's always been the only one that can do this to you."

I shrugged. "I'm so tired. I want to turn it off."

Mom's mouth tilted down into a concerned frown. She wrapped her arms around me, pulling me close, and stroked my hair. "Sounds like you've had this nightmare more than just tonight."

I sighed heavily against her. "Just a couple times recently," I admitted. I didn't want to tell her the truth, because I didn't want to lay a guilt trip on her.

Before she could press me about it, I moved out of her embrace and over to the refrigerator to open the door and peer in. "Want some cocoa?" I asked, trying to change the subject.

There was a pause then she said, "Sure," and I heard the chair slide back from the table. I busied myself for a few minutes at the stove, hoping she'd let it go.

"How long have you really been having the dream, Lily?" Mom asked again, her tone serious.

I stirred the milk, avoiding her gaze. "Ever since we moved in here."

I heard Mom's breath catch, but she managed to hold her tongue. I sighed as steam lifted from the milk in the pan. After pouring the milk into two mugs, I brought them to the table.

"Tell me about it," she said, her eyes creasing in the corners with worry.

So I did. And Mom listened in patient silence. At the end she simply studied my face while our cocoa cooled, before reaching across the table and putting her hand on mine. "It's been a tough couple of months, hasn't it, kiddo?"

I sighed, staring into my mug. "Yeah. For both of us."

"You know that the dream is probably about the divorce, and your breakup with Tanner, right? Maybe it's time to see someone professionally, Lily, you know, to talk about all that you've been going through."

I'd balked at her earlier attempts to enroll me in therapy. Mom had first made the suggestion shortly after she and Dad filed for divorce. Dwelling on all my problems in some stranger's office didn't sound very therapeutic to me.

"I don't know how the dream connects to all that, though, Mom. I mean, I started having it when I was a little kid. How could it be about your split with Dad or my breakup with Tanner when it started happening twelve years ago?"

That seemed to stump her. "Is it exactly the same dream?"

I nodded. "In every way."

Mom tapped her finger on the tabletop. "Well, that's odd," she said. "And maybe even more of a reason to talk to a therapist."

I shook my head. "Please don't make me."

Mom smiled patiently. "I've been talking to one."

My eyes widened. "You have?"

"Yes," she told me, as though that was hard to admit. "It's helping, Lily. It's how I managed to swallow my pride and accept Maureen's offer."

The feud between my grandmother and Dad was something of a mystery to me. Mostly I think that it had to do with the fact that my grandmother was really, really wealthy, and she liked to control people through her money.

I suspected that at some point in the past my grandmother had tried to control my dad one time too many, and he'd rebelled enough to cause her to cut him off. He'd gone on to become successful anyway, and I think that irked her.

It worried me a little that Mom had accepted Grandmother's offer to live on her estate and work at the hospital where she was so influential, but even this situation beat staying in Richmond.

"I didn't know," I told her.

She smiled and sipped at her cocoa. "He's good," she said. "Dr. Carson. He's nice, and he helps me figure things out. He's given me some perspective about what happened between your dad and me, and he's helping me to cope with the fallout."

I looked down at my hands. I knew exactly what Mom meant by "fallout." Three months ago, in May, Mom and I had been in the car on our way to a boutique on the other side of Richmond when we'd spotted Dad at an outdoor café with his girlfriend. The PDAs between them were disgusting, and Mom had had to pull the car over, she was so upset.

That afternoon, our family had crumbled like an old ruin. Dad had admitted to the affair, and in the next sentence, which I'd overheard because they were shouting at each other, he'd said that he was leaving Mom for his pregnant girlfriend. He never told me if he was also leaving me; I think I'd assumed at the time that that was implied.

"What's your doctor say to you?" I asked, genuinely curious.

"Well," she said, "he's helped me see your father in a more compassionate light." My brow furrowed. Was she kidding? "I know that may sound strange," she said, "but it helps to see him as a flawed human being rather than my son-of-a-bitch ex-husband who had an affair and got his girlfriend pregnant. It helps me feel less angry toward him. And Dr. Carson also helps me to see how I was complicit in the demise of our marriage."

My mouth fell open. "*You?* How were *you* to blame?"

Mom sighed but there was a sad smile playing at the corners of her mouth. "It's complicated, Lily, and I'm not going to burden you with the details, so you'll have to trust me that it takes two people to make a marriage either succeed or fail."

I frowned at her. "It still doesn't excuse what he did," I said stubbornly.

"No," she agreed. "It doesn't. But it's helping me sleep better at night."

I shook my head and stared down at my hands again. Her hint was well taken. "How long would I have to see Dr. Carson?"

Mom smiled. "Well, I wouldn't send you to my therapist, Lily. I'd send you to one of his colleagues. He shares a practice with a Dr. White, and I've heard very good things about him. Maybe you could go see him."

"What if I don't like him?"

"Then we'll find you someone else."

"Can I think about it?"

"Of course," she said easily. And then she got up and took our mugs with her to the sink. "For now, though, how about we both go back to bed and get another two hours of sleep before your first day?"

"Yeah, okay," I said, grudgingly. Even though I felt super-tired, I still wasn't sleepy, but maybe I'd get in an hour if I didn't think about it too much.

Mom walked me back to my room and kissed me on the forehead before squeezing me into a comforting hug. "You're a great kid, you know that?" she whispered as she held me.

I smiled and squeezed back. "Thanks, Mom."

"Now, just lay your head on the pillow and think about something nice and pleasant. You'll be back to sleep in no time."

With a kiss on the cheek she left me at the door to my room, and I turned to watch her walk away, wishing it were that easy. Moving over to the bed, I got in and sighed wearily. But maybe Mom was right. Maybe if I focused on happier thoughts, I could keep the nightmares at bay. Trouble was, I was hard-pressed to come up with anything good.

Amber

TRYING TO THINK ONLY GOOD THOUGHTS, I SMILED brightly and turned from side to side in front of the mirror in my room, looking at my reflection. It was my first day of high school, and I so wanted to make a good impression. I dropped the smile, but I had to admit I was pretty satisfied with the final wardrobe selection. The skirt and top I'd gotten at Esprit were flattering, and they went perfectly with the wide belt I'd stolen from Momma's closet. My thick socks, new high-tops, and big canary-yellow earrings, bracelet, and headband really pulled the whole look together.

"You ready?" Daddy said from the doorway.

I jumped a little. I hadn't heard him in the hall. With a nervous laugh, I said, "Yeah. Sorry."

I blushed, then blushed deeper as I watched Daddy glance at the clothing scattered all over my room.

"Sorry!" I said, hastening to straighten up.

Daddy came forward to put a hand on my shoulder. "It's okay, baby girl. Don't worry about it. You can clean this up when you get home. I won't tell your ma. It'll be our secret."

I wrapped my arms around him. "Thanks, Daddy."

We headed out and Daddy drove the four miles to Chamberlain High. The school was undergoing a renovation, expanding because Fredericksburg would be including a freshman class next year, adding to the existing model of tenth through twelfth grades at Chamberlain High. I understood that this was in line with a lot of high schools across the country transitioning from the traditional elementary, junior high, high school model, to the elementary, middle school, high school curriculum. A year from now my old junior high would be called a middle school, and be made up of sixth through eighth graders, instead of seventh through ninth. I remembered when they announced the timing of all the changes that I'd been a little miffed that my class had been the one shorted out of the extra year of high school and stuck one more year in junior high. Heading to high school just felt so mature.

Daddy pulled up to a line of cars parked alongside the drop-off lane leading to the high school. There was a big banner there that read WELCOME, CLASS OF 1987!

My stomach bubbled with nerves and anticipation. My sophomore class would be made up of the graduates of three separate junior highs around the district. I wondered how I'd adjust to all those new kids. At least I had my two best friends at my side. It'd been Britta Cummings, Sara Radcliff, and me since kindergarten. We always looked out for one another.

Out of the corner of my eye I saw Daddy glance at me. "Don't worry, buttercup, high school isn't any different from junior high except that the building is bigger and there's more homework."

I turned hopeful eyes on him. Was it as easy as that?

"Hey," he said, pulling to stop at the curb and reaching over to cup my face. "You're gonna do great. It's your first day, and you look beautiful, so just go have some fun. There'll be plenty of time to figure it all out later."

He always knew what to say. "Thanks, Daddy," I said, leaning in to give him a big hug before taking a deep breath and getting out of the car.

Walking toward the entrance, I looked around for Britta and Sara. We'd agreed to meet by the oak tree to the left of the front entrance.

"Look out!" I heard someone call, and I turned my head just as something very hard thudded into my back. I cried out and stumbled, feeling myself losing my balance as if in slow motion, but at the last second an arm reached out and caught me around the middle.

"Mind if I have this dance?" a mirthful voice said as my new school supplies slipped out of my hands and clattered to the sidewalk.

I pushed my hair out of my eyes and turned slightly to stare up into the most beautiful face I'd ever seen. The boy who'd caught me before I could sprawl to the pavement hovered above me, wearing a smile and an intriguing glint in his bright blue eyes. His hair was light blond, nearly platinum, with no wave, and contrasted beautifully against his darkly tanned skin. He had broad shoulders, and, from the way he was bent over me, I suspected he was several inches taller than my five foot seven inch frame. The rest of his features were square, chiseled, and perfect.

"You okay?" he asked me.

I opened my mouth but no words came out. I couldn't take my eyes off him. He continued to hold me like that, his arm cradling me in a sort of dancer's dip while I held on to his biceps. His very firm, well-defined biceps.

"Uh...yes," I finally managed. "I'm good."

He pulled me toward him as he stood the pair of us up straight, and he took his time letting me out of his embrace. I heard footsteps running toward us, and only when two other boys arrived did his arms release me.

"Oh, man! I'm really sorry! Did that hurt?" said one of the boys. He was also tall, with very neatly combed brown hair and a polo shirt with the collar turned up.

"I'm fine," I said, rubbing a sore spot on my back. The boy who'd saved me leaned down and picked up a football, and I realized that'd been the thing that'd hit me.

"I'm really sorry," repeated the guy with the brown hair, and I had to give him credit. He looked very sorry, and also a little worried. "Please don't turn me in."

I smiled to let him know it was all right. "It's fine," I repeated. "Besides, I don't even know your name, so I can't actually turn you in."

The anxiety furrowing his brow lessened and he grinned back at me. "I'm Jamie," he said offering me his hand.

I took it. "Amber."

The boy with the blond hair and blue eyes nudged Jamie in the shoulder and offered his own hand.

"Spence," he said. "The guy who *didn't* hit you with the football."

I laughed, taking his hand. My midsection fluttered at the feel of his touch. My God, he was gorgeous. He idly tossed the football to Jamie and said, "I'll catch up with you guys in a minute."

It was a not so subtle hint, and I felt my cheeks heat.

Jamie cleared his throat and motioned to the other boy, whom I'd never been introduced to, and the pair of them moved off, leaving me still holding on to Spence's hand.

I let out another nervous laugh and attempted to pull away, but he held on to my fingers for an extra second, and in that moment it felt like fireworks in the air between us.

"Are you a sophomore?" he asked.

I nodded.

"Me, too," he said.

From a distance I heard my name called and turned to wave to Britt. She and Sara were waiting for me with eager smiles. I knew they couldn't wait to hear about my conversation with the gorgeous boy in front of me.

Spence looked over at them, too. "I should let you get back to your friends."

I wanted to protest, to keep him there longer, to gaze on his beautiful face and stand in the light of his smile, but I couldn't think of a single thing to say.

"Maybe I'll see you around?" I said to him.

His smile broadened. "Around? How about right here?" Pointing to the ground he added, "I'll be right in this spot at three o'clock."

My breath quickened. "You will?"

"Yep," he said confidently. "I'll be waiting to see if you'll let me to walk you home."

"Is that so?" I said, thrilled with the little spark that seemed to light up between us.

"Think you'll let me?" he asked. "Walk you home?"

I couldn't stop smiling, but I didn't think it was smart to appear too willing. "Guess we'll find out at three."

He let out a low, throaty chuckle. "Guess we will."

With that, he tipped an imaginary hat at me but made no move to turn away. I felt his gaze on my back, like a warm ray of sunshine, all the way until Britt, Sara, and I walked into school.

Lily

THE FIRST RAYS OF THE SUN WERE JUST PEEKING over the horizon when Mom drove me to school. My stomach fluttered with nerves and there was an empty hollowness in my chest. I suddenly felt very homesick for my old high school in Richmond. Sophie would probably be meeting our other two friends, Michelle and Quinn, at the bench next to the bike racks. And Tanner would be pulling into the parking lot in his parents' old BMW. He'd park in the spot third from the left in the last row, next to Dylan and Grant, and he'd walk all the way around the building to find Sophie. . . .

"You okay?" Mom asked, pulling me from my thoughts, as she eased her car into the line of vehicles slowly making their way up to the front of Chamberlain High School.

"Yeah," I said, sitting up a little straighter in the seat. Unwilling to confess how much I missed my friends, especially Sophie, which was really messing with my head, I added, "I'm just nervous. I've never been the new kid before."

And it was true. Even in kindergarten I'd had my neighbor Carrie to accompany me to the first day of school. And I'd known other kids from the neighborhood back then, too. This was the first time I'd ever faced the first day of school knowing absolutely no one, and it made me feel supervulnerable and alone.

Mom moved us over to the curb and put the car in park. Placing a hand on the back of my head, she looked me in the eyes and said, "I know this is really scary, lovey, but you can do this. The kids might be a little standoffish at first, or they might welcome you with open arms, but either way I know what an amazing person you are, and before long you'll fit right in."

I gripped her free hand, trying to draw on her strength. Mom had just started her new job, where she didn't know anybody, either. If she could do it, I could, too.

"Thanks, Mom."

I wanted to say more, but I was aware of the long line of cars behind us, and the fact that we were holding things up. Taking a deep breath, I reached for the door handle.

"Your grandmother is sending a car for you this afternoon," Mom said as I got out and turned to shut the door.

I winced. "I can walk home, you know."

"Lily, it's nearly three miles."

"I can walk it," I told her, putting a little more steel in my voice. No way did I want my grandmother's town car pulling up to the curb after school.

Mom sighed. "We'll have to see about getting you some transportation."

I closed the door, but kept my hands on the open window. "A car?" I asked hopefully.

She smiled. "I was thinking about a Vespa."

"A car would be better," I said. Dad had promised me one for my sixteenth birthday and then he'd reneged on the deal when he found out I was going to live with Mom in his mother's guesthouse.

"Maybe your grandmother will cosign for a loan," Mom said.

My stomach muscles clenched. The thing with my grandmother was that nothing was given without the expectation of something in return. Everything had strings attached: she'd been more than willing to help Mom get her residency at the hospital, but Mom had to agree to bring me to live with her on the estate, and even though Mom had never said it out loud, I knew it irked her that she'd been given little choice about where we'd call home.

And, if I were being completely honest, I'd have to admit that I didn't really like my grandmother. I'd tried to like her, but she was a cold, rude snob of a woman, and she thought she could control everyone through her money.

Given our current situation, she was partially right, and that really bugged me.

"That's okay," I told Mom. "A Vespa would be fun. I'll look around for something used."

I had money saved from the generous checks my grandmother had sent every year on my birthday. Maybe I could swing a Vespa on my own.

Mom tried to hide it but I saw a bit of relief in her eyes. "That's my girl," she said. "Call me when you get home, okay?"

I nodded and shut the car door, turning to face the school.

Chamberlain High was a big place, built in that style that most high schools are constructed—like a prison. I had to tamp down the urge to turn and run.

Squaring my shoulders, I took my first steps away from the car, and resisted the temptation to wave at Mom. I knew she was watching me climb the steps up to the front door, but I couldn't look at her or I'd lose my nerve to keep putting one foot in front of the other.

Once I was through the double doors, I pivoted to my right. Mom and I had come here the week before for student orientation, which I'd been forced to take along with four hundred incoming freshmen. Not that I have anything against freshmen, it's just that, as a junior, I felt really out of place. It'd been a long day.

Still, it had been good if only for the fact that I'd figured out the general layout of the school and thought I could navigate it with a little help from the map they'd given me.

I thought wrong.

The warning bell sounded, and I found myself in some section of the school I didn't recognize. I tried the map, but it was no help. Kids all around me were ducking into classrooms, and I felt my palms grow moist. I didn't know what the penalty was for being late, but I did know that coming through the door after the bell would draw a lot of attention to myself, which was the last thing I wanted on the first day.

I looked up from the map to see the hall all but empty. My heart started to race.

"Where the hell am I?" I muttered, flipping the map around to view it from another angle. My vision started to blur as my breathing quickened. God. In a minute I'd have to knock on a classroom door and ask a teacher how to get to my first period. How would I ever live that humiliation down?

"You lost?" asked a deep, slightly smoky voice.

I stiffened, and glanced up to stare into the most impossibly blue eyes I'd ever seen. The sight of the guy they belonged to stole the breath from my body.

"I...uh..." I said, blinking furiously.

"Where're you headed?" he asked, moving a few steps closer to look sideways over my shoulder at the map and my schedule.

His nearness filled me like honeysuckle invading the senses of a bee. For a moment, I was dizzy with it.

"Mr. Rennick," I managed as he leaned close enough to brush my arm.

He cocked his head at me, his smile sending another wave of dizzy disorienting wonderfulness through my system.

"You're on the right track. Just around that corner." Pointing ahead, he added, "First room on the right."

"Ah," I said, feeling my cheeks heat. What the hell was wrong with me? I'd never had a reaction to anyone like I was having to the boy at my side. I slid a sideways glance at him, and took in his tall frame—the tight fit of his T-shirt against a well-defined torso, the ripple of biceps stretching the fabric around the sleeves, the square line of his jaw with a bit of stubble on his chin and the ash-blond hair. It was cut close on the sides, while fuller on top, and styled in a slight peak toward the middle. I focused again on the map and found myself blinking furiously just to try to clear my head.

"Better hurry, though," he said, mindless of the spell he was casting on me. "Bell's about to ring."

Stepping away and tilting his head to the classroom on my right, he offered me another gorgeous smile.

"Thanks, Spence," I said, trying to play it cool and fold up the map. And then I realized what I'd just said.

For a second I held my breath, but when I looked at him, his expression was one of surprise. "What'd you call me?"

"I . . . I . . ." Where the hell had *that* come from? Spence? I thought. I didn't know anyone named Spence, and yet, it'd flowed right out of my mouth as smoothly as if I'd spoken it every day of my life.

He stepped toward me again and offered his hand. I took it out of reflex, and it felt right and warm and wonderful against my palm. "Cole," he said to me. "Spencer is my middle name."

Whoa! I thought. *That* was weird. Still, I nodded again, hoping I didn't look too much like a bobblehead.

"Lily," I said quickly, embarrassed and wishing I could duck away. "Sorry, I don't know why I called you Spence. Maybe it's 'cause you look like a Spence."

Stop. Talking. I mean, what was I even saying? What did a "Spence" look like, anyway?

Cole continued to grip my hand, and he eyed me curiously. As if there was something about me he might recognize. "Do I?"

"Totally," I said, but how the hell did I know?

Just then the bell rang, and the spell between us broke. I forced a small laugh and said, "Saved by the bell."

Cole released me, motioning again to the classroom just around the corner.

"Rennick's cool," he assured me. "He won't give you a hard time about being late on your first day. But don't push it. I'd hurry."

I nodded, waved shyly at him, and rushed away. It was several minutes later, after I'd gotten to my first period, apologized to Mr. Rennick, and been assigned a seat, that I realized my birthmark was burning.

After last period I made my way through the mob of students to the front door, and out into the bright sunshine. The day was hot, the sun blinding, but I welcomed it because I'd officially survived my first day. As I made my way down the steps to the sidewalk, I paused next to a streetlamp to fish around for my sunglasses and had just put them on when a car slid up to the curb.

The chatter around me went abruptly quiet, and I looked up to see a white Rolls-Royce idling next to me. "Oh, crap," I muttered.

The window rolled down and an elderly man with silver hair, partially covered by a chauffer's cap, winked at me. Arthur—my grandmother's driver.

"Good day, Miss Bennett," he said, touching the brim of his hat.

Arthur reached for the door handle. He was about to get out of the car and come around to open the door for me.

"Don't!" I said as my heartbeat ticked up.

Glancing subtly to my right and left, I took in the dozens of kids standing nearby, and even some not so nearby, all of them speechless. There were lots of dropped jaws and wide eyes. And then my own gaze came to rest on a familiar figure twenty feet away. Cole stood next to a couple of other guys, all of them staring in shock at the car. Except for Cole, whose brow was furrowed, like he couldn't quite figure out how a Rolls-Royce and I went together.

I wanted to dissolve. To turn into vapor and float away on the breeze. Except there was no breeze. Only the gleaming polish of the pearl-white Rolls to act like a spotlight on me. My mind raced with options. Walk away and pretend the Rolls was there for someone else? Open the door and get in as fast as possible? Point down the street and yell, "Ohmigod! Look at that!" before making a run for it in the opposite direction?

I was about to go with option three when Arthur said, "Miss Bennett?"

I bit my lip and saw movement out of the corner of my eye. Cole was laughing at something one of his friends said, and I could just imagine that he and his buddies thought my situation hilarious. Awesome. Just awesome.

Yanking the door open, I hustled inside as fast as possible. "Go! Please, Arthur, just go!"

"As you wish, miss," he said, without a hint of irritation. Arthur was a sweet old guy; at least, that was my impression from the little I'd been around him.

My early-morning encounter with Cole aside, the rest of the day had been a crapfest of repeatedly getting lost;

sensing that with each new classroom, all eyes were locked on me; enduring whispers of, "Who's the new girl?"; and struggling at lunch to find anywhere to eat that didn't make it conspicuously obvious that I didn't have any friends. It'd been miserable.

And, as if all that wasn't bad enough, Sophie had texted me ten minutes earlier, putting a capper on an awful eight hours. Once we'd driven past the school, I sat up and pulled out my cell to look at her message again:

> Lil I know you don't want to talk to me but you're not anywhere in school today and there's a rumor going around that you've moved out of Richmond! Is it true? I can't believe you'd do that without telling me!

I hadn't told a soul that Mom and I were moving to Fredericksburg because I was still too hurt over everything that'd gone down, and it wasn't like anyone had tried to reach out to me over the summer. Michelle and Quinn had taken Sophie's side in the dissolution of our friendship, and those guys and Tanner had been my whole inner circle—my four closest friends.

Over the summer, I'd kept myself busy by volunteering at Clover Hill—a rescue ranch for sixteen horses and about a dozen dogs and cats. I'd felt as lost and abandoned as many of the animals that had come to live there, and in helping to take care of them, I'd discovered a kinship and an affinity for them that surprised me. By the end of the summer, I'd come to prefer the company of the animals over any of the humans I knew. In fact, one of the perks of moving in with Grandmother was that she owned four Thoroughbreds, and I'd already spent more time down at her stable than anywhere else. I liked horses especially because they never wanted you to be something that you weren't.

I pocketed my phone and let out a sigh, content with the decision not to reply to Sophie. Let her sweat both that I'd moved, and that I wasn't replying. My smug satisfaction was a little short-lived when I realized I might've been rude to poor Arthur.

"Sorry about yelling at you back there," I said.

"Think nothing of it, Miss Bennett," Arthur said kindly, his British accent delicately affecting his diction. "Are we to journey straight home?"

"Yes, please," I told him. I couldn't wait to get to the guesthouse and shed this car. It fit me like a diamond tiara fits a duck.

"Oh," Arthur said next, as if just remembering something. "Your grandmother wishes an audience with you at three thirty. She says to save room for tea and cookies."

I frowned. Grandmother was big on tea and cookies. The tea was usually bitter, and the cookies were very hard vanilla wafers coated with grainy sugar she had imported from somewhere. I worried that someday I'd break a tooth on one.

"Do you know why she wants to see me?" I asked. Grandmother never sent a summons unless she had an ulterior motive.

"No, miss," Arthur said.

I leaned my head back against the soft leather and tried to relax, but I was wound pretty tight. We arrived at the very edge of my grandmother's vast estate, and I looked out over the rolling green hills that made up Maureen Bennett's property with little interest and barely veiled disdain.

Grandmother had written to me when I was about eleven, telling me that she'd decided that I was going to be the one to inherit her entire fortune and all of her properties, and then she'd asked me to come for a visit. I'd shown the letter to my parents, and when my dad had read that part, he'd become angrier than I'd ever seen him in my eleven years. He'd forbidden me to visit his mother. But one Sunday, Mom had told Dad that we were going shopping, and, instead of the mall, we'd gone to see Grandmother.

The visit had been forced, awkward, and uncomfortable, but thereafter, about four or five times a year, Mom sneaked me off to spend an afternoon with my grandmother because, as she said to me, it was important to get to know the only living grandparent I had left.

Still, I never looked forward to those visits, even though Grandmother seemed to be trying her best to entertain me. Most of the time together involved eating out and shopping, and what should have been fun wasn't. It was the way that Grandmother treated people, as if everyone were beneath her. She seemed to enjoy making them feel small, or like she were doing them a big giant favor by being in their presence. No one who waited on her ever looked her or me in the eye, and that really bothered me. Even Mom struggled to maintain eye contact with Maureen, which was why I made sure to always look directly at her whenever I was with her.

She'd made a comment about it once, staring at me with a flinty glare after I'd refused to back down on some minor point about my attire and her disapproval of it. I was tall and on the thin side, and I wore a lot of skinny jeans and spaghetti-strap tanks. After I refused to change, Grandmother had said, "You're much like your father, Lily. I don't know that I especially like it." At the time, I'd been kind of proud of that, but after everything Dad had pulled lately, I wasn't so sure I'd ever want to be compared to him again.

"Beautiful day," Arthur said, rousing me from my thoughts.

"It is," I agreed, looking out the window at the passing fence posts that marked the borders of Grandmother's estate. I wondered again what she wanted with me.

Even though I didn't have any homework for tomorrow, there was a small research project that I wanted to look into, and I wouldn't have time to get into it before tea. Also, I needed to call Mom to tell her about my first day, but no way was I going to call while Arthur was around. Mom had warned me that Grandmother regularly grilled the staff about our overheard conversations. We'd learned very quickly to keep any talk between us to the guesthouse or her car.

Arthur drove up to the gates, which took their time parting enough for us to slide through, and we headed down the long drive to the main house, which was enormous. I'd seen photos on the Internet of European estates, and they had nothing on my grandmother's home.

The place was nearly as big as my high school, and even more like a prison. Lucky for Mom and me that the guesthouse was at the back of the property not far from the stables, and much more modest in size. Arthur was taking us to the left to steer clear of the main house when I saw someone coming out of the front door. Recognizing who it was, I reached forward to grip the back of Arthur's seat.

"Wait!"

Arthur applied the brake. Turning in his seat to offer me a startled look he said, "Miss?"

"What the hell is *she* doing here?" I nearly yelled. My blood boiled as I pointed to the woman making her way carefully down the steps. She wore stilettos, despite being six months pregnant.

Arthur blinked. "I've no idea, Miss Bennett."

We watched my dad's girlfriend get into a shiny black Lexus that he'd probably bought her, and in short order, begin to drive toward us. I wanted to scream as she came closer. And then she happened to glance at us, her eyes widening like a hungry lynx. Belatedly, I realized she was more interested in the Rolls than she was in who was in it. A cool smile spread across her lips, and I saw her hand drop from the steering wheel to the top of her belly. And then, she was gone.

"May I continue on?" Arthur asked me gently.

"Sure. Sorry, Arthur," I muttered.

"No need to apologize, miss," he said, offering me a kind and understanding smile.

We stopped in front of the guesthouse and I opened the door of the car before he could get out to help me. He was sweet and old, and I felt uncomfortable having him wait on me like that.

With a wave to Arthur, I headed inside to the kitchen, grabbed a bag of carrots and some sugar cubes, and hurried over to the stables. On the way, I stopped to pat Gus, the stable hand's dog. He was a grizzled old coonhound who now preferred the shade of a tree to hunting. He offered me a dozy tail wag and I set a small dog treat at his feet, then moved on inside the stables, which smelled sweetly of hay and horse musk.

As I approached one of the stalls, I heard a nicker, and Apollo, a fifteen-hand, chestnut-colored gelding, stuck his considerable muzzle out of the stall.

"Hey, boy," I said softly. He nickered again and kicked the door of the stall to let me know he was happy to see me.

I opened the bag of carrots and angled my shoulder underneath his muzzle to feed him, but he pushed at my pocket, more inclined toward the sugar. I dug it out for him, and he settled contentedly against me.

Stroking the white star on his forehead, I said, "Sophie texted me today."

Apollo snorted, and I glanced sideways at him. Sometimes, he had great timing.

"I didn't text her back," I said. He rubbed the side of his head against my shoulder, and I fed him a carrot. "And I don't think I'm going to." Apollo nodded, as if he completely agreed with that decision.

That's the thing about horses: they have an almost eerie ability to make you feel understood. I'd been pouring my heart out to Apollo ever since setting foot inside the stables, and I know it sounds weird, but he always made me feel heard and validated, and I knew that every time he saw me, he'd greet me with the same eager enthusiasm.

Horses are loyal to the core. They'll never throw away

your friendship for another human. Show them kindness and they'll be yours. Forever.

Unlike Sophie, who'd promised that we'd always be best friends until she betrayed me in the worst possible way.

"She can stare at that phone until the end of the school year," I told him. "No way am I answering her back!"

Apollo rubbed my shoulder again, and I figured that he understood how hard it would be on me to keep that promise. The truth was, I missed Sophie more than I could say, and I knew myself well enough to understand that I wanted to forgive her . . . I just didn't know how.

With a sigh, I fed Apollo several more carrots before I looked at the time on my phone.

"Gotta go," I told him. He nickered again and set his lips around my forearm, as if he didn't want me to leave. I leaned in for a last hug and said, "Thanks, buddy. I needed that."

After dropping some carrots into the buckets of Easy Ed, Lady Finger, and Roger Boy—Grandmother's other horses—I dashed back to the house and up the stairs to my room. Taking a seat at my desk, I propped up the mirror that I used in the mornings to do my hair and makeup. For a minute, I peered at my reflection with a bit of alarm. I didn't look so good. Dark circles underlined my eyes, and there was a pale weariness to my skin that made me look like someone on the verge of getting sick. My hair could have used some attention, too. How long had it been since I'd seen a stylist? Three months?

"Yikes," I said, and my thoughts drifted to the encounter I'd had that morning with Cole.

A flush touched my cheeks when I took in my simple

white shirt and skinny jeans. That morning I'd been focused on not calling a lot of attention to myself on the first day, so I'd muted my look considerably. But now I could see how that plain-Jane plan had backfired, because *this* had been Cole's first impression of me. And then my mind recalled how I'd ducked into Grandmother's pearly Rolls-Royce to get away from all the stares. I had no idea what Cole's overall impression of me might be, but I was betting it wasn't, "Hey, that new chick is awesome!"

I started to reach for my makeup, but stopped to take note of the time and grimaced. If I took a few extra minutes to work on my appearance, I risked being late for tea. But then, if I didn't and went to her looking like this, Grandmother would probably be displeased anyway. Making up my mind, I took up a bottle of foundation and got quickly to work.

Amber

MOMMA WASN'T AT ALL PLEASED THAT I WALKED into work at her salon fifteen minutes late. I could hear it in her tone.

"Amber?" she called as I tried to duck behind the reception desk. Pulling up the neck of my shirt so it didn't hang off my shoulder so much, I approached her chair, and nearly stopped in my tracks when I noticed who was sitting there.

Clearing my throat, I said, "Hey, Momma. Hello, Mrs. Bennett. Nice to see you."

Fredericksburg's wealthiest woman narrowed her eyes and looked at me in the mirror as if she couldn't quite place me. She'd been a regular of Momma's for a while now, coming in once a month to get her hair dyed jet-black, and done up like Alexis from *Dynasty*. She did look a bit like Joan Collins—the actress who played Alexis—with her thin, angular features, dyed hair, and green eyes, but she lacked the classic beauty of the Hollywood star. Still, that didn't stop her from throwing out the occasional crisp line laced with a slight British lilt.

"Who's this?" she said, looking down her nose at me. Never mind that I'd greeted her at the reception desk for the past year and a half every time she came in.

"This is my daughter, Mrs. Bennett. Amber," Momma said.

"Sorry I'm late," I told her.

"Late?" Mrs. Bennett repeated, eyeing me a little more crossly now. "Why were you late, young lady?"

I cleared my throat again, nervous around such a sharp-tongued and powerful woman. "I got held up," I said. "I'm sorry, Momma. It won't happen again."

"It's fine," Momma said, but she was frowning at me. I suspected she knew that I'd been late because I was trying to decide what outfit to wear for my date with Spence that night. He'd be picking me up at six, right from the salon. I'd gone with a short jean skirt, torn black stockings, lots of bangles, a thin off-the-shoulder heather-gray cutoff sweatshirt cinched at the waist with a red belt, and my new Reebok high-tops with thick bright-white socks. It'd taken me two hours to come up with the combo, do my hair, and apply my makeup, and even though I'd thought I'd left plenty of time, I'd still been fifteen minutes late to work.

Saturdays were the busiest days at the salon, but things didn't really get going until around eleven, so I'd figured it'd be okay to come in a tiny bit late. But if I'd known that Mrs. Bennett was going to be there, I'd have made sure to arrive on time. She always demanded Momma's sole attention and often had some harsh criticism for her that left

Momma a wreck the rest of the day. Mrs. Bennett was a mean woman, and her husband, Dr. Bennett, wasn't any nicer. They both came to Momma to get their hair done, and why she put up with them, I couldn't say.

"You're not going to teach your daughter anything by allowing her to break the rules, Gina," Mrs. Bennett said tartly. "You should ground her."

I sucked in a breath, but Momma laughed lightly. "Oh, now, Mrs. Bennett. I don't think that being a little late warrants a grounding. Amber's a good girl. I'm sure she won't make a habit of it."

I watched Mrs. Bennett's expression in the mirror go from merely displeased to something closer to anger. She didn't seem to like that Momma was letting me off the hook. And, seriously, what business was it of hers anyway? Not that I'd ever say something like that to her, but I could sure think it.

The long red fingernail of her right index finger tapped on the arm of the salon chair as she glared first at Momma, and then settled her gaze on me, as if I were an evil young lady who'd gotten away with something.

The air around us gathered tension and Momma said, "Well, then, Amber, you'd best get over there and help Darcy cover the phone."

"Yes, ma'am," I said.

As I turned to leave, Mrs. Bennett said, "Wait," and I stopped in my tracks. That red fingernail continued to tap, tap, tap on the arm of the chair. "I would like a glass of Tab," she said, her words clipped and crisp. "With a fresh squeeze of lemon. Not lime. Lemon."

My eyes widened. The Tab was no problem—I'd just get it out of the vending machine—but where was I supposed to get a lemon? I looked at Momma, who shifted her shoulders uncomfortably.

"Mrs. Bennett," she said gently. "I'm afraid we don't have any fresh lemon here at the salon, but Amber would be glad to get you that Tab."

Mrs. Bennett twisted in her chair and pressed her lips together in a fine line. "How long have I been your customer, Gina?"

Momma blinked and her hand holding the comb hovered in the air. "Well, let's see . . . about five years or so." I could tell she was trying to keep the conversation light, and I could also tell that she was a little rattled by Mrs. Bennett's angry tone and flinty glare.

"Yes," Mrs. Bennett said. "I've graced this establishment of yours for five long years, and I've referred at least a dozen people to you. Why, most of my friends from the country club come to you and likely keep your business afloat! The very *least* you could do to show your gratitude for all that goodwill is to send your daughter out to get me some fresh lemon for my cola. And remember, it would only take one phone call from me for half your clientele to find another beautician."

Behind me the salon's phone rang. I heard Darcy on the other line booking an appointment and I knew she probably had yet another customer on hold. Then, the bell over the entrance rang, too. Someone had just come in for their appointment. The Saturday rush had arrived.

Momma stepped forward and swiveled the chair slightly

to turn Mrs. Bennett back toward the mirror. "Amber, would you please head down the street to the grocery store and bring back some lemons?"

I couldn't believe she was backing down when she knew Darcy was already struggling because I'd been late, *and* we were just starting to get busy. But Momma didn't look at me. Instead she focused on combing out a section of Mrs. Bennett's hair.

I glanced in the mirror and saw Mrs. Bennett studying me with a crocodile smile.

"Yes, ma'am," I said woodenly.

"Be quick about it," Mrs. Bennett said. "I'd like to be sipping my cola by the time your mother puts me under the dryer."

The grocery store was a half mile away, and I had no transportation other than my Reeboks. The day was already hot and humid, and by the time I jogged to the store, collected the lemons, and got back, my makeup was running and my hair had gone completely flat.

Darcy shot me a pained look as she checked out a customer while trying to book a client at the same time. The phone was lit up with people on hold, and there was a line at the door of people waiting to be checked in.

I knew Darcy really needed help, but I also knew that Mrs. Bennett would throw a fit if she didn't get her Tab right away, so I held up a finger to Darcy and raced to the back with the stupid lemons.

After using my own change to get a Tab from the vending machine, I sliced the lemon quickly, hung it over the edge of a glass, and darted over to Momma's station. Doing my best to push a smile to my face I said, "Here you are, Mrs. Bennett."

She made a face at the glass. "Is that clean?"

"Yes, ma'am," I said.

"It doesn't look clean," she said.

Behind me I heard a customer complain loudly to Darcy that she'd been standing at reception for several minutes and hadn't been checked in yet.

"I promise it's clean, Mrs. Bennett," I said, looking to Momma, who I hoped would back me up.

"Amber," Momma said softly. "Please get Mrs. Bennett another glass."

I pressed my lips together and turned to hurry to the back and dig out another glass. My heart was racing with anxiety, and I could hear both the constant ringing of the phone and the bell above the door dinging. Still, I took an extra twenty seconds to wipe down the glass with a towel and hold it up to the light to make extra sure that it was smudge-free, then rushed it back out to Mrs. Bennett.

"No ice?" she asked me when I again attempted to hand her the glass.

I bit my lip hard enough for it to hurt, and instead of arguing with her I turned on my heel and went to the back again to grab a few cubes from the ice tray.

The third time I headed to Momma's station I got there just as Mrs. Bennett was getting up. She refused to take the glass from me and instead walked over to the dryer Momma pointed to, waited for her to lower the hood over her rollers, asked for a magazine to read, rejected the one Momma offered her, then, at last, took the glass from me, only to hold it up and say, "I said *lime*, not lemon."

I sucked in a breath and beside me Momma did, too. Mrs. Bennett eyed us as if daring either one of us to challenge her. Everyone knew she'd told me to get her some lemon.

I looked at Momma, whose face was flushed with her own anger. In the background another customer was getting angry with Darcy, who sounded like she was on the verge of tears.

"Amber," Momma said. "Please go back to the store and get some limes for Mrs. Bennett."

I stood rooted to the spot, so angry my hands curled into fists. Mrs. Bennett was being ridiculous, punishing both Momma and me, and for what? Because Momma hadn't taken her suggestion to ground me for being fifteen minutes late?

"Amber!" Momma said sharply. "Do as I say, child."

"But Darcy—"

"She'll manage! Now, go, and remember, bring back some *limes* for Mrs. Bennett."

She emphasized the word to let Mrs. Bennett know she couldn't change it to oranges or grapefruit when I got back.

Mrs. Bennett actually chuckled; she thought the situation was so funny. I turned to leave, but not before she got in a parting shot. "Next time, Amber, perhaps you'll remember to be punctual."

Lily

"THANK YOU FOR BEING PROMPT, LILY," GRANDMOTHER said. Somehow I'd managed to fix myself up and hustle over to the main house in time for tea, coming through the door at three thirty on the dot.

"Yes, ma'am," I said, a little out of breath. Hoping she hadn't noticed that I'd rushed over, I went directly to one of the chairs in her elegant—if slightly dated—parlor. We were surrounded by an overflow of printed fabrics, wood buffed to a reflective sheen, and the smell of lemon-scented furniture polish. The large room overlooked her extensive gardens, and the staff made sure to include several fresh flower arrangements all around the room. Grandmother sat erect in her wing chair, her silver hair styled in an asymmetric bob and her bichon frise, Hamlet, settled on her lap.

"You're a very pretty girl, Lily; why do you have to wear

so much makeup?" she said, her face pulling into a frown as she handed me a cup of tea.

"I was just playing around," I told her, twirling a lock of my hair around my index finger and suddenly feeling foolish.

My effort to take more care with my appearance had ended in a smoky eye, lots of blush, and false eyelashes look that might have been better suited to a night out at a New York club. Sophie and I used to play around with this exact look when we wanted to feel glamorous and grown-up. I think she'd been on my mind a little too much that afternoon, and I might've been influenced both by fond memories of Sophie, and maybe seeing Dad's pregnant girlfriend in Grandmother's driveway.

"I saw Jenny," I said.

My grandmother made a sound of disgust while I stirred sugar into my tea with a small golden spoon. "Can you believe that little tramp actually came here looking to get her paws on the family money?"

I could believe it. "What'd she say?" I asked, feeling a bit smug that Grandmother had referred to Jenny as a tramp.

Grandmother rolled her eyes. "She came here on the pretense of delivering the news that she and your father are engaged," she told me. "They're getting married in December, right after the baby is born."

I nearly choked on my tea. "Was he going to tell us?"

"I doubt it," she said.

I dropped my gaze to my lap. I don't know why, but it stung that he hadn't even tried to contact me about his plans. I mean, I was really, really mad at him, which should've acted like a barrier to anything hurtful he could've said or done, but I was quickly learning that anger didn't make my heart bulletproof.

"Lily," Grandmother said, leaning forward to peer closely at me. "What is it you'd like to do with your life?"

Apparently, we were off the subject of Jenny and onto the subject of me. I hesitated while I thought about my answer. It felt a little like Grandmother was offering me a trick question. At last I decided to tell her the truth.

"I'd like to become a behavioral scientist," I said.

Her lids closed in a protracted blink. "A . . . what?"

"A behavioral scientist," I repeated. "I'd like to work with animals, study their behavior, and try to figure out how to communicate with them."

This was an idea that'd formed over the summer and solidified in my mind when I was working at the horse sanctuary. Many of the animals that came to the rescue had been terribly abused, and I'd felt such a connection to them. I'd also been so impressed by two of the women who worked there—trainers specializing in assisting the animals to get over their traumas.

One of the trainers, a woman named Rachel, had told me that she felt it was always the responsibility of the animals to try to assimilate themselves into the world of the humans who took care of them, and when the humans were poor communicators, the animals often felt the brunt of that miscommunication in the form of abuse. Rachel had shown me how simply watching a horse or a dog or a rabbit for an hour or so could teach me a lot. She'd been so right and I'd come away with a much bigger curiosity about the world, and why we all behaved the way we did.

Grandmother, however, appeared less than pleased by my aspirations. "You want to study...*animals?*" she said, as though that was something vulgar.

I squared my shoulders. "Yeah. I think I might go into veterinary science first, and then continue on to become an applied animal behaviorist."

Rachel had had those exact credentials, in fact.

Grandmother's next reaction left me cold. She laughed. She actually laughed at me.

"Oh, come now, Lily," she said, as if she'd just gotten the joke. "If you're interested in medicine, then at least go to medical school and become a doctor or something similarly palatable. I can't imagine a *Bennett* mucking around with the livestock, for God's sake."

I pressed my lips together and heat seared my cheeks. When I'd first told Mom about my experiences at the animal sanctuary, and how I was thinking about pursuing a career in the behavioral sciences, she'd encouraged me wholeheartedly, and I'd felt really good about wanting to go into something unique and intriguing. Grandmother's reaction wasn't something I'd been prepared for.

"I'm not interested in becoming a doctor," I said, careful to rein in the bitter and angry response I wanted to spout. I knew that Mom and I had to be nice to Grandmother until Mom got on her feet.

Grandmother made a *tsk*ing sound. "Lily," she said, touching her gray hair with a light hand, as if to check that it was still perfectly coiffed. "No heir to the Bennett fortune will be schooled in *veterinary science.*"

I stared at her, forcing myself to display no emotion

whatsoever. I didn't give a rat's ass about her fortune. Money had never bought anyone in my family any form of happiness. Instead, I'd seen it used like a weapon to control and limit the choices of the people that I loved, and it sickened me.

Still, I did care about Mom, and knew that if I balked, Grandmother would remind me that the roof over my head, and Mom's residency, were all her doing.

"I'm not totally sold on it," I lied. The taste of the subtle deception was bitter on my tongue.

It seemed to satisfy my grandmother, though.

"I thought as much," she sniffed. "You will study business—at Yale, of course. We need a savvy business-woman in this family to take over for me someday." She paused to consider me. "How are your grades, Lily?"

I had a 3.8 GPA coming into this year, but I definitely didn't want Grandmother to know I had my sights set on UC Davis in California, which was the best school for the field of study I was interested in.

"They're okay," I said, playing it off like I was a little embarrassed.

Grandmother made a face. "We'll get you a tutor. I suppose you can always attend Georgetown if we can't get your grades up enough. I've got a close friend on the board there. She owes me a *substantial* favor."

I took a sip of my tea and kept in the sigh I desperately wanted to exhale.

Grandmother prattled on. "Yes, business at Georgetown will be an excellent direction for you. I have a great many enterprises that you will be taking over once it's time to 'pass the torch,' as they say. I think it's also prudent for you to study the law, Lily. We've never had a solicitor in the family, and I find that the more money I make, the more my attorneys try to lay claim to it. I'd like someone at the helm to keep those sharks in check."

I nodded, like I was on board with the whole plan, then sat back and listened dully as she laid out my future. After twenty minutes, she finally talked herself out and went back to focusing on my appearance.

"What is happening with your hair, Lily?" she asked, waving a hand at the top of my head.

Heat once again spread through my cheeks. "I need to get it highlighted," I said, reaching up to swipe a strand behind my ear.

Grandmother's disapproving frown returned. "You'll go see my stylist, Gina," she said. "She's very good, and she'll take care of you. You'll come home looking like a proper young Bennett."

I sat forward. No way did I want the same person who made my grandmother look like an elderly Anna Wintour anywhere near my hair.

"That's okay," I said quickly. "Mom can drive me to Richmond this weekend to see my old stylist."

Grandmother was too busy picking up and dialing the phone next to her to pay my protest any attention. A moment later, she was ordering someone on the other end of the line to book me a session with Gina.

"Seven o'clock? That's perfect. My granddaughter will see you then."

Once Grandmother finally released me, I headed back

to the guesthouse to mutter unkind things to myself about her and get something to eat. Thanks to my nerves, I'd had very little at lunch that afternoon. After making myself a sandwich, I washed a lot of the extra makeup off and sat down at the computer.

Grandmother was such an overpowering force in our lives now, and I knew that if I told Mom about our conversations, she wouldn't hesitate to march over there and tell Grandmother to stuff it. That wouldn't be good for anyone, so I decided to keep the conversation over tea to myself.

Because I was squarely in pouting mode, I decided to snoop around Sophie's Instagram page. She'd posted a ton of selfies from the first day of school—of course. I dabbed at the subsequent tears, and I went back a little further to the photos of the two of us on our first day of our sophomore year. God, we were so excited to start school then. Sophie had braided our hair in matching fishtails, and I thought we'd looked so pretty that morning. In a weak moment, I considered responding to her text.

But after staring at my phone for a good minute, I didn't feel brave enough or forgiving enough. She'd betrayed and hurt me too deeply for me to trust her ever again. Instead, I gave in to another temptation. Digging through my backpack, I pulled out the folder I'd been given at orientation. In addition to the map of the school, it also held a directory of students and instructions to Chamberlain High's Intranet. After locating the directory, I flipped to the pages where all the students were listed in alphabetical order by grade.

There were three Coles. Cole Drepeau, Cole McDonald, and Cole Stewart. I turned to the computer and logged into

Facebook, hoping that the Cole I'd met that morning had a profile. After plugging *Cole Drepeau* into the search field I let out a little whoop when I hit the jackpot on the first try. Then my breath caught as I took in the sight of him. His account settings were very private but at least I could look at his profile picture, which was so flattering. It showed him standing in a sleeveless tee; his tan, gorgeously defined arms flexing slightly while slung casually around the shoulders of two other guys to his right and left. All three boys were laughing into the face of the camera, as if the photographer had just told a particularly funny joke.

Around Cole's neck, he wore a dark leather cord strung with a yellow bead, and around his wrist he wore a similar cord also strung with more yellow beads. The accents were subtle, but they definitely added to his level of hotness.

Hey! my bossy, rational side thought. *What the hell are you doing looking up some new guy when Tanner just cheated on you?!*

To which the side of myself that is a general admirer of hot guys replied, *There's no harm in looking.*

My bossy side wasn't fooled, but I still couldn't force myself to turn away from Cole's profile.

I studied the photo, only slightly ashamed of myself for cyber-stalking him, but I loved that he'd chosen this image to use as his profile pic. It clearly showed Cole's lightheartedness. He looked like the kind of guy who laughed easily, held deep friendships, and was generally well-liked. Maybe that was me doing a whole lot of projecting, but there was just something friendly and kind about his face. I found myself sighing a little as I looked at his photo, and immediately rebuked myself again because I was being an idiot.

No way was I ready to be thinking about getting involved with somebody else—I was still smarting from the breakup with Tanner.

But then I wondered: was I really heartbroken over losing my boyfriend, or losing my boyfriend to my best friend?

If I was being honest with myself, I was far more hurt by Sophie's betrayal than Tanner's. The truth was, I missed her way more than I did him.

But even that admission didn't make me ready to start something new. At least, that's what the practical side of me thought. And yet, when I stared at Cole's photo, I couldn't shake this feeling of familiarity. I couldn't quite reconcile the sense that I knew him from somewhere. It felt like we'd met before this morning.

On impulse, I switched over to Google and plugged in a search on Cole's name and Fredericksburg, Virginia. What came up made me gasp. The first link I found led to a news report about a murder from 1987. Investigating further, I discovered that the case was unsolved; the victim an eighteen-year-old boy who'd been shot to death the night of his prom. His name had been Ben Spencer.

I got through maybe two paragraphs of the story before I started to hyperventilate. I'd had one panic attack in my life. It had come the day Dad had tried to introduce me to his girlfriend. He and Mom had already filed for divorce, and he'd taken me to lunch like he wanted us to bond one-on-one. Instead, Jenny had been at the table, waiting for us.

It'd been so unfair, so underhanded, and I'd felt a sudden rush of panic and fear take hold of my insides and threaten to rip me apart. Dad had gotten me through it by rubbing my back and helping me regulate my breathing. The bastard.

There was no accounting for why this panic attack came on, though—it just did. I slipped out of my chair, gasping for breath, and got on all fours to try to temper the force of it.

It took a long time, and I came close to reaching for the phone to dial 911, but at last it subsided. When it did, I was damp with sweat, even though I was shivering with cold. Trembling, I crawled over to the bed and sat against it, wiping the hair out of my eyes and pulling an afghan off my bed.

"What the hell, Lil?" I asked myself.

This time I'd had to fight it all on my own. I wondered if the appearance of Dad's girlfriend at the door of my grandmother's house had somehow triggered a delayed reaction. But when I glanced toward my desk and the still-lit computer screen, I knew this one hadn't been about her.

Something about that article had set me off. But what was it? And why was Cole's name attached to a thirty-year-old murder?

Cautiously, I got up, hugged the afghan close, and hobbled over to the desk again. Taking a seat, I scrolled to the top and began to read.

At the end of the first page I found Cole's name. A few months earlier, on the day of the thirtieth anniversary, he'd been asked to comment on the death of his uncle.

"Whoa," I whispered when I read that part. I'd never known anyone who'd been murdered, not even by extension.

Cole had told the reporter that it was still hard for his family to talk about. He'd been born well after his uncle was killed, but it hung over his mother and his grandmother like a dark cloud. He said he wished that the case would be reopened and looked at again, if only to confirm the general suspicion that Ben had been murdered by his then-girlfriend.

I felt my brow furrow. I read the line again, and something about it seemed off. Like the panic attack, it hit me wrong, but I couldn't explain why. I read on, even though the details were few.

Ben Spencer had been shot twice in the chest. Police suspected his longtime girlfriend of the crime. A girl named Amber Greeley, who had killed herself four days after Ben's murder. A note had been found at her home, which suggested that she'd been the one responsible for Ben's death, and she'd taken her own life, but questions remained. Namely, the murder weapon had never been recovered, and she and Ben had appeared to be a happy couple that was very much in love. There were no signs from their friends that anything had been wrong between them that evening, but both had gone missing from the dance at about ten o'clock in the evening, and a half hour later, Spence was discovered dead in a field next to the high school. The reporter alluded to other inconsistencies, and it wasn't hard to see that he thought someone else might be responsible.

The article ended with a question, which was: why would someone want to murder the popular captain of the football and track team, a good student, and a boy about to head off to college where even more greatness likely awaited him? What could've been the motive?

I sighed and shut the lid to my laptop. The article left me feeling profoundly sad on top of the fact that my eyelids were heavy and my limbs like lead. I was exhausted. Glancing at the clock I saw that it was only a little after five. I could take a nap and still make it to the salon appointment Grandmother had set up for me.

Moving back to the bed, I pulled the afghan over myself and closed my eyes. I was worried about having the dream again, so I focused on happy thoughts. It wasn't lost on me that over and over my mind kept drifting back to Cole.

A few minutes later, I was sitting on a bed in a strange room. Alarmed by the unfamiliar surroundings, I looked about and realized I did somewhat recognize where I was, but for the life of me I couldn't place it.

I had the distinct impression I'd been in that room before, but when and where? I wondered. The room itself was spacious, painted a soft, soothing yellow with bright-white trim. The bedspread was dotted with sunflowers, and a large white desk occupied one corner. I sat on the edge of the bed, facing one of two windows, and outside the sun was setting, the last rays of the day bathing the room in a soft blush.

The setting was soothing, and yet, my heart was racing. I felt tense with the knowledge that I was in danger.

Behind me, somewhere deeper in the house, I heard a dog bark, and it, too, sounded familiar, even though we'd never owned a dog.

Could it be one from the animal sanctuary? I asked myself.

As I was trying to sort it all out, I heard footsteps from beyond the door, as if someone in the hallway were approaching. I felt the immediate urge to get up and hide, but instead an unseen force held me there. I was suddenly completely paralyzed. And then, the door behind me creaked as it opened, and footsteps closed in. I was filled with panic but I couldn't move. Not a limb, not a finger, not even to blink my eyes. It was as if my whole body had been taken over and reprogrammed to sit still and wait for an attack I knew was coming. I tried to scream, but couldn't get my lips parted. My vocal chords refused to work. Behind me, I felt the bed depress with the weight of an unknown intruder, and then my shoulder was gripped with pain.

I tried to fight that paralyzing sensation, but no amount of strain or effort could break the hold. And then, I saw an arm snake around my other shoulder, and a dwindling ray of sunlight flashed against silver. Too late, I realized the intruder had a knife, and in the next horrible moment, that knife arced up, and then straight down again to plunge into my sternum. In the final second, my whole chest exploded in a fireball of pain as the knife drove mercilessly into my heart.

Amber

BEN SPENCER PUT A HAND OVER HIS HEART AND gave his chest a few pats. "You," he said dramatically, "look incredible."

I laughed, holding open the front door, and ducked my chin, both pleased and a bit flustered. Since I'd shown up to our first date looking frazzled and stressed from the day spent catering to Mrs. Bennett, I was determined to look my absolute best tonight when he took me out a second time. I was glad that the bright-pink denim dress with the high collar I had on was working its charm.

"How're you?" I asked him as he came close to put his hands on my hips and stare down at me. I felt flushed and giggly in his presence. So uncool.

"Better now," he said. For a moment I thought he was going to lean in for a kiss, and a surge of excitement coursed through me. I sucked in a breath, because I was unprepared for it. Spence caught my reaction and immediately dropped his hands to step away.

"Sorry," he said. "You just look so hot in that dress."

I laughed again. "You're forgiven. Should we go?"

"Amber?" Momma called. I held in a groan. I'd been hoping to avoid having to introduce Spence to my parents. Momma was going to pepper him with questions, and Daddy was probably going to try and scare him off. It'd be humiliating.

But Spence waved and then extended his hand when my parents appeared. "Mr. Greeley, Mrs. Greeley, it's very good to meet you. You have a beautiful home here."

It was a pretty formal introductory speech, but as I watched Spence make small talk with my parents, Daddy's expression changed from barely veiled suspicion to one of surprised delight. And within a matter of a few minutes, Spence had totally won both my parents over.

At last we were free to leave, and Spence held my hand as he led me down the walk to his car. I loved that he was old enough to drive!

"Madame," he said, opening the car door for me with a flourish.

"Why, thank you, kind sir," I said, laughing as I turned sideways to scooch into the seat. Spence closed the door and got in. The second he turned the ignition, Yes's "Owner of a Lonely Heart" blasted from the speakers. Spence jumped to turn the volume down.

"You like it loud, huh?" I asked.

"Naw," Spence said, with a wink at me. "I'm just the owner of a lonely heart."

I smiled and tried to hold in the giggle bubbling up again. He was so clever, he kept surprising me. But then he reached to his back pocket and made a face.

"Aww, crap," he muttered, covering his eyes with his hand.

"What's the matter?"

Lifting his face, he said, "I left my wallet at home."

I held up my purse. "I can cover us."

He winced. "No way, Amber. And if I ever let you pay for me, break my heart and dump me, okay?"

I frowned at him. "What is this, caveman times? Are you going to drag me into the movie by my hair and buy me a brontosaurus burger later?"

It was Spence's turn to chuckle. "Hey, don't knock the brontosaurus burger. It tastes like chicken." Then he sighed and said, "I really want this to be on me, okay?"

I pointed to the digital clock on the dashboard. "It's still early. We have tons of time before the movie starts."

He smiled again and said, "My house is on the way. We can make a quick stop and not be late."

We talked easily as we drove to Spence's house, and I was eager to see where he lived, but as we got close, the neighborhood changed to something a bit seedier.

Spence stopped in front of a two-story white home with black shingles. For a moment he seemed to look up at the house, which had a light on in the front window, and I saw the flash of a grimace there.

"It'll just be a sec," he said, and hurried out of the car.

He bounded up the front walk and rushed inside. While I waited, I tried to find the charm in his house, because how could someone like Spence live in a place that didn't have a little appeal?

But the more I looked, the more neglect I noticed. There was a flowerpot on the front porch that held only dry, dead flowers. Two weatherworn plastic chairs stood slightly askew, and one had a broken leg, which caused it to list to the side. A pink bike leaned up against a tree in the front yard, but even it looked like it'd seen far better days.

With a sigh, I rolled down the window and tried to figure out what was taking Spence so long. Maybe he couldn't find his wallet? That's when I heard an eruption of noise coming from inside his home and I flinched in alarm. Two voices, one male, one female, were shouting at each other, and while I couldn't hear the words, the sentiment was loud and clear.

The male voice had to be Spence's dad—it was too deep to be Spence's—and I thought that maybe the woman's voice was his mother. I covered my mouth with my hand, wondering if there was something I could do. Was the argument about Spence? The male voice was so angry and so loud that I was worried it might lead to violence, and then, abruptly, it stopped.

I waited a moment and heard a loud bang, like a door slamming shut, and then the sound of an old engine turning over. The front door opened just as a station wagon backed jerkily down the driveway, narrowly missing Spence's car before it squealed off down the road.

I glanced back at the porch and saw Spence standing there with hunched shoulders and fisted palms. Next to him stood a woman as tall as Spence, wearing disheveled clothes and slightly crooked glasses. She stared angrily down the road in the direction of the moving car, then turned her gaze on me, and I swear her glare became harsher.

Spence said something to her and she headed back inside, slamming the door in her wake. Spence stood still for a moment before walking down the steps and over to his car.

When he opened the door, the overhead light came on and I saw a red welt on his cheek before he got settled into the driver's seat.

I was speechless. The whole thing was so shocking. My parents never yelled like that at each other. Even in their most heated arguments, their tone never rose to the levels that I'd heard Spence's family use. But even worse, had Spence's dad punched him?

"Are you okay?" I asked when Spence didn't say anything. It appeared he was trying to get his emotions under control.

"Yeah," he said curtly. And then he took a deep breath and said, "Sorry. My dad can get a little intense."

I bit my lip. I wanted to touch the welt on his cheek, but I also didn't want to further upset Spence by letting him know that I'd noticed it.

"We can skip the movie," I said.

His shoulders sagged. He leaned forward and let his head fall to the steering wheel. "You want me to drive you home, Amber?"

"No!" I said quickly. "No, Spence. I mean, if you want to drive me home, that's okay. But we don't need to go to the movie if you're not up for it."

He sat back again and turned to me. All that cool confidence and engaging personality had vanished, and in its place I saw a hurt and vulnerable guy. It moved me more than I could say.

"I'd really like to see the movie," he said. "With you. If you still want to go?"

I reached out and put my hand on his arm. I could feel the muscles relax under my fingertips and saw his expression soften.

"Then let's see the movie. And after, maybe you could treat me to that brontosaurus burger you keep talking up."

He gifted me with another one of those oh-so-gorgeous smiles. "Deal," he said, and we set off.

Lily

WE WERE LATE SETTING OFF FOR THE SALON. AFTER
the nightmare I'd had during my nap, it'd taken me a while
to pull myself together and meet Arthur for the ride over.
On the way there I nervously wondered if I was going crazy.
The dream had felt so vivid and *real*. And when I'd jolted
awake, my birthmark didn't so much burn as radiate a pain
that felt like an actual stab wound.

"Here we are, Miss Lily," Arthur said, pulling up to the
curb in front of a cozy olive-green house with a maroon
door and a sign that said simply GINA'S. The salon was a
surprise; I'd been expecting something more in line with a
traditional-looking commercial salon. After collecting my
purse, I told Arthur I'd call him when I was done and headed
inside.

Coming through the door, I looked around at the interior, which was dimly lit, but welcoming. The salon itself
was coated in a lighter shade of dark, woodsy green, with

pops of bright orange. A large Asian-inspired coffee table dominated the waiting area, and it was artfully adorned with fashion magazines. In the center was a square glass vase filled to the top with lemons and limes. The vase made me do a double take, and I had a weird déjà vu moment, but then it passed. I realized belatedly that the salon appeared to be deserted. Moving a little farther into the space to peek around a wall, I saw all the salon chairs were empty and there was not a stylist in sight except for a girl, maybe in her early twenties, with jet-black hair tipped in bright blue, sweeping the floor. She glanced up just as I spotted her.

"Can I help you?" she asked.

"I had a seven o'clock appointment with Gina?" I said, more as a question than a statement.

The girl tilted her head. "At seven?" she repeated. "We close at seven."

I opened my mouth to apologize, but was interrupted.

"That's okay, Rebecca. I booked it."

I turned around and a surge of dizzy disorientation overtook me. A woman with wavy auburn hair, who I'd put anywhere between sixty and seventy, but who still appeared beautifully youthful, approached, wearing a long knit gray tunic with chunky jewelry. I knew her. I could swear I *knew* her, but for the life of me, I couldn't place her face.

She smiled broadly. "Hello, Lily, I'm Gina. I'll be taking care of you. Won't you come this way?"

My mouth was opening and closing as I tried to form words, but each attempt got stuck in my throat. I felt wobbly and unsteady and didn't know if I could walk. Sweat broke out across my brow, and I wondered if I was having yet another panic attack.

Gina seemed to notice because she stopped, pivoted back to me, and cupped my elbows. "Sweetheart, you don't look so good. Are you okay?"

Her touch was my undoing. I felt my knees give out and I sort of sagged against her. She managed to catch me, and I heard her call for her assistant. Another pair of hands got under me, and they eased me to a sitting position on the floor.

Gina swept my hair back from my face and studied me. "Lily, can you hear me okay?"

I managed a nod.

She put a hand to my forehead and said, "You're very pale; are you sick?"

"No," I whispered. I didn't feel feverish, just . . . over-whelmed. But from what? What had caused this ridiculous and humiliating reaction? I couldn't imagine what Gina and the other girl must be thinking. Still, I leaned into the cool of the stylist's palm and closed my eyes for a minute.

"Rebecca, go to the back and bring me a glass of ice water and a damp washcloth." I heard the girl behind me scramble to her feet and hurry away.

"I'm sorry," I told Gina, so embarrassed I could hardly stand it.

"Shhh," she said gently. "Honey, did you have anything to eat today?"

I opened my eyes and leaned away from her to show her I was better. "I had a big sandwich for dinner. I'm sorry; I think it's because I haven't been sleeping."

She laid a hand on my shoulder. "Oh, well, I know all about how that can mess you up."

Rebecca came back with the water and the wet washcloth. Gina took both and offered me the water. I took a few sips, breathed in deeply a few more times, and let Gina pat at my forehead and cheeks with the washcloth. Her touch was kind and gentle.

"Thanks," I told her. "I think I'm okay."

Gina stood and leaned down to take my arm and help me up, even though I felt fine again. "Did you want to go home and rest?" she asked me. "I can call your grandmother to have Arthur come get you."

I was surprised that she knew Arthur, but then, maybe Grandmother had mentioned him over the years. "I really am fine now," I told her.

She studied me for a moment.

"You do look better. At least you've got color back in your cheeks. Why don't you come over to my chair and sit awhile, though, okay? We can play with your hair, and if you start to feel dizzy again, you tell me and we'll send for Arthur."

"Okay," I said, allowing her to lead me over to a mirror.

After easing me into a seat and sending Rebecca to get me a smock, Gina began to run her fingers through my hair and asked me what I had in mind.

I told her that I just wanted to add some highlights, and I watched in the mirror as her lips pursed in a way that said she might have other ideas.

"You know," she said, "this style isn't doing you any favors. Have you always worn it so long without layers?"

I gulped and nodded. My hair was down to the middle of my back and I'd always worn it like that; one length, no bangs, and long. I had a feeling she wanted me to let her change it, and change can be hard for me. Plus, I'd had so much of that lately.

Gina must've picked up on my reservations because she said, "Lily, you have a lot of things going for you—these cheekbones, that gorgeous skin, those bright-green eyes— but this cut and this color isn't showing any of that off. If you'll trust me, I promise to turn you into a goddess. I swear; I'm good."

There was just something about how confident she sounded, because in the next moment I heard myself consenting. "Okay. If you promise."

She beamed at me. "Just wait till you see yourself, honey."

With that, she gave me a pat and told me she was off to mix up some color. I was left to stare at the now entirely empty salon. And then I remembered what Rebecca had said, that the placed closed at seven. Immediately, I felt ashamed as it dawned on me that Grandmother had probably thrown her weight around to get Gina to agree to see me tonight. I should've taken the opportunity to leave when Gina had offered it, if for no other reason than to spare her from working past closing.

When Gina came back with a roller table topped with bowls of dark hair color and brushes, I was quick to apologize.

"I'm really sorry about the time. I didn't realize you'd have to work late to see me."

"Don't sweat it," she said easily as she swirled the color around with one of the brushes.

"My grandmother is pretty used to getting her way," I said a little bitterly.

Gina stopped swirling, looked at me, and said, "I owe your grandmother a tremendous debt of gratitude, Lily. It was nothing to accommodate you after all she's done for me." I attempted a smile. It felt like I'd overstepped. "Sorry," I said.

She laughed. "There's no reason to be sorry, honey. I know how Maureen can be. Hell, I've been doing her hair for thirty-five years so I know all the stuff she pulls when she wants something her way."

I fell silent after that, wondering what debt of gratitude Gina owed my grandmother.

"I guess I've just never seen her be kind," I said. Maybe that was bold of me, but it was true.

Gina, however, was nodding as she swept the cool color through my hair.

"I've only seen her express some genuine kindness once," she said. "But it was the most incredible gift anyone had ever given me, and it came at a time when I needed it most."

Silence followed as I mulled that over, curious. Finally, I worked up the courage and asked. "What was it? What'd she do?"

Gina exhaled. "She was there for me when my daughter died," she said. "At a time when no one else in this damn town showed me any sympathy, your grandmother was there for me. She probably even saved my life."

"Wow," I said, stunned. I couldn't understand how anyone could deny a grieving mother some sympathy. "I'm sorry about your daughter."

"Me, too, honey."

I searched for something appropriate to say. Nothing came to me. "How old was she?"

"Eighteen."

That shocked me. I'd imagined a toddler or an infant, not a girl my age.

"What happened?" I asked, knowing I was probably out of line, but unable to resist the temptation to know.

Gina smoothed the brush over more of my hair with an almost cool detachment.

"She was murdered," she said.

I put a hand to my mouth. "Oh, Gina..." I said, now really ashamed of myself. "I'm...that's...God, I'm so sorry!"

How was it possible that this small, quaint town had seen so much violence? This was the second murder I'd heard about in just a few hours.

"It's okay," Gina said, lifting her gaze to look at me. "Really. I've had thirty years to get strong enough to talk about it."

"Did they catch who did it?"

"No," she said. "They never did."

She didn't elaborate any further, and I let the topic drop. No way was I gonna press her for more details, and I still felt bad for even bringing it up. And yet, I wondered what specifically it was that my grandmother had done for Gina during that time.

"I'm really glad my grandmother was there for you," I said at last.

A faint, sad smile played at the corners of Gina's lips.

"Maureen used to come to my home, you know. After my daughter died, I was so depressed I spent nearly a year in bed. I lost my salon, my husband left me, and all my clients found other stylists to do their hair, and I didn't even care. And then one day your grandmother shows up at my door, demanding that I get out of bed and do her hair."

My mouth fell open, but Gina laughed and shook her head.

"She saved my life," she said. "I mean, that day I wanted to sock her in the mouth, but she acted like barging into my home and demanding I take care of her was her God-given right as a Bennett. So, just to shut her up and get her out of my house, I did her hair. It came out awful, but she went on and on about how gorgeous she looked, and then she left.

"The next day, one of her friends from that snooty country club shows up and says that she's got some sort of hair emergency. And the next day, two more friends of hers came by. Pretty soon, I didn't go a day without doing some friend of Maureen's, and then after about two months of that, she presented me with a deed to this place."

"She *gave* you this shop?" I asked. I couldn't imagine Grandmother being so generous—unless of course there were strings attached.

"She did," Gina said, but then laughed again. "Oh, it didn't look like this, though. No, it looked like something that should've been condemned. It was an old house that'd been commercially zoned before the last tenants abandoned it, and Maureen said she wanted it off her books because she couldn't sell it or rent it out, so she deeded it over to me.

After seeing it for the first time, I didn't think it was much of a gift, but Maureen called me the next morning and said some people were waiting for me here. When I arrived, there were two trucks fully loaded with supplies, from paint to tile to drywall, and a crew of volunteers to help me whip this place into shape. It took a long time to fix it up, but all that hard work was really good for me. It helped me through the grief and gave me my life back."

Gina's story stunned me in a way that made me feel ashamed all over again. Had I pegged my grandmother all wrong?

Gina switched the topic over to me, asking me about Richmond and school there, and I found myself telling her things that normally I'd keep private. I confessed to losing both my best friend and my boyfriend at the end of the previous year, and she was nicely sympathetic. She also told me to hang in there at my new school.

"It might take a week or two, Lily, but the kids will warm up to you. I promise."

By the end of my appointment, I felt better than I had in a long time. There was just something about being in Gina's presence that soothed me. It struck me how like Mom she was—gentle and kind, but strong and determined.

When she turned me around for the final reveal, however, my jaw dropped and I stared at my reflection, almost unable to process it.

Gina had taken my ash-blond hair and turned it a chestnut brown with light auburn highlights that framed my face. She'd cut a good eight inches off the length, which had brought back some of my natural wave, and she'd added layers and bangs. I hardly recognized myself.

"Oh . . . my . . . God!" I gasped. I looked amazing. Like, seriously, the best I'd ever looked in my whole life.

Behind me Gina beamed. "You're a knockout, sweetheart, and now all those gorgeous features aren't hidden and they can come shining through."

"I can't believe I look like this," I said, running a hand through my hair and turning my head from side to side. I felt like a movie star. Whipping out my phone, I indulged in a selfie, immediately posting it to my Instagram account.

"Take that, Sophie," I said meanly. But there was also that accompanying pang, because I knew that she would've raved about the new me. Still, I told myself that it was a good thing to show her that I was moving on without her. To show her that I didn't need her. Or miss her. Even if that wasn't exactly true, it was still the message I wanted to send.

As I sat and thought about all that, I saw someone heart my photo, but I didn't recognize the name. It felt a little creepy, so I clicked off the image and immediately realized that Gina was waiting.

"Sorry," I said with an embarrassed blush.

"Oh, honey, take all the time you need. There's a hamper behind that curtain to throw your smock in. I'll call Arthur and tell him to pick you up."

"Thanks, Gina," I said. I couldn't wait to get home and show Mom. I moved into the area behind the curtain and there was a small dressing room there. I heard Gina on the phone as I came back out and casually walked around the salon, noticing how cozy it was. Here and there were some personal touches that really made it feel more like a home than a salon.

"Come on, girl," Gina said, calling to me. "Arthur's going to be here in twenty minutes, which is enough time for us to have a snack."

Leading me through a corridor toward the back of the salon, Gina opened a door with a key. I figured she was taking me outside, but instead, when she opened the door, I realized that it *was* actually her home.

The door opened to a whole new space, with a living room, kitchen, and bedroom off to the side. It mirrored the salon in style, but the palette was softer, less harsh, done in a dusky rose with a tan trim.

"Wow," I said, coming through the door. "You live here?"

"I do."

I walked into her living room and took it all in. There was a seating area done in rich mocha, and a shaggy white rug, which was a beautiful contrast to the dark-brown floors. Everywhere I looked, there were artistic touches that seemed to fit the space perfectly. Gina invited me to sit at the counter in her small kitchen, which had a white-and-black marble countertop and bright-white cabinets.

"I love your place," I said as I sat.

"Thank you," she said, turning to the fridge. "I've got veggies and hummus, will that do?"

"Sure," I said.

"How about iced tea or cranberry juice for something to drink?"

"Cranberry juice, please."

Gina set out my drink first, then busied herself with the veggies and hummus, and I leaned toward a series of frames on her counter. One was a photograph of another woman who looked similar to Gina—I guessed it was a sister. Another was a framed prayer that talked about grace and forgiveness, and a third was tucked a little bit behind the others. Curious, I reached out and nudged it forward. When it came fully into view, my grip loosened and the glass of cranberry juice slipped through my fingers. I tried to grab it again and managed only to prevent it from shattering, but all the cranberry juice spewed out onto the counter, the chair, the floor, and me.

"*Ohmigod!*" I cried, mortified that I'd been so clumsy. "Ohmigod, Gina, I'm *sooooo sorry!*"

She was next to me with a wad of paper towels in an instant. "Don't sweat it, honey," she said calmly.

I stood there, hunched over and dripping, and my mind seemed to blank on how to help. "I . . . I . . . I . . ." I stammered.

Gina mopped at the mess, then stood up to get a garbage can and the whole roll of paper towels. "Lily, really, it's just a little juice and it cleans up quick. We're lucky the cup didn't break or you might've gotten cut."

Tears blurred my vision. Here she'd been so nice to me, and I'd made a total mess of her kitchen—and even though she was saying it was no big deal, I knew it was. "I'm really sorry," I whispered.

Gina paused to look at me. "Lily," she said gently. "It's just juice. It's okay. I promise. Now, why don't you head down the hall to the bathroom and use one of the washcloths in the basket to clean yourself up. You'll be a sticky mess on the drive home, otherwise."

I was breathing hard and still unsure, but at last I managed to turn and do as she instructed. After closing the door to the bathroom, I sat on the rim of the tub and covered my face with my hands. I was so rattled and upset, and not just about making a mess. When I'd first looked at the photograph on the counter, I'd been stunned to see that it was a photo of *me*. I'd been weirdly dressed, and my hair was totally different, but I swore it was me pictured there, and then I'd felt the glass slipping out of my hand and I'd blinked and the image had been replaced by someone else—a girl about my age—and as all the synapses in my brain had been firing, I'd known that she was Gina's daughter. But the *really* weird thing was that I'd also known her name as clearly as I knew my own. I knew that her name was Amber.

With a deep breath I got up from the tub and moved to the sink to stare at my reflection. What the hell was happening to me? Why was I having all this crazy déjà vu? And *how* did I know names of people I'd never even met? Yeah, I'd gotten Cole's middle name instead of his first name right, but still . . . Spence wasn't a common name. How had I pulled that out of thin air? And why was I so sure that Gina's daughter's name was Amber?

I shook my head. I was being stupid. Of course her name wasn't Amber. And then another thought occurred to me. Hadn't Cole's uncle been murdered by his girlfriend whose name was Amber?

Sweat broke out across my palms. Could it be the same girl? But the paper had said that Amber committed suicide, not that she'd been murdered. And how could the girl from the article be Gina's daughter? I mean, that really would be a freaky coincidence. Wouldn't it?

"Only one way to find out," I whispered. After hurrying to clean myself up, I stepped back out to the kitchen. Gina was rinsing her hands under the faucet and no sign of the mess I'd created remained. "Again, I'm so sorry," I said.

She shut off the faucet and turned to me as she wiped her hands. "Sweetie, after you've had a life like mine, you learn not to sweat the small stuff."

"Thanks," I said. "But I still feel bad."

"Well, don't. Now, have a seat and try my hummus. I make it myself."

I nibbled at a little pita bread dipped in the hummus, and it was, in fact, delicious. "Gina?" I said carefully as she sat down next to me.

"Yes?"

"Can I ask . . . what was your daughter's name?"

Gina's gaze moved to the set of framed photographs next to me. "Amber," she said. "Her name was Amber."

I blinked. I'd been right. For a moment I wondered if maybe I was developing some sort of psychic ability. I mean, all of the day's coincidences just seemed so freaky to me. But wouldn't I know other things besides just a name or two? Wouldn't I have visions of events that had yet to happen?

I had no idea how that stuff worked, and I was on the fence about whether or not I believed in it, but no other explanation came to me to account for pulling out two random and somewhat unique names associated with two people I'd never met before.

As I pondered that, the doorbell rang and Gina hopped off her chair. "That'll be Arthur."

I followed her back out to the salon, and she undid the lock for me. Arthur stood by the car, holding the back door open. I turned to Gina to say good-bye, but she beat me to it.

"It was a pleasure to meet you, Lily," she said.

"Thank you," I told her.

And then I did something that was totally unlike me, and impulsive, and...well...weird. I reached out and hugged her. She gave a startled laugh, but she hugged me back, and as she did so a wave of sadness overtook me that I couldn't explain. It came out of nowhere. I felt my eyes well up, and as I hugged Gina, I had the urge to hold on tight and never let go. She laughed again and patted my back, obviously a little thrown by how fiercely I was hugging her.

Feeling a fresh blush touch my cheeks, I said, "I should go.... I'm sorry...I..." and then I simply pulled away and ran for the car.

Amber

SPENCE'S CAR RUMBLED A LITTLE IN PROTEST AS HE pulled to a stop in front of my house. He'd asked me to come be his good luck charm at the varsity football game, and then we'd hung out with our friends in the parking lot of the local Burger King afterward. By the time we got back to my house, it was late, but still a few minutes before my curfew, and I glanced nervously toward the front window, hoping neither of my parents were peeking out to spy on us.

This was the third time Spence and I had been out together, and we still hadn't done more than share a light kiss good night. I'd been hoping for more. I longed to feel his lips linger on mine, to feel his arms embrace me, to melt under his touch, but none of that had happened yet, and it was causing a mounting frustration, not to mention making me feel a little insecure. I was beginning to wonder if Spence actually liked me, or if he was already losing interest.

My anxieties weren't helped by the fact that Britt and

Sara grilled me for details the morning after each date and read into everything that Spence either said or didn't say, did or didn't do. For Sara and Britt, boys were like some sort of military secret they were constantly trying to decode. Still, of the three of us, only Britt had ever been French kissed, and from the way she'd described it, it sounded awful. I wanted Spence to kiss me with more passion than the light pecks he'd been giving me, but I didn't want him to shove his tongue down my throat. What if he was a terrible kisser and I had to pretend that I liked it?

"That touchdown pass you threw in the final seconds was amazing. The whole team played so well," I said, trying to hide how nervous I was about the next few minutes alone with him in the car. Would we make out? Was he interested in that? And if he was, and he did kiss me, would I know what to do? I was still a little unclear about how to move my own tongue, and I was terrified I'd get it wrong and that he'd know that I was inexperienced.

"Yeah, we did," Spence agreed. "Except for Walker's fumble in the fourth," he added. "He almost cost us the game."

I'd heard about Brent Walker's fumble all night. An endless discussion about what a terrible player he was. How Coach Danvers played favorites because Brent was his cousin's son or something. Why Walker should've been kept on the bench, etc., etc.

Of course, the rest of us girls knew that the discussion was driven by spite—Brent Walker was the only sophomore besides Spence playing varsity, and while I could understand their point, because Brent really wasn't that good, it seemed to be the only thing the boys could talk about.

While I mentally fished around for another topic, because I didn't want to hear any more about Brent Walker, Spence tapped his index fingers in time with the music coming from the radio. Yes's "Owner of a Lonely Heart" was playing again, and I thought of the week before when there'd been that terrible fight at his house. We hadn't talked about it. I thought Spence might've wanted to, but he acted like nothing at all had happened, and I just figured he was embarrassed about it and wanted to pretend like everything was fine.

"So..." I said, too nervous to come up with anything interesting to talk about.

Spence chuckled.

"What?" I asked, smiling, too.

He laid his head back against the headrest and looked up at the roof of his car. It took him a long time to answer me, and I got the feeling he was trying to work out what to say.

"Amber, tonight I wanted to kiss you, like *really* kiss you, but..."

"What?" I said suddenly afraid. Was he turned off? Had I done something? What was the rest of that sentence?

He inhaled deeply and let out a sigh. Turning to look at me he said, "I wanted to kiss you, but I...I haven't kissed a lot of girls, and no one I like as much as you." Spence paused for a minute, obviously embarrassed by the admission. "Anyway, I guess what I'm saying is that I don't know if I'm any good at the whole making-out thing, and I'm worried that if I kiss you the way I want to, you won't want to go out anymore."

I sat there stunned for a minute, but then it was my turn to laugh. And once I started I couldn't stop. He eyed me curiously and that made me laugh even more. Finally, still giggling, I leaned toward him and gripped him by his leather jacket. Pulling him close, I shook my head a little before I said, "Oh . . . the irony."

And then I boldly kissed *him*.

And it was amazing. My lips met his, softly, gently, and his then pressed a little against mine until his mouth parted, and mine with it. His hand came up to cup my cheek and sweep back through my hair, and then our tongues met and his caressed mine so sweetly, so gently, that it ignited a fire within me. I felt a sudden and swift desire for him that was both longing and satisfying, and then he moaned and I was lost to everything but an overwhelming awareness of him. His breath. His heat. His physique. His caress. It all seemed to go on and on as though he filled a universe of unexplored stars, and I was swept up into his night sky and drifted across his constellation, until we both became aware of a strobe of light flashing on and off against the interior of his car. I pulled away first, breathing heavily and confused by the bouncing light, but then I realized the source and turned to look over my shoulder. The porch light was flickering. On and off. On and off.

My parents obviously knew that Spence and I were parked out front. "Oh, God," I said, glaring at the house. "Why? Just, why?"

Spence cleared his throat, and I turned back to him.

He had beads of sweat across his forehead and his face was flushed, but his lips were also beautifully swollen.

"I'd better walk you to the door," he said.

"Sorry," I told him, ready to get out of the car, but he caught my arm and leaned in toward me to kiss me sweetly and ignite those embers all over again.

At last his face lifted from mine, and as he stroked my cheek tenderly, he said, "I can't believe I waited so long to do that."

I grinned. "*You* didn't."

He chuckled. "Right. How about, 'I can't believe I waited so long to let *you* do that'?"

We both laughed, and Spence took my hand. "Come on, before your parents open the front door and ask why all my windows are fogged."

We got out of the car and headed up the walk, holding hands. I thought about how perfect a first kiss that was, and how I couldn't wait to set the record straight with Britt and Sara.

As we got to my door, the light flickered again, and I groaned. My parents were still at it. Turning hopefully to Spence, I said, "See you later?"

He leaned in one last time and kissed me lightly. "Definitely," he said before turning to head back down the porch stairs. On the way down, however, I heard him say again, "Definitely."

Lily

I WAS DEFINITELY LOSING MY MIND. I HAD TO BE. AN hour before, I'd walked into my sixth period class, only to discover it wasn't my sixth period. It wasn't anyone's sixth period. It was an unused classroom filled with old desks, chairs, and other storage items.

And then I'd had a very disorienting few minutes of trying to find my *actual* sixth period class, which had been on the other side of the school. I'd barely snuck in before the bell.

To make a bad day even worse, Sophie had texted me again.

> I saw your new look. You're soooo beautiful! I miss you, Lil. I really do. Just wanted you to tell you that.

Knowing that she'd had a glimpse of my new hairstyle hadn't felt like I thought it would. I thought I'd feel . . . I don't know... vindicated in a way? But all I really felt was sad. It was just like her to tell me I was beautiful. Back when we were friends, she always made me feel like I was the smartest, prettiest, most special person she knew. And maybe that's why it hurt so much—all that validation had just been ripped away from me when she started seeing Tanner. It was like everything nice she'd ever said to me had been a lie. Like I'd been played.

Except... maybe I hadn't. Maybe Sophie really did miss me. Maybe she really was sorry. It was impossible to know the truth. At least, at the moment it was. I was way too exhausted to have any hope of figuring out how I felt about my ex–best friend.

A little shaky and out of it, I leaned against my locker while the other kids hurried to grab their stuff and leave for the day. I wondered if I could even make it home. Mom had left me the keys to the car, which was nice of her. She said in a note that she'd had to stay at the hospital an extra six hours so she was headed to bed, but she'd found another resident to carpool with. I'd been happy about getting the car, but I'd wanted to talk to her before school because I'd had the dream about the boy in the field again, only this time it'd been even more intense.

For as long as I could remember, the dream had always begun with me walking through a field. Last night had been different: the dream had opened with me running through the corridors of Chamberlain High, caught like a rat in a maze and frantic for a way out. Finally, I'd found the exit and I'd walked right out to the field, which already fully engulfed in flames. The rest was like always, and I woke again at two A.M., covered in sweat and sobbing.

I got back to sleep around three, and slept fitfully for the next two and a half hours, then woke feeling like I hadn't rested at all.

To add to the misery, at school, no one had tried to talk to me or be friendly, and I felt too shy and vulnerable to make any attempts myself. What's more, I'd been unable to catch a glimpse of Cole, and I didn't even know if he'd been in school today. It would've meant a lot to see a friendly face.

With a sigh, I pushed myself away from my locker and worked the combination to open the door. The bustling of students around me had noticeably thinned. Nobody drags their feet to leave school. Tugging open the locker door, I began to gather books and my laptop.

"Hey, Cole," I heard someone say from just around the corner.

I stiffened. "Hey, Coop," he replied. "Are you in Rennick's first period?"

"Yeah."

"Have you seen the new girl?" Cole asked.

"You mean that hot new piece of ass from Richmond? Yeah, I've seen her. Why? You lookin' to tap that, bro?"

My face bloomed with heat. Ohmigod. They were talking about *me*!

"Naw," Cole said. "It ain't like that."

"Really?" Coop pressed.

Cole said, "Nope. Hey, do you remember if she was here today?"

And just like that, my pride and my ego took a one-two

punch. The first from Coop, who'd just described me as a piece of ass, and the second from Cole, who clearly wasn't at all interested in me. I was left hurt and rejected even though Cole should've meant nothing to me. I mean, I'd talked to him for, what, two minutes the day before? I wasn't just losing my mind; I'd now become pathetic as well. Pulling the last book out of the locker, I shoved it into my backpack and slammed the door.

The voices, which had been approaching, abruptly stopped, and out of the corner of my eye I saw them turn the corner almost right next to me. I made eye contact with Cole and a boy I vaguely remembered sitting an aisle over in Rennick's class. I thought his full name was John Cooper. I glared at both of them to let them know I'd heard everything they'd said.

Cooper nudged Cole with his elbow. "There she is."

"Whoa," Cole said, his jaw dropping and his eyes widening as he stared at me.

I pivoted on my heel and walked angrily away. A furious dialogue started in my head. *Boys! Stupid, dumb, asshole boys! "It ain't like that." You bet it ain't like that, you asshat!*

"Hey!" Cole called after me.

Ignoring him, I quickened my pace.

"Lily!"

I kept walking.

"Hey!" he said again, trotting forward to come up next to me.

I lifted my chin a little higher and refused to look at him. "What?" My tone was sharp enough to cut glass.

He chuckled. "Seriously," he said, "you walk crazy-fast."

I halted and glared hard at him. "What do you want, Spence?" And then I covered my mouth. Oh, shit, I'd done it again. I'd called him Spence.

Cole didn't seem to mind the slip. "Uh, it's Cole, remember? The guy who saved you from being marked late yesterday?"

I tossed my hair and rolled my eyes. Angry as I was, I had to admit that I was a tiny bit pleased he'd come after me.

"What can I do for you?" I said, throwing my backpack over one shoulder so I could cross my arms. No way was I letting him off the hook.

He cocked his head at me the way a puppy does when he's unsure why you're mad at him. "First of all, I'm sorry about Cooper," he said, waving his hand back down the hallway. "He's a douche."

I continued to glare at him, refusing to let it go. Lack of sleep and the terrible day I'd had could've been a factor in how mad I was.

"Second of all..." He looked me up and down slowly. "Wow."

I blinked. "What's 'wow'?"

Cole shook his head as if he were amazed or a little chagrinned. "For real, Lily, I've been looking for you all day, and the whole time I was searching for a blonde, and now I find you and you're...this..." He waved his hand at me again, his gaze darting all over me as if he couldn't quite believe it.

I tensed and my brow lowered to the danger zone. "What's. This?" I demanded, mimicking his hand motion.

Cole's gaze stopped roving. Looking me dead in the eyes,

he said, "*Hot.* Like...yesterday, you were...you know... whoa, but today...I mean, damn, woman. Damn!"

I burst out laughing. I totally hadn't been expecting anything like *that.* He started to laugh, too, and then all that tension and anger I'd been feeling just melted away.

I tucked a strand of hair behind my ear and said, "Were you really looking for me today?"

He nodded. "Yep."

"Why?"

It was Cole's turn to become a little shy. "I...uh..."

"Yeah?"

He shrugged. "I wanted to know if you were up for hanging out sometime."

I blinked again and my pulse quickened. "Sometime?"

He made a funny face and tried again. "Today. I wanted to see if you wanted to hang out today."

A rush of fluttery adrenaline pulsed through my veins. I was flattered and excited and nervous and still trying to remind myself that I'd basically *just* had my heart broken.

"Or, you know, tomorrow," Cole added, and I realized I hadn't answered him.

"What'd you have in mind?" I asked, aware that I seemed to be far more interested in Cole than I should've been.

"Uh..." he said, and his face turned red. Clearly, he hadn't thought his plan all the way through. "We could get a couple of slices at Sam's Pizza."

I hitched my backpack up a little farther on my shoulder. "That could work," I said.

He broke into a broad grin. "Yeah?"

"Yeah."

"Cool," he said. I stepped forward, and he tucked in next to me. We emerged from the school to find all the busses gone and most of the parking lot empty. Cole pointed to the back of the lot. "I'm at the end of the last row."

"Get here late this morning?" I asked as we began to walk. Mom's car was in the middle of the lot.

"Nah, I just like that spot." Cole then changed the subject. "How's it going at school?"

"Oh, you know," I said, trying to make light of the fact that I hadn't made a single friend yet and I'd spent my lunch hour hunkered down in Mom's car.

He eyed me sideways like he knew I might be having a tough time. "The girls here can be kinda cliquey."

"Yeah, so I noticed."

He frowned. "I'll introduce you to some people."

Some of the tension I'd carried the past two days eased from my shoulders. "That would be very cool of you."

I heard someone call his name from behind us and we both stopped to see a kid maybe a year or two younger run across the parking lot toward us. "Cole!" the kid called again.

"Hey, Rory," Cole said when the young man caught up. "What's going on?"

"I can't do Mrs. Kingsley's tonight," Rory said, his face twisted into an anxious knot. "My mom has to work late, and she needs me to watch my sister."

"Don't sweat it," Cole told him. "I'll cover for you. Did you get my text about the new lawn on Mercer this Saturday?"

Rory bit his lip. "I lost my phone," he admitted. At the mention of his lost phone Rory looked so sad.

Cole reached into his back pocket and pulled out his wallet, which was fat with cash. He tugged out several twenties, handed them to Rory, and said, "Take it."

Rory shook his head, but Cole pushed the money into his chest. "You've been doing a great job, bro. Take the cash and get yourself a phone, okay? Text me when you get it, and I'll send you the address for the new lawn."

Rory reluctantly took the money. "It's a loan," he said, clearly uncomfortable with the offering.

But Cole merely squared his shoulders and said, "No, bro. It's a bonus. Don't fight me on this or I'll fire you."

Clearly, he was joking because Rory broke out into a relieved grin. "Thanks, man. Sorry about tonight."

"It's cool," Cole said, as though it was nothing. Rory then bolted away and I was left to put the puzzle pieces of their conversation together.

"He works for you?"

"Yeah," Cole said as we started walking again. "I mow a bunch of lawns in the area. Been doing it since I was, like, twelve. It started to take off when I was a sophomore, and I had to hire a few friends to help me. Rory's a good guy. I hired him last year. His dad walked out on the family, and money is always tight, so I give him some extra lawns and pay him a little more than some of the other guys on my crew."

"And hand him a bonus when he loses his phone," I said. Cole's generosity had moved me. Tanner, my ex, used to caddy during the summer. He was always complaining about having to split his tips with other caddies, especially the younger ones, and I knew for a fact that he would often skim a little off the side of his daily tip total.

But Cole shrugged it off like it was no big deal. "He's worth it. Like I said, he's a good guy."

We got to his car, which was impressive. The vintage black Mustang with a raised cowl hood, waxed to a glossy sheen. No doubt his lawn business was fairly successful.

Cole paused next to the car to dig into the pocket of his backpack, presumably fishing for his keys. I waited as he ran his hand around the inside, but there was no telltale jingle to indicate that he'd found them.

He shifted to another pocket, and I leaned against his car. That's when I noticed a something glinting in the sunlight. "Uh, Cole?"

"Yeah?" he said, still searching through his backpack.

"Are you looking for those?" I pointed into the car, and he leaned forward to look at the keys dangling in the ignition.

"Aw, shit," he said. I stepped out of the way so he could try the handle. The car was locked.

"Do you have a spare set?" I asked.

Cole rested his forehead on the roof of the car. I felt for him. It had to be embarrassing. "I do. They're at home."

"I can take you there to get them," I said, pulling my mom's key fob out of my backpack.

"You have a car?"

"It's my mom's," I said, pointing the fob at the car in the middle of the lot to unlock it. "Come on."

Cole and I settled into my mom's Subaru and I drove us out of the lot. He still seemed really embarrassed so I tried to make light of it. "At least you didn't try to take me out on a skateboard," I said.

"A skateboard," he repeated. "What does that even mean?"

"My ex," I told him. "He first asked me out on his skateboard."

Cole snorted. "What were you, eight?"

"Fourteen," I told him.

He laughed. "Okay, but you still said yes, right?"

"I did," I admitted. "I was dumber back then."

"Why'd you guys split up?"

I shrugged. "Oh, you know, girl meets boy, girl dates boy for two years before boy dumps girl for girl's best friend."

Cole stared at me. "He hooked up with your best friend?"

I stared straight ahead. "Yep." Thinking of Sophie and Tanner brought a fresh stab of pain, which I was trying hard to brush off. I didn't want Cole to see that I was still hurt.

"That had to suck," he said.

"It did."

He was silent for a minute, then said, "Want me to beat him up?"

I smirked. "I don't know. He's a pretty big guy."

Cole made a show of flexing both his arms. "I could take him."

I laughed. "You know, you probably could. Tanner was pretty lame when it came down to it."

"So why'd you go out with him for two whole years?"

"That's a good question," I said. Why *had* I gone out with him? The past few days I'd been reflecting on Tanner with clearer eyes. It was like the minute I met Cole I subconsciously began comparing the two, and I kept finding Tanner more and more pathetic. Or maybe I was finally able to see him for who really was—an insecure guy with a huge ego who'd never really cared about me. "Anyway," I said, shrugging it off, "he's Sophie's problem now."

"That your best friend?" Cole asked.

"*Former* best friend," I corrected.

Cole eyed me critically. "I'll never understand women," he said. "I mean, we bros don't ever cross that line. There's a code."

"Bros before hos?" I said, quoting the familiar, yet incredibly insulting, phrase.

"Not that," he said, with a roll of his eyes. "It's the bro code. You just *don't* hook up with one of your bro's girlfriends. And if you break the code, no other bro will trust you. You're voted off the island if you pull that shit."

I sighed wistfully. Wouldn't it have been easier if I could've voted Sophie off the island? Instead, all of my former friends had rallied around *her,* which I figured was probably because Tanner was super-popular and nobody wanted to get on his bad side, but still. It hurt.

We were silent for another moment or two when I turned a corner and pulled to a stop, putting the car into park. "We're here," I said, turning to Cole.

He looked at me incredulously, then at the house I'd parked next to, then back at me.

"Lily," he whispered. "How the hell did you know where my grandmother lives?"

"What?" I said. And then I realized we'd been so engrossed in our conversation that I'd driven the entire way to this house without him once giving me any direction.

And yet the house we were parked in front of felt like some-place I'd been to a thousand times before.

But then I took in the surrounding neighborhood and I didn't recognize where we were. Nothing except the house we were sitting in front of was familiar. I wasn't even sure what street we were on.

"Ohmigod," I said, gripping the steering wheel tightly as my heart started to race. I felt the oncoming panic attack take hold and knew I'd be powerless to stop it. My breathing was labored and my chest felt like it was filling with hot lava. "I...I...don't...how did I...?"

"Hey," Cole said. I felt his hand on my arm. "Lily, are you okay?"

I shook my head. Tears formed in my eyes, and I couldn't catch my breath. The car felt claustrophobic. Like a coffin. I clawed at the door handle. It took several tries, but I finally managed to pull it up and get the door to open.

Stumbling out of the car, I sucked in great lungfuls of air, but no matter how much I tried to take in, it fell far short of what I needed to breathe. I tried to make up for it with the next breath, but that fell even shorter.

I bent over and wobbled unsteadily to the curb. Maybe if I could get down on the ground I could breathe. Firm hands gripped me by the arms to steady me, and guide me over to the grass.

When I sat down, I pulled at the collar on my shirt. This was something entirely different from my other panic attacks—a whole new level of agony and fear. I tugged again at my collar. Why did my clothing feel so restrictive? Why couldn't I get any oxygen into my system when all I was doing was heaving in lungfuls of air? My heart sped up even more and pounded so hard against my chest it hurt. Blood throbbed out the frantic beat of my pulse in my ears, and then I started to see stars in my peripheral vision. I could hear Cole talking to me, but I couldn't make out any of his words, and I avoided looking at him at all costs, because on top of everything else, what was happening to me was so humiliating.

In desperation I reached into my back pocket for my phone and thrust it at him.

"Ma...Ma...Mom!" I gasped. She was a doctor. She'd know what to do. If only she could get to me in time.

And then I sank forward onto the grass, too weak and frightened to do anything more.

Amber

I FOUND SPENCE LYING IN THE GRASS IN THE CENTER of the field adjacent to the track. I nearly cried out when I saw him. His left eye was swollen shut, and he had a fat lip that was still bleeding. Sinking down next to him, I reached out to lace my fingers through his, my heart hammering for him. I hated seeing him like this.

"You okay?" I asked gently.

For a long time he didn't reply. He simply squeezed my hand and lay there, his one good eye staring up at the late afternoon sky and a tear or two leaking down the side of his face every now and again. He made no noise, and I could only imagine what tumbled thoughts he might be having.

I wanted so much to wrap my arms around him, cover him with love, and protect him from any further harm, but in the year and a half that we'd been together, I'd learned to give Spence his space after one of these fights. So I sat there and leaked a few tears of my own until, finally, he cleared his throat and that one good eye focused on me.

"How'd you know?" he asked.

"Your sister called, looking for you."

Spence's gaze moved back to the sky. "And you guessed I'd be here?"

I looked around at the large circle of trampled grass where Spence and I would go sometimes to be alone with each other. This little circle was ours, close enough to the school to get back quickly, but hidden from just about everyone by the field it was centered in.

At the beginning of junior year, we'd been lucky enough to be assigned the same study hall, and it was easy to sneak out here on occasion, twenty minutes before the bell rang when Mrs. Rutledge slipped out for her smoke break. If she knew we also snuck out, she never marked us as absent, and none of the other kids ever told on us.

"I had a feeling," I said, pulling his hand to my stomach. I'd had a bad feeling all day, and then at three, when his sister called, I knew why. This was the first place I'd thought of when I came looking for him.

"Where's your car?" I asked him. Spence lived a good three miles from the school. I'd already checked the parking lot, and there was no sign of his beat-up old Mustang.

"At home. I felt like walking."

After a lengthy pause I said, "What happened this time?"

Spence shook his head. "The usual. He found out I got that D on that chemistry quiz, and he wouldn't let go of it.

He kept telling me it was proof I wasn't cut out for college. No college was gonna give a D student a football scholarship. I mean, God, Amber, it was one quiz!"

"I know," I said, gritting my teeth against the anger I held in my heart for Mr. Spencer. Spence had been working late the night before the pop quiz—which barely counted toward his overall grade. Spence was a decent student. I had no doubt that, with his skills on the football field, he'd get a scholarship somewhere.

"Anyway," Spence continued, "Mom tried to intervene. He raised his fist, I got between them. . . . It got bad. . . ."

I breathed deeply and tried to hold my emotions in check. It was hard. Spence's home life was so unfair because he was such a good guy: he got decent grades and worked weekends and after football practice to bring home a little extra money. He was also kind and protective of his little sister, and he was a rising football star. It infuriated me that his parents could be so completely horrible and abusive to him in the face of all of that.

About three months earlier I'd told my parents what was going on within the Spencer home, how his father drank and became violent and often struck Spence. They'd been far more alarmed than I'd been prepared for, and they'd very nearly gone to the police.

I'd managed to stop them only after telling them that Spence's family was barely getting by, and they couldn't manage without Mr. Spencer's income. I knew that for a fact because that was the reason Spence always gave me when I asked him why his mom didn't throw his dad out. I'd been tempted to call the police once or twice myself, actually, but Spence had always talked me out of it.

This time, however, I didn't know how I could hold back. "Isn't it time?" I asked him.

He exhaled loudly, like he knew exactly what I was about to say next. "Amber," he said gently, "please don't."

"Don't what, Spence?" I said as my temper flared. I couldn't take it anymore. "Don't do anything while your father uses your face like a punching bag? Don't say anything when I know what's happening at home is killing you? When would you like me to say something? At your funeral?"

Spence sat up abruptly and wrapped me in his arms, pulling me to the ground on top of him to hold me there against him. "It looks worse than it is," he said.

I pushed at his chest. "Well, that's fantastic," I snapped. "Because you look like Rocky Balboa at the end of twelve rounds with that Russian."

Spence actually laughed. "I look that good, huh?"

"It's not funny."

He seemed to sober. "You're right. It's not." Sitting up with me still cradled against him, he said, "But there's nothing I can do to make it better."

"You could call the police," I said. He began to shake his head and I reached up and held it still. "Spence, please. He could kill you."

Mr. Spencer was an ox of a man—at least six foot four, and solid. Spence was also big and strong, but his dad had the upper hand on him in both size and weight.

"How would that work, Amber?" he asked me gently. "If my dad went to jail, what would we live on? Mom doesn't work; I only make so much cutting lawns. I mean, how would we survive?"

"We could help you," I offered. I had no idea if my parents would be open to the idea, but I could ask. They loved Spence, so maybe they would be willing to help his family make ends meet.

He laid his forehead against mine and sighed sadly. "There's no way I'd do that to your parents," he said. "And no way my mom would ever take charity. You know how she is."

I did know how Mrs. Spencer was. From the moment I'd met her there'd been tension between us. Secretly, I disliked her only slightly less than I disliked her husband.

"But what if someday he hits your mom?" I said to Spence, knowing how loyal he was to her. "Or your sister?"

"He won't," he told me, and it hurt so much to think that he believed that. He really believed that as long as he was there to take his father's physical abuse, Mr. Spencer wouldn't harm his wife or his daughter.

"But, Spence, what if after you go away to college, he *does* hit your mom or Stacey? What if without you there to take the punishment, he moves on to the next convenient target?"

Spence hugged me tightly again. "I'd have to kill him," he said.

A chill went through me. I knew when Spence was kidding, and when he'd said that, he wasn't.

I started to cry, because the whole situation seemed so

hopeless. "What about talking to Mr. White?" I asked him, desperate to find a better way to deal with what was happening at Spence's house.

"The new school counselor?"

"Yeah. I met with him last week about Britt and—"

"What's up with Britt?" he interrupted.

I shook my head impatiently, annoyed that he was trying to divert me. "She's not eating, and she keeps saying she thinks she's fat. Anyway, the point is Mr. White seemed really nice, and he didn't try to pull Britt out of school or anything dramatic. He just set up a couple of meetings with her, and I swear she's better. I mean, she ate most of her lunch today. And that was just after a couple of meetings with him."

Spence rocked me back and forth in his arms. It was so soothing. "I don't know what meeting with him would do, Amber. I mean, I've been eating all my lunch every day."

I pushed against his chest again, my temper back. "Why are you making fun of this?"

"I'm not, babe, I'm not," he said, holding up his hands in surrender. "It's just . . . this is bigger than a school counselor, okay? I know it. I do. But it's either put up with my dad's bullshit for another year and a half, or send him to jail and we're out on the street."

"But what if it keeps getting worse?" I asked him, pulling back to look at the bruises on his face. Spence told anyone who asked that he'd been learning how to box. During football season no one even mentioned his occasional black eye or bruised jaw, but I could always tell the difference between a mark he got on the football field and one he got at home.

"It won't," he said without conviction.

Again I thought about going home and telling my parents to call the police. What I didn't know was if Spence would ever forgive me for it, which was the *only* thing that was keeping me from making that call.

Then Spence was shifting me off his lap and helping me to my feet. "Come on," he said. "It's getting late. I'll walk you home."

We made our way off the field and began walking toward my house, which was only a mile from the school. Spence held my hand and we were mostly silent, each lost in our own turbulent thoughts. About five minutes later, the quiet of the Sunday afternoon was shattered by the high-pitched squealing of tires and a thunderous noise.

"What the hell?" Spence said.

And then, just above the tree line, we saw the curling rise of black smoke. In the distance, a woman screamed and that was followed by more cries of alarm. Spence took off running, and I ran after him. He was much, much faster than me, and within moments I'd lost sight of him, but I kept going. It was an agonizing two-block run, by the end of which I was completely out of breath, but I finally made it to the street where a crowd had gathered.

A station wagon had plowed into a telephone pole and erupted in flames. I searched the crowd for Spence, but couldn't see him anywhere. The sound of sirens grew loud enough for me to cringe, and I stepped onto the sidewalk as the fire trucks roared past. At last I reached the crowd and called out for Spence, but I couldn't find him. My heart began to race, and I felt so panicked and afraid. I kept my eyes averted from the car and the blackened form inside; it was all too horrible a scene to take in.

"Spence!" I cried as an intuitive fear mounted. *"Spence!"*

And then, someone, I'm not even sure who, took me by the arm and pointed me to the front of the crowd where a small commotion was taking place. I pushed my way forward and found Spence wrestling with two firemen, his hands badly burned and his hair singed.

"Dad!" he screamed, his voice ragged and agonized. *"Daaaaaad!"*

And then it hit me: the barely visible blue tint to the car's back quarter panel with a dent that I'd seen a hundred times before, and which marked it unmistakably as Mr. Spencer's car. I sank to my knees as flames ten feet high fully engulfed the car.

It was the last thing I saw before I blacked out cold.

Lily

"SO," DR. WHITE SAID AS I SAT NERVOUSLY ACROSS from him, "your mom tells me you've been having panic attacks and that you blacked out yesterday while in the middle of one."

"Yeah," I said, thinking that what I'd experienced felt way more intense than a simple dose of panic.

Dr. White twirled his pen along his knuckles. It had a slightly hypnotic effect. "What's been triggering those, do you think?" he asked.

I squirmed in the leather chair, worried that at any moment I'd say something that would make him think I was crazy, because by now, I was convinced that's exactly what I was. Still, meeting Dr. White a few minutes before had been a surprise. He was older than I expected, with hair that matched his last name, but his eyes were youthful and kind, and his manner was easy and relaxed. Maybe this wouldn't be so bad.

"I don't know," I said. So much was overwhelming me lately, and the day before, when I'd driven Cole not to his house, but to his *grandmother's*—with whom he didn't even live—had just blown my mind.

Dr. White smiled at me. "Can I tell you a secret?"

"Uh...sure. I guess."

He pointed to me then back to him. "This works better if you tell me what's going on with you. Otherwise, we'll have to play charades, and, fair warning, I'm awesome at charades."

That broke the ice, and I laughed a little. "Okay, so, like, where do I start?"

"Anywhere you want."

So I did. I told him about my parents' divorce; my breakup with Tanner; how he'd hooked up with my best friend; how we'd moved out here to live with my domineering grandmother, who decided to plan my entire future; about going to a brand-new school for my junior year and how I hadn't made a single friend until yesterday when the hottest guy I'd ever laid eyes on asked me to hang out, and at the end of a short drive with him I'd had a full-on, completely humiliating panic attack and blacked out.

"Whoa," Dr. White said, that pen still sliding up and down and over his knuckles. "That's all kind of intense."

"Tell me about it."

"Okay, so is there anything else that's been happening? Your mom said that you've been having a recurring nightmare. Want to tell me about that?"

I'd purposely left out the dream—and a few of the other really freaky details—because, again, I didn't want to appear too cray-cray on the first visit. But it felt good to talk about all the other stuff, so maybe I could tell him just about the one dream, and leave out the other super-freaky nightmare I'd had during that nap I'd taken before heading to the salon. I figured revealing one glimpse into my clearly disturbed subconscious per session was probably best.

As I told Dr. White every detail of the dream where I was in the field searching for the boy, he stopped twirling his pen and sat forward slightly. He seemed intrigued.

"How long have you had this dream, Lily?"

"Since I can remember."

His brow furrowed. "How old would you say you were the first time you had it?"

"I think I was, like, four."

Dr. White sat back in his chair again and tapped on the armrest. "Really?"

"Yes."

"Huh," he said.

"What?" I asked, afraid I'd just revealed that I was someone who should be sent off to the asylum.

"It's quite unusual for a four-year-old to have such a vivid dream where they are represented as an adult."

"Oh," I said. "Well, the dream has never changed... until two nights ago, actually. It did change a little."

"How so?"

"Well, instead of it starting out in the field, it started out in my high school."

"Really?" he said, his brow lifting. "Where in your high school?"

"In a hallway, but I couldn't find the exit. Every time I

turned a corner I ended up in another section of the school that I didn't know well enough to find my way out, but eventually, I found the exit and, when I ran outside, the field was totally on fire."

"I see," he said, jotting another note. "Have you ever noticed that this dream occurs more often during certain times of the year?"

"I almost always have it in the spring," I said. "Well, except for this time. This is the first time it's come up in the fall, but usually, it's every spring in, like, late April or early May."

Dr. White pursed his lips.

"That's interesting," he said. He slowly made a long note on his pad, and then he inhaled deeply, as if gathering his thoughts. "It's quite remarkable, really. The fact that the dream has been occurring for all of these years, with such consistent regularity, and without significant changes to the events within the heart of it is intriguing. The subconscious speaks through images, and it's most vocal when we're asleep, so dreams are like a visual dialogue of what's going on in our minds. The thing that is absolutely fascinating to me is that you began having the dream when you were four. By all rights, even if your subconscious was capable of creating such a complex dream with so many adult themes at that time, it should have evolved over the years, morphed into something else."

"So what does that mean?" I asked him.

"Well," he said, sitting forward and setting aside his legal pad and pen to clasp his hands in front of him, "normally, I'd recommend seeing you for several sessions to help you work through the most troubling symbols in the dream, and by talking them through, help you figure out what they mean, and make peace with your subconscious, so to speak, which, hopefully, would be how we'd be able to get them to stop. But all I need to do is take one look at you to see that you're exhausted to the point that you're having panic attacks, and otherwise you're having a hard time functioning. I think a more aggressive approach might be in order."

I frowned and shook my head. I was afraid he'd say something like that. "I don't want to take any drugs," I told him. I'd said as much to my mom, too.

He smiled. "I wasn't going to suggest a prescription, Lily. Not unless your mom pushed for it."

That surprised me. "Then what?"

"I'd like to try hypnotherapy."

"Hypnotherapy?" I repeated. "What? Like, you're getting *sleeeeeepy*?"

Dr. White offered me a sideways smile. "Not quite like that, but you're close. It could be very effective in your case, because through hypnotherapy we would be able to speak directly to your subconscious and find out what, exactly, it was trying to tell us."

It sounded creepy. I shifted in my chair, envisioning Dr. White dangling a pocket watch in front of me.

"Your mother would be present, of course," he told me, as if reading my mind.

That helped, but still it sounded weird. "I'm not gonna cluck like a chicken every time a bell rings, will I?" I'd seen a YouTube clip of a Vegas act where a professional hypnotist made some poor guy from the audience do that for nearly ten minutes.

"No," Dr. White said with a smile, but I got the feeling he'd been asked that before. "I promise not to make you do or say anything embarrassing. We're just going to speak directly to your subconscious by bypassing your more dominant conscious mind. That's all hypnosis does—it takes a shortcut around the conscious mind to find out what's truly at play here."

"When would we do it?"

"Given the fact that you're not sleeping and you'd prefer not to take a sleep aid, I'd suggest right now."

"Now?"

"I have time if you do."

"Can my mom really come in?"

Dr. White got up and crossed the room. He opened the door and called to Mom. A minute later he was explaining what was going to happen next. She seemed uncertain.

"Will this really work?" she asked him.

"It might," he said. "At the very least it's worth a try."

Mom looked at me. "You really want to do this?"

"If it'll get rid of the nightmare and let me sleep?" I said. "Let's do it."

She smiled, but she still looked worried. Turning back to Dr. White, she said, "Okay, then."

Dr. White explained how the whole hypnotizing thing would work. I'll admit I was really skeptical. I mean, I wasn't even sure that hypnosis was a real thing.

Dr. White also explained that he would record the session on his laptop so I could have it as a reference should the dream continue to interrupt my sleep.

"We'll attempt to re-create the dream in your hypnotic state, and once we do that we'll alter it so that it'll become something pleasant, rather than a thing that upsets you to the point of waking you up," he said.

"Okay." I rubbed my palms against my jeans. I was anxious to get started, but also nervous.

Dr. White told me to close my eyes and take some deep breaths. Mom sat in a chair behind me, and I felt better for her presence. I listened to Dr. White as he talked me through creating a space in my mind where I was very relaxed. He told me what the room would look like, where to put the furniture, and then he had me take a seat in the room I'd created in my mind. It was an odd experience because the longer I listened to his soothing, calm voice, the easier it was to imagine myself in this room. By the time I'd taken a seat in the imaginary chair, I could practically feel its warmth and comfort. I felt myself closing my eyes and starting to drift. There was a slightly dizzying sensation, and then I was out like a light.

I woke up to someone gently shaking my shoulder.

"Lily?" Dr. White said.

Blinking, I sat up with a start. "Oh!" I exclaimed. "God, I'm sorry! I think I fell asleep!"

Dr. White stood up straight from his bent over position. He looked... concerned. "How do you feel?"

I blinked again. "Uh... fine. Sorry," I apologized again,

rubbing my eyes. "I was just so tired.... I didn't mean to ruin it." I twisted a little in my chair and saw Mom sitting behind me. Her expression made me do a double take. She looked shaken and upset.

"What?" I asked her. "Mom, what's the matter?"

Instead of answering me, she got up, moved her seat next to me, and took up my hand to kiss it and squeeze it tight. Something was off, and my pulse ticked up.

"What happened?" I demanded.

Dr. White took a seat in his chair. "Lily, what do you remember from being hypnotized?"

I frowned. "What do I remember from being hypnotized? I wasn't," I told him. "I mean, I fell asleep, right?"

"What was the last thing you remember?" he pressed.

I sighed, frustrated. Mom squeezed my hand again, and it rattled me that both of them were acting so weird.

"I . . . I remember sitting in that chair you told me to put in the room we built in my mind, and then I laid my head back and closed my eyes like you told me, and then I fell asleep."

Dr. White's gaze shifted to my mom, and I didn't like the pensive expression he wore.

"Lily," he said next, and I thought his speech sounded a little too careful, like he was speaking to someone frightened or crazy, "do you know who Amber Greeley is?"

That took me by surprise. "Amber Greeley?" I said.

For just a moment my mind went blank, and I felt goose pimples line my arms. I knew full well who Amber Greeley was, but why did Dr. White want to know if I knew about her? "She's that girl who killed her boyfriend thirty years ago."

Mom's hand jerked slightly. "How do you know that?"

Before I could answer, Dr. White said, "Lily, is that all you know about Amber?"

My brow furrowed as I looked back and forth between Mom and Dr. White. Something was going on, but they weren't telling me. It was creepy and unnerving.

"Why are you asking me about her?" I demanded.

"I'll tell you," he said. "But first, please answer my question. It's important."

I sighed. "Well, I read an article about the boy she killed, and it mentioned that she was his girlfriend and she'd killed him the night of their senior prom, and then she committed suicide." I didn't tell Dr. White about getting my hair done by Gina, who was Amber's mom, because I still didn't know why he was asking me about her.

He studied me for several seconds before he said, "And that's all you know about her?"

"Uh, yeah," I said, exasperated. "Why?"

Dr. White wiped his brow. I noticed that he'd broken out into a slight sweat, and although he tried to cover it, I swear he, too, looked rattled. "Do you have a birthmark, Lily?"

I turned to Mom again. Her eyes were big round Os, and she stared at Dr. White in a way that seemed to ask him how he knew.

"Yes," I said as she nodded.

"Where?" he asked.

I put my hand over my sternum. My shirt covered the

blemish, but I knew exactly where it was under my fingertips. "Here."

Dr. White nodded. "What scares you the most?" he asked me next.

I was starting to get really impatient with him. What the hell was going on? "What does that have to do with anything?"

"Please. Indulge me, Lily," he said.

I sighed again. I was getting really freaked out. "What scares me?"

"Yes. What're you afraid of?"

I shrugged. "Well, ever since I was a little kid I've been really afraid of knives."

Dr. White sat back in his chair, and his gaze went to Mom. Her eyes welled up, and tears began to spill over down her cheeks as she nodded her head. "When she was little she used to hide them," she said in a choked whisper. "We'd find them under the sofa, outside hidden in the dirt, behind the bookcase. It was the oddest thing, because she didn't like us using them and she couldn't be in the same room with us when we did."

I half smiled at the memory. I'd been a little weird when I was a kid. But then I focused on Mom's expression, and how frightened she seemed. "Please tell me what's going on."

"You fell into a deep hypnotic state, Lily," Dr. White said. "And when you did, you seem to have divorced yourself from being Lily Bennett and you became Amber Greeley."

My mouth fell open. "I *became* Amber Greeley?" I repeated. "What does that even *mean*?"

Dr. White moved to the side of his desk and tapped at the computer to bring up the screen. There was a frozen image of me there, and I remembered that he said he was going to record the hypnosis session.

"I think the only way to tell you what happened is to show you."

Amber

I BLINKED IN THE DIM LIGHT, UTTERLY SHOCKED AT the change to my surroundings. A moment before, I'd been in my bedroom, and now, here I was, sitting in a chair in a foreign room in front of a stranger.

"Do you know where you are?" he asked me.

"No," I said, more than a little frightened. And then I remembered, and my hand flew to my chest. There was a slight burning feeling there where the knife had struck me, but nothing like it'd been a moment before.

"Lily, you're breathing a little too hard. Try to slow it down for me," the man said, his voice even and calm, as if attempting to soothe me.

It took me a moment to realize he was speaking to me and there was something very familiar about his voice. I squinted at him. He looked a great deal like our guidance counselor, Mr. White, but much older.

"Who are you, and where am I?"

"I'm Dr. White," he said patiently. "And this is my office."

"Dr. White?" I repeated. "Are you any relation to Mr. White? The counselor at Chamberlain High?"

Dr. White pulled his head back, as if I'd shocked him. "How do you know about that?"

"About Mr. White?"

"Yes," he said.

"Because he's my counselor at school. I just talked to him, actually."

Dr. White studied me; he seemed somewhat startled. "What did you and Mr. White talk about, Lily?"

I frowned. "My name is Amber," I told him, so confused by all this. "Am I in a hospital?"

I looked down at myself and realized that I was in strange clothes. I was wearing light-mint–colored jeans that were entirely too tight and sitting too low, and the silk blouse I was wearing had an odd neckline. Then I turned my attention to the room I was sitting in, which was nice enough, but there was something off about the style. It seemed a little futuristic for my taste. And then I noticed a woman sitting quietly behind me. She smiled when I took her in. Her appearance startled me, too, but mostly because she wore her hair so flat, almost like something out of the seventies. I had the sudden urge to tell her to go see Momma for a better, more flattering haircut.

"Hello," I said to her.

"Hi, honey," she replied. "Focus on Dr. White, okay?"

I turned back to the doctor only to see that he now looked...stricken. "What?" I asked him.

"What...What did you say your name was?"

"Amber," I reminded him. "Amber Greeley." He sat back in his chair, his eyes wide, but there was something even more unsettling there...disbelief? "That's my name," I insisted. Why didn't he believe me? I looked toward his desk, but all I saw was some futuristic-looking metal plate with a white apple on it, that looked like the Apple logo on my dad's computer, but absent the rainbow of colors. Clipped to the top was a round ball with a black lens in the middle. At first I thought it resembled a camera, but it was entirely too small. "Don't you have my chart or something?"

Dr. White cleared his throat and said, "Yes, I'm sorry. I misspoke. Amber, can you tell me today's date?"

It came to me immediately. "May twenty-seventh."

"And the year?"

"Nineteen eighty-seven."

"And your address?"

"One-seven-one Beverly."

"Tell me about yourself," he said next.

I took a deep breath; where to start? "Well, I'm an only child, and my parents are really cool, except my dad can be a little goofy sometimes. He likes to try and square dance with my mom in public places. It's so embarrassing."

Dr. White sat forward, and put his elbows on the desk. "That would be embarrassing," he said. "What else?"

"Um...I'm a senior," I said, trying to gather my thoughts. For some reason my mind felt a little foggy, as if I'd just woken up and was trying to recall the details of my dream, but couldn't. "I have an amazing boyfriend, and two best friends."

"What're their names?"

"Spence is my boyfriend—well, actually, Ben is his first name and Spencer is his last name, but everyone calls him Spence. And Britta and Sara are my best friends."

Dr. White shook his head ever so slightly. It seemed as if he didn't quite believe me. "What's Britta's last name?" he asked.

I thought it a weird question, but I answered him anyway. "Cummings," I said. "But we usually call her Britt."

"You mentioned a Mr. White from your high school, Amber—"

"Do you know him?" I asked him again.

"I do," he said.

"I knew it," I told him. "You look a lot like him. Is he your son?"

Dr. White nodded. "He's the one who referred you to me," he said. I blinked. I didn't remember Mr. White telling me he was sending me to a doctor. "Mr. White told me that he also worked with one of your friends. Do you remember?"

"Britt," I said. "She's obsessed with thinking she's fat, and she's always on a diet. She's starting to get really skinny again, and Mr. White has been talking to her about it."

Dr. White made a note on the pad of paper on his desk. "Do you remember the last time you spoke with Mr. White?" he asked.

I thought back. "Last week," I said. "It was our final meeting before graduation. He wished me luck, and gave me the letter of recommendation for my summer job he'd promised me."

Dr. White paused in his scribbling to look up at me again

with those wide, disbelieving eyes. "Do you remember the last thing he said to you, Amber?"

I thought back again and laughed at the memory.

"Yeah, he said, 'See you around campus, Miss Jung.' I want to study psychiatry, and Mr. White gave me that nickname because I've been reading up on Carl Jung and I think he was amazing. Mr. White is a Freudian, and he likes to debate me about whose theories are truer. Anyway, he's going back to school for his doctorate next year, so maybe we'll run into each other."

Dr. White set his pen on the tablet and stared at the woman behind me. I turned to look back at her and she appeared puzzled.

"Amber," Dr. White said, calling my attention back to him, "I want to take you forward to today. Do you remember what happened?"

I turned back around. "Today?"

"Yes. Specifically, tonight. Take me through the hours between six and nine P.M. What was going on?"

A rush of memories flooded me, and it was like being doused with a bucket of cold water. "Spence..." I whispered. "Ohmigod...Spence!"

"Amber," Dr. White said sharply. "No matter what you remember, you will feel calm and relaxed. No matter how upsetting the memory, you will breathe deeply and feel no fear. All tension will leave you, and you'll feel like you're floating in a calm, safe place. Okay?"

The icy panic left me, just like that, and I felt calm, centered, and light as air. "Okay," I told him.

"Excellent. Now, tell me what happened between six and nine on May twenty-seventh, nineteen eighty-seven."

"I was in my bedroom, waiting..." I began.

"Waiting for what?"

I blinked sleepily. "Waiting for Momma and Daddy to leave. Waiting for..."

"What?"

I closed my eyes. The sensation of floating weightlessly was very intense. It was making me drowsy. "For the end. For death to find me."

"For death to find you?" he repeated. "Or the other way around?"

The irony brought a tiny smile to my lips. "A little of both. I knew it'd come. But I didn't know how it would happen until I saw the knife." I put my hand over my heart; the wound still burned.

"Did you take it from the kitchen?" he asked me. "Did you use a blade from the knife block?"

"Did...I?" I said, confused. "No. No, not me. Not me. I wasn't brave enough to do it. I didn't know how else to get to Spence, so I set it up so that everything would be taken care of. Otherwise, it all would've come undone."

"Amber, please explain what you mean by that," said Dr. White.

I let out a long breath, that floating feeling was intensifying, and I felt so tired. So sleepy. And yet, I still had enough awareness to be wary of his questions. So many secrets I needed to keep.

"It's not important," I told him.

There was a lengthy pause, and then Dr. White said, "Did you kill yourself, Amber? Did you use the knife to kill yourself? Your parents will want to know: Was it your doing?"

I opened my eyes; his question had jarred me back for a moment. It'd never occurred to me that my parents would think I'd killed myself. "No! Do they think that's what happened?"

"Many people do," Dr. White told me.

That made me angry. "I didn't," I assured him.

"Did you kill your boyfriend?" he asked me next. "Did you kill Ben Spencer, Amber?"

I actually laughed. Was he kidding? "Did I...?" And then I realized he was quite serious. "I could never hurt Spence," I told him. "Never."

"Then what happened, Amber? Tell me, and I'll let everyone else know."

I sank wearily back in the chair. I felt like I was drifting farther and farther away from Dr. White and this room. It was like being sucked backward by an unseen and powerful force. I had to focus very hard simply to talk.

"Let them know it wasn't me," I managed to say. "Tell Momma and Daddy it wasn't me. Tell them that it was very fast. The pain didn't last long."

"Amber, they'll want to know who was responsible," Dr. White said. "Tell me who it was who murdered you so that I can tell them."

I shook my head and sank back into the chair, closing my eyes and drifting further and further away. "I'm so tired," I said. "I'm so tired...."

"Amber," Dr. White called to me, his voice urgent. Insistent. "Do you know who Lily Bennett is?"

A wave of awareness came over me, and a flood of memories formed instantly in my mind. Memories that weren't my own, and yet were. It was as if I'd teleported through time and suddenly remembered that I was someone else entirely. Someone without the memories I had. Someone vulnerable.

"Lily," I whispered. "Lily Bennett."

Of course, that was her name. In that moment I knew I needed to protect Lily. I realized my error then, that I'd left poor Lily vulnerable. She was in danger. Without the knowledge of what'd happened to Spence and me, she was in very real danger. I tried to open my mouth to warn Dr. White, to beg him to talk to Lily and tell her what I knew, but the drifting feeling was too powerful and I couldn't seem to speak.

Distantly, I heard Dr. White call my name again, but it was too late. I was already gone.

Lily

DR. WHITE HIT A KEY ON HIS KEYBOARD AND MY image was gone. He then pivoted his laptop back around and regarded me soberly.

"In nineteen eighty-six I took a job at Chamberlain High School as the school counselor," he began. "It was the height of the Cold War, and many young people were struggling with the idea that a nuclear holocaust was imminent and schools were starting to see that fear manifest in destructive ways. I was brought on as something of an experiment, to be there for kids who were struggling with personal issues or who just wanted to talk, and Amber Greeley was one of my regulars.

"She was a bright and engaging young lady, and she developed an interest in psychology her junior year, so she came to me to ask about the profession and where the best schools were to pursue a career in that field. I knew her well enough to never believe she took her own life, or had a hand in Ben Spencer's murder, and in our last meeting I *did* give her a recommendation letter for her summer job and wish her well at school the following fall. On occasion I also referred to her as Miss Jung. I can't imagine how you'd know exactly what I said to Amber at the end of that last meeting, Lily. I can't believe that anyone but she and I would."

I was stunned mute. "You think I'm possessed by Amber Greeley?" I finally managed to ask.

Dr. White smiled kindly at me. "No, Lily. I believe you *were* Amber Greeley. I believe that you've reincarnated and are now Lily Bennett, but for whatever reason, the soul of Amber Greeley is having a hard time letting go of her past life, and has brought some of that forward to your reality."

"You're serious?" Mom said. She looked as scared and shaken as I was.

"I am," he told us. "Take Lily's dream. The dead boy in the field? The field on fire? Ben Spencer's father was killed in a terrible car crash and burned to death. Amber arrived at the scene shortly after the crash. What she saw traumatized her, and that's when she started coming to me once a week. Fire equated death to her psyche, and when, in Lily's dream, she steps out into the field and sees that it's on fire, she knows that what she'll discover will be something traumatic.

"In addition, Ben Spencer was shot to death in a field behind the high school on May twenty-third, nineteen eighty-seven. Amber died four days later. Her death was ruled a suicide, and no one questioned the coroner's report because she'd been so obviously distraught over losing Ben, and because only her prints were found on the knife. Somewhere in the ensuing days after Amber died, a rumor began to circulate that Amber had killed Ben because he'd wanted to break up with her. Not being able to handle her guilt, Amber took her own life by stabbing herself in the heart with a blade from her kitchen. The rumor stuck, and most people who remember that far back take it as a fact.

"The point, however, is that I believe the dream that Lily has been having from as far back as she can remember is actually a manifestation of Amber's memory of that spring night when she discovered her murdered boyfriend in the field at the school."

I looked down at my lap. My head was full of information I couldn't quite take in. It was overwhelming and disconcerting. I felt like I'd just been told that my entire life was a lie.

Mom seemed to sense how it was affecting me, and she pulled my hand up to her heart protectively. "But how, Dr. White? How is that possible? I mean . . . reincarnation? *Really?*"

He nodded like he understood her skepticism. "I know it's a lot to process, Dr. Bennett, but you witnessed your daughter's hypnosis. All the details that she as Amber gave us, the things that Lily couldn't possibly know or have access to learn. She didn't get a single thing wrong. Not Amber's address, not the names of her best friends, not the details of our final meeting. And I should mention that only the conscious mind is capable of producing a lie. The subconscious is the most honest part of ourselves—it's where all the truth is hidden. It would be impossible for Lily to have created a ruse under hypnosis, and it's not possible, in my opinion, that she faked that, either. She presented all of the telltale signs of being in a hypnotic state."

Mom shifted in her chair, I stared at my lap and concentrated on taking deep breaths. "But how can this reincarnation stuff be real?" she said softly, as if she needed actual, scientific proof.

Dr. White tore off a piece of paper from his pad and began to write on it.

"Reincarnation isn't my area of expertise," he said. "But I do have a colleague at UVA who's spent twenty-five years devoted to proving its existence. Dr. Van Dean is part of a collection of doctors devoted to the study of reincarnation at UVA's Division of Perceptual Studies. I've read a few of his published papers, and both their methods and findings are fascinating.

"From what I've read, the department and Dr. Van Dean devote their research exclusively to young children, and normally Lily would be about ten years too old for him to consider seeing. However, I'm hoping that if I send him the copy of her session under hypnosis—with your permission, of course—he'll agree to evaluate her and talk to the both of you."

Dr. White handed Mom the folded piece of paper and she took it. "He'll be able to help us?" she asked.

Dr. White leaned against his desk and folded his arms. "He will."

"Okay, but what do we do in the meantime?" Mom asked next.

"Go home and try not to let this upset you. I know it's a shock, but Lily isn't alone in her experience. Far from it, according to Dr. Van Dean. If the nightmares persist and she's unable to sleep through the night, call me and I'll write her a prescription for a sleep aid. I'm hopeful that, now that Lily knows the dream's source, it will interrupt her sleep less."

"That's it?" I said. "Just go home and hope that this other doctor will see me?"

Dr. White reached out to put a hand on my shoulder. "Yes, Lily. But try to remember that all the terrible events that happened to Amber happened to *her*. In another life. At another time. In *this* life, you're safe and protected and alive and well."

I stared at him in disbelief. I felt anything *but* safe. I felt totally freaked-out.

Mom got up and, as she was still clinging to my hand, I got up with her. "Thank you, Dr. White," she said.

I knew I should've thanked him, too, but I just didn't have it in me.

Amber

I HOPED THAT I HAD ENOUGH COURAGE IN ME TO face Spence and tell him the news. I hoped even more that he'd find a way to be happy for me, because I was ecstatic. Also nervous and anxious, but most of that was due to the fact that I didn't know how Spence was going to react.

I'd gotten the letter three days before, but it'd taken me this long to get up the nerve to talk to Spence, and as my birthday was a week and a half away, I figured maybe I should tell him the news before he did anything big and romantic for me.

Not that I thought he'd break up with me. At least I hoped he wouldn't. That thought gave me pause as I neared the gym where I knew he and Jamie and a few of the other football players would be racing back and forth doing their sprints to keep in shape for track season in the spring.

The track was currently covered in snow, and track season didn't even start until April, but Spence and his buddies never took time off from their training. Most of them fully intended to play college ball, but only Spence was being actively recruited by scouts. I slid quietly into the gym and made my way over to the bleachers while watching a line of boys race each other across the basketball court to touch the wall, then back again.

"Did you tell him, yet?" I heard from behind me as I took my seat. Turning, I saw Sara making her way down from the top of the bleachers to me.

"No," I said. "I'm afraid he'll get mad."

She sat down next to me and pushed at her curls, which were extra full today. Taking a scrunchie off her wrist, she bound up a section of her hair, causing her bangle bracelets to clink together pleasantly.

"You look cute," I told her, realizing she'd made an extra effort.

She smiled and nudged me with her shoulder. "Thanks, but let's not get off track." Pointing to Spence she said, "What's he gonna do? Tell you not to go?"

I didn't answer her, because I didn't know what Spence would say. The truth was, I didn't know if I truly had the courage to leave him. I couldn't imagine us being apart, but I also couldn't imagine giving up such an amazing opportunity.

"I don't know," I admitted.

"Amber, he's gotta support you," Sara said, leaning in to hug me sideways. "I mean, this is an awesome thing, right?"

"It is."

"Well, then, there you go," she said easily. "And if he

says something stupid, signal me and I'll come over and kick his ass!"

That made me laugh. "You will, huh?"

"Yep," she said confidently. "Just give me a week or two to get an army together."

I laughed again. "You're a good friend," I told her.

"Aww," she said, giving me an extra squeeze. "Takes one to know one."

I patted her arm, and we watched in silence as Jamie and Spence lined up at the start to race each other. They streaked down the wood floor, their arms and legs pumping so fast they looked blurred.

"Whoa," Sara whispered as the pair halted at the padded wall, touched it, then whirled around to run back the other way. As they neared the finish they both strained with effort, leaning forward, neither yielding to the other. They crossed the finish line neck and neck, and I swore Spence edged Jamie out by a toe, but the other guys declared a tie.

The two boys bent double to catch their breath, then Spence reached out a hand and Jamie slapped it good-naturedly. At that moment Spence seemed to notice us and he stood up tall again to walk limply over.

"Hey!" he said, taking a seat and wiping his sweaty brow with his arm.

"Hi, sweetie," I said, surreptitiously motioning to Sara to let us have a moment alone together.

She nodded and leaned in to whisper, "Remember, if he says anything stupid, my army and I will smack some sense into him." I giggled and pushed at her. She laughed, too, and added loudly, "Gee, maybe I'll go *waaaay* over there and listen to some music." Then she put on her Walkman and strolled casually up to the top of the bleachers.

"Did I miss something?" Spence asked.

My palms were sweaty with nerves. "No. I wanted to talk to you in private. I need to tell you something."

Spence cocked a curious eyebrow. "What's up, Bambi?"

Spence's new favorite nickname for me was Ambi-Bambi. I liked it, but not in public. "I got an acceptance letter this week."

"You did?" he said. "Wow, that was fast."

"Yeah. I was surprised, too."

"Actually, I'm not," he said, wrapping an arm around my shoulders for a sideways hug. "With your grades and SAT scores there's no way UVA would pass you up."

I bit my lip. This was the hard part. "Actually," I said. "The acceptance letter was from UCLA."

Spence pulled his head back in surprise. "UCLA? You mean, California's UCLA?"

"Yeah. Their school is one of the best for psychiatric studies."

Spence's eyes pinched at the corners. "I didn't know you'd applied there."

"It was a last-minute thing," I told him. "I sent it in the same time I applied to UVA. I just got the letter. I'm in."

Spence studied me for a minute and then he suddenly broke into a grin. "Congratulations!" he said, and pulled me up to my feet for a real hug.

I was so relieved I started crying.

"Hey." He leaned back to look at me and stroked a tear from my cheek. "Bambi, what's the matter?"

"I don't want to leave you," I confessed. "Spence, I really want to go, but I don't know how I can go to a school on the other side of the country from you."

"Are they still taking applications?" he asked as we both sat down again.

I gazed hopefully at him. "Yes, until the end of this month. You'd have to hurry."

"*Can* I get in?" he asked next, and I knew he was worried that his aptitude test scores wouldn't be high enough.

"You'd probably have to retake your SATs," I said honestly. "But, I was going to try to talk you into applying anyway, so I've already looked into it. There's an SAT exam at the end of the month, and, according to the UCLA admission guidelines, as long as you've taken the test before sending in your application, they'll wait on the test results before they make their final decision. Your grades are good enough, though, Spence. As long as your SATs come up you could totally get in."

"Will you help me study for the exam?"

I put both hands on his chest, never more in love with him. "Yes, I'll help you study, absolutely."

"Well, okay, then," he said. "We'll work on the application this weekend and I'll sign up for the SAT at the end of the month. I'll also talk to Coach and ask him to send out a letter to their coach right away. They've got a bitchin' team, Bambi. I could play for them."

"Oh my God, Spence, you mean it?"

"Shit yeah," he said, cupping my cheeks. "We're in this together, remember? You and me. Forever."

My eyes blurred with fresh tears. "What about your mom and Stacey?"

I knew it was the one thing that could break the spell, but it wouldn't do me any good to give into the fantasy if it never had a chance of happening. The only way that Spence's family had been able to make ends meet was with the addition of Spence's income from all the lawns he mowed. His plan had been to go to UVA and live at home to help his mom cover expenses.

"Mom's been talking about picking up a couple of extra houses now that Spunky can stay home by herself," he said. "And I can always work a job out there and send money back. As long as I can get a football scholarship, we could make it work."

And of course he'd get one. UVA had already offered him a full ride, and a few other schools were also showing interest. UCLA would probably jump at the chance to have someone as good as Spence on their team. So, could it be that easy? I wrapped my arms around him and kissed him over and over. "You're the best boyfriend *ever*!"

He laughed, but then he sobered and cupped my cheek. "We're in this together," he said again. "Don't forget that, okay?"

"Never," I told him. "I'll never forget that, Spence."

Lily

I FORGOT MY COMBINATION. STANDING AT MY locker, I spun the dial around and around but couldn't remember the first digits. Putting my forehead against the cool metal door, I closed my eyes and took a deep calming breath.

"Come on, Lily," I whispered to myself. "Think."

"Not enough coffee this morning?" I heard someone say.

My eyes popped open, and I glanced over my shoulder. Cole stood there looking a little shy, but beautiful all the same.

"Hey," I said, surprised to see him. "I . . . uh . . . the locker . . . the combo . . . it . . . something." My shoulders sagged. I was almost too tired to talk.

He cocked his head as if trying to figure out my secret language. "Wow," he said. "You picked the wrong day to give up caffeine."

"I can't remember the locker combination," I said, pointing to the stupid knob.

"All three numbers or just the first one?"

"Uh…just the first one," I told him, wondering how he knew.

"Maybe I can help," he said. "Answer these questions as fast as you can, ready?"

I stared at him for a beat. "Okay."

"Close your eyes; it works better that way."

I felt a little stupid, but I did as he suggested.

"What's your birthday?"

"October fifteenth."

"What's your phone number?"

"Eight-zero-four-five-five-five-seven-one-three-four."

"How old is your mom?"

"Forty"—I had to think—"three."

"How many cousins do you have?"

"Seven."

"What's eight plus fifteen?"

"Twenty-three."

"What's the first number of your locker combo?"

"Seventeen." My eyes flew open in surprise. "Ohmigod, seventeen! Thank you!"

Cole beamed at me. "I had a feeling that'd work out," he said.

I turned and quickly opened my locker, realizing that at some point I was going to have to face the music and explain to him about the panic attack.

"So, about yesterday," I said.

He leaned against the locker next to me and played with his phone. "You okay?" he asked me.

His question caught me off guard. "Yeah," I said. "Totally."

"I would've sent you a text," he said. "But I didn't have your number."

"Oh, sorry. I . . . it's . . ." And then my phone pinged with an incoming text. Momentarily distracted, I took it out and saw that it was from a number I didn't recognize. The text read:

> Hi Lily. It's Cole. Checking on you. You okay?

It dawned on me that Cole had gotten me to say my phone number out loud. "Pretty clever," I said with a grin.

"Works every time," he said. Then he got serious. "So . . . what happened, exactly?"

I hesitated, still more than a little embarrassed about having a panic attack right in front of him. "My parents' split and the move and all the other stuff has been really hard. I started to have panic attacks about a week ago."

"Whoa," he said. "That sucks."

"Sorry I freaked out on you," I told him as my gaze shifted to the floor.

"Hey," he said to get my attention. When I looked up he smiled sweetly at me, as if he totally understood. "Don't sweat it, okay? It's cool."

Relief washed over me. "Thanks," I said. "For everything."

"Sure," he said easily. And then he seemed to want to say something else, but hesitated. I had a feeling I knew what was coming, but I hoped that maybe he'd let it go.

He didn't. "There's just one thing that I don't get, Lily. How did you know where my grandmother lives? And, how did you know that my middle name was Spencer?"

Of course everything that'd happened in Dr. White's office had given me an explanation, but it just seemed so out there, so crazy, so unbelievable to think that Amber Greeley and I were connected through reincarnation. And yet...

"I swear I'm not some weird stalker," I said quickly. Just then the warning bell for first period sounded. "Listen, can we talk later? After school? I promise I'll explain everything."

Cole studied me for a moment, his expression unreadable. "That's cool," he said, but something had shifted. "Meet you here at quarter after one?"

The school district had given us a half day of school at the end of our first week, so we'd get to go home early.

"Yeah, that'll work," I told him.

He offered me a quick nod and headed off. I had no idea what I'd say to explain everything to him. What *could* I say to him that he'd not only believe, but accept?

I'd been thinking and thinking about it ever since leaving Dr. White's office, and considering myself the reincarnated soul of a girl who'd lived and died in Fredericksburg, Virginia, some thirty years ago was almost more than I could process. But, much as I tried to figure out another explanation, I just couldn't. Nothing else could fully explain what'd been happening to me. And if I took it from the standpoint that I was Amber Greeley reincarnated, then almost everything clicked into place. In fact, the more I thought about it, the more I had to admit that it simply *felt* right. I hadn't absolutely accepted it as fact, yet, but I was pretty close.

Still... I didn't know how Cole would react to the theory, and I especially didn't know how he would react to the concept of my being the reincarnated soul of the person who'd supposedly murdered his uncle. I pulled out my phone as I walked to class and thought for the hundredth time about calling Sophie to tell her what'd been going on. I needed an ally, someone to tell me I wasn't totally crazy, someone who'd believe me simply because I said I was telling the truth... but I knew that I couldn't reach out to her. There wasn't enough time to explain it all, and she was probably in class, and I was still so hurt and angry with her. So I was on my own with this until I talked it out with Cole, and *that* was certainly something to sweat about until the end of the day.

A few hours later I hurried to my locker and checked my phone. Mom had sent a text to call her right away.

"Hi," I said, cradling the phone between my shoulder and ear while I shoveled books into my backpack. "What's up?"

"Hi, baby," she said, with a pitch of excitement in her voice. "I got a call from Dr. Van Dean himself about an hour ago. He's seen the recording of your session last night, and spoken with Dr. White, and he said that he's anxious to talk to us. Can you pick me up from the hospital at three thirty and we'll drive into Richmond together?"

My breath caught. "Today?" I said. "He wants to see me today?"

"Yes." There was a pause, then: "I think it's a good idea, lovey. You had the nightmare again last night, and I'm worried about the restorative sleep you're supposed to be getting and aren't. Plus, these panic attacks keep catching you by surprise, and I think with all the added stress of the divorce and the move and the new school, it's just too much, baby. If Dr. Van Dean can help us figure this out, and give you some peace of mind, then I think we should go see him as soon as possible and hear what he has to say."

I leaned wearily against the locker, reminded about the intensity of the dream from the night before. I hadn't told Mom, but the nightmare had morphed into a combination of the boy in the field and someone murdering me in a yellow bedroom, and I had to really wonder if that was the way Amber actually died. It was so horrifying, so painful, so terrifying. Nobody deserved to die like that. Nobody. But I had the strong sense that that's *exactly* what had happened to Amber, and it was so awful that I'd woken up screaming. Mom had held me most of the night to comfort me. She'd also gotten very little sleep herself, and I knew she, too, was already running on empty.

"Okay," I agreed. "I'm in."

We made arrangements about where to meet and then I clicked off with her to go back to shoveling books into my bag. "Hey, Lily," said a familiar voice. I turned.

"Hi, Cole," I said, offering him a smile.

"You hungry?" he asked.

"Yeah, I could eat."

"Cool," he said. "I'm starving. Wanna get lunch?"

I nodded eagerly. I was actually famished. We walked together and Cole said, "Mexican work for ya?"

"It does," I told him.

"Okay if I drive?" he asked, and there was something about the way he said it that suggested he was making light of what happened yesterday.

"It is as long as you didn't lock your keys in the car." I grinned and nudged him with my elbow.

He chuckled and held up his hand to show me the keys in his palm. "I've got both sets on me, just in case."

"Phew," I deadpanned. "That could've been awkward."

Cole took me to a small shack of a place a few miles south of school. It didn't look like much, which was fine, because I was pretty anxious, and if he'd taken me someplace fancy, that would have felt like a date. When we sat down, I simply stared at my food, trying to find the words to explain what was going on with me.

"Hey," Cole said. "I know it doesn't look like much, but I swear it's awesome."

Obviously, he mistook my hesitation for skepticism about the food, so, to set his mind at ease, I bit into the burrito, and couldn't help the small moan that was inspired by the burst of flavors in my mouth. "Ohmigod," I mumbled, and placed a hand in front of my lips as I chewed.

"Right?" he said with a smile.

We both chewed in silence and that moment of awkwardness I'd been dreading seemed to have arrived.

"So, what did you want to tell me?" he asked almost casually.

I set down my burrito. It was time to fess up. I'd come up with a plan during school, and it was super-risky, but I didn't think I could convince him any other way.

"Okay," I began, having rehearsed my speech a number of times in my head. "This is kind of a long story, and you're probably gonna think I'm nuts, but just promise that you'll hear me out before you decide."

Cole furrowed his brow and cocked his head slightly, as if waiting for me to deliver a punch line. *"Okaaaaaaaay..."* he finally said.

I took a deep breath and dove in.

"I started having this recurring nightmare when I was about four years old," I told him. "It was always the same dream, starting out with me wearing a light-blue dress and entering a field that was on fire. There was always this feeling that I needed to reach the middle of the field or something terrible would happen, and I had to dodge the flames as I went. Each time, I tried to get there as fast as I could, but no matter what I did, I was always too late. Every time, once I reach the center of the field I find this boy—he's about our age—and he's dead. He's staring up at the sky lifelessly, and each and every time I discover him, it's like a knife right to my heart. It's the most heartbreaking thing I've ever felt. It destroys me, and I sink down next to him and try to hold him close to me, but I always wake up at that exact moment, and I can't shake the feeling that I've just lost someone I loved more than anyone else in the world.

"Now," I continued, "the really weird thing is that, until yesterday, I had no idea who the boy was."

I snuck a quick glance at Cole and he was looking back

at me, intrigued. "I'm with you," he said with a nod of encouragement.

I took another deep breath. "I used to have the dream only once or sometimes twice a year. It always cropped up right around spring. But then, when we moved here, I started having it every night. Like, *every* night. And I couldn't figure out why. And there've also been small things that I haven't been able to explain. Like, there are parts of Fredericksburg that seem so *familiar* to me, but I swear I've never seen them before. And that goes for some of the people, too."

I bit my lip, staring once again at my lap. Man, it was hard to say this stuff out loud to somebody who I was really beginning to like. I didn't know if my recently broken heart could take it if Cole ended up thinking I was crazy.

"Anyway," I continued, "a few days after we moved here and the nightmare started showing up every night, I also started having panic attacks. Mom thought they were from all the stress of the move and lack of sleep and the divorce and stuff, but when I had that really bad panic attack at your grandmother's house, Mom took me to see a shrink."

My lip quivered with the arrival of unexpected emotion. Even though I knew it was misplaced, there was a part of me that felt a little ashamed at having to go see a psychiatrist to talk about what was going on with me. I cleared my throat.

"So we saw this guy, Dr. White, yesterday. He said he wanted to hypnotize me to see why my subconscious kept creating the nightmare. I thought it was a little weird, but I'm so tired from not being able to sleep that I figured it couldn't hurt. He recorded the session, which I don't remember at all.

It was like I was listening to his voice one second and then I was asleep and he was waking me up again. It felt like I'd just nodded off, and then I jerked awake, but that's not what really happened."

Again my lip began to tremble and my vision blurred with tears. I didn't know if Cole could tell I was close to losing it or not because my gaze was fixed on my lap. I tried to get ahold of myself, but I couldn't seem to push back the wave of emotion enough to risk speaking again. So I sat there for a minute and just focused on breathing in and out.

"Lily?" Cole said gently.

I swallowed hard and said, "Yeah?"

"What really happened?"

I lifted my chin and found Cole leaning toward me, his expression earnest and sincere. Instead of answering him, I lifted my phone out of my backpack along with a set of ear-buds. Dr. White had sent me home with a copy of the video, and I figured the only way to convince Cole that I wasn't flat-out crazy was to have him see it for himself.

"Here," I said, crossing my fingers that I was about to do the right thing by tapping the screen to call up the session. "See for yourself."

Cole cocked his head again curiously, but he didn't hesitate to put in the earbuds and press PLAY.

I waited anxiously as he watched the recording. I kept trying to read his facial expression, to brace myself for that moment that he threw off the earbuds and told me I was nuts. Worse, what if he didn't say anything at all? I could just imagine the terrible scenario where he'd avoid making eye contact with me at school, and what if he told everybody else what I'd confessed to him here? What if everyone ultimately thought I was the crazy new girl?

All of these thoughts swirled round and round in my mind as Cole stayed riveted to the screen. At last he sat back in his chair, and pulled out the earbuds. "Whoa," he said.

I dropped my gaze to my lap again. What did that even mean? "Pretty freaky, huh?" I said, forcing myself to look up at him again. "He thinks I might be Amber... reincarnated."

Cole pushed a hand through his hair. "This is so crazy," he whispered.

I nodded, my gaze returning to my lap. It was crazy. It totally was. It was also overwhelming and scary and, well, *big*. "I think that's why I called you Spence the first time I met you," I confessed. "I think that ever since I moved back to Fredericksburg, Amber has been creeping into my mind. You look a lot like the boy in the field from my dream."

"That's why you drove us to my grandma's house?" he said. "You were going to Spence's?"

I risked looking up again. His question gave me a little hope that maybe he believed me, or that he was at least open to the idea. "I think so," I said. "I mean, I was just driving, I wasn't even thinking at the time. The route felt like something I'd driven before, and it wasn't until you asked me how I'd gotten us there that I realized I'd never actually been to that house in my life.

"And I know I probably shouldn't believe in something like this, Cole, but what other explanation could there be that isn't also just as insane?"

He seemed to study me critically. "I can't think of one," he admitted.

I nodded and looked away again. It all made me feel so weird, so separate, and yet, there was a tiny part of me that accepted the concept and was even relieved to have some kind of an explanation for the dreams and the déjà vu. "Mom and I are going to see an expert in reincarnation today," I told him once I'd gathered the courage to look at him again. Cole's brow furrowed and I rushed to tell him about Dr. Van Dean.

After I was done, Cole wadded up his napkin and turned in his chair to get our waitress's attention. When she came over he asked her for two boxes and the check. A bitter hurt hit me in the solar plexus. He didn't believe me, and he couldn't even stand to finish his meal in my company.

But then Cole fished into his wallet to pull out some bills and said, "Would you be willing to come to my house and look at something?"

"What?" I asked, warily.

Leaning in to whisper he said, "It's something nobody else knows about, but I think you should see it."

I started to get nervous. What was his intention? "I have to meet my mom soon," I said.

Cole handed me one of the boxes the waitress had brought and said, "It won't take long. Please, Lily? I think it's something that could help."

I didn't know what Cole had in mind, but nothing about his manner seemed like he was trying to trick me, so I put the rest of my lunch in the box and followed him out the door.

We didn't talk much on the way to his house. I was mostly consumed with thoughts about what he might be thinking. I wanted to ask him if he thought I was crazy, but I didn't know if I could keep my emotions in check if he said yes.

We arrived at his home about ten minutes later. It was a low ranch, painted dark brown with light tan accents. He parked his Mustang to the far right of the attached garage, and I followed him inside.

Cole led me through the side entrance and into the kitchen, which was bright white with black granite countertops and chrome fixtures. It was pleasant and clean. A soft *wuff* greeted us as we came into the kitchen, and after setting my leftovers on the counter, I heard the click of dog's paws against wood floors. Into the kitchen trotted a gorgeous golden retriever.

Dropping to one knee as the pup approached, I put a hand on her head and said, "Hey, Bailey!"

In another one of those jarring déjà vu moments, I realized Cole had never told me he had a dog, or her name.

Looking up, I took in his shocked expression. "How did you...?" he asked, pointing to the dog.

I shook my head. "I don't know," I told him. "I swear. I don't know."

Amber

"CAN YOU GUESS WHERE YOU ARE?" SPENCE ASKED. I laughed nervously as he led me, blindfolded, through a narrow corridor where I bumped into a wall to my right. "No clue," I said.

"Oh, come on, Ambi, you gotta have some idea."

"I swear, Spence, I don't have any idea!" Our surroundings felt familiar, but I was a little dizzy from the car ride where he'd insisted I wear the blindfold.

The narrow space felt like it opened up suddenly and then Spence was guiding me to sit down. I did, and knew he'd just deposited me on a couch. And then I got a whiff of something like Pine-Sol, and felt the rough scratch of the fabric beneath my fingertips, and heard a suppressed giggle somewhere off to my left, and I knew exactly where I was. "I'm at your house?"

Spence eased the blindfold away from my eyes and I had

to blink a few times to get them to focus, but finally I saw that I was, in fact, in his living room and staring at me were about twenty people wearing party hats.

"Surprise!" they all yelled.

I let out a small squeal. "You guys! I had no idea!"

That was a lie, but Spence had worked so hard to put together a surprise party for me that I didn't want to let on that I knew. Britta grinned knowingly at me, because she'd been the one to tell me, but only after I'd grilled her about it.

Spence's little sister stepped forward from the crowd and handed me a small wrapped package. "Aw, Stacey! What'd you get me?"

Stacey smiled wickedly and twitched with excitement. "Open it!"

I offered it out to her. "Help me with the paper?"

She eagerly came to sit next to me and pulled at the bright yellow wrapping paper. I took out the present and studied it curiously. It was a pink rhinestone collar.

"Oh!" I said, careful to keep the confusion from my expression. "This is awesome, Stacey! Thank you!" I wrapped the collar around my wrist. "I love it," I said to her, and she burst into a fit of giggles.

Next I was handed a present from Britta and Sara. "Here!" they said in unison. "It's not much, but we think you'll *really* like how it'll come in handy," Britta added, with a conspiratorial wink at Sara. Sara pressed her lips together, as if trying to hold in a secret, and nodded with vigor.

Eyeing them curiously, I tugged open the wrapping paper

and discovered a leash that matched the pink in the collar that Stacey had given me. For a long minute, I was really confused. I mean, I could make the dog collar into a nice bracelet, but what was I supposed to do with a leash?

"Uh..." I said. "Thanks, you guys. I love it!"

Everyone in the room laughed, and next to me Stacey laughed the hardest. I had a feeling they were laughing at me, but for the life of me I couldn't understand what I'd done that was so funny. "What?" I asked Spence.

Instead of answering me, he nudged Jamie, who was standing next to him.

"Here," Jamie said, handing me yet another present.

"Did you wrap this yourself?" I teased. The package had more tape than it had wrapping paper.

"That obvious?" he said.

"No," I mocked as I struggled to get the thing open. At last I got my thumbnail under a corner and pulled it open to discover a doggie dish. Holding up the dish I said, "Okay, you guys, what gives?"

The crowd of people standing in front of me parted. Spence came up through the middle and in his arms was the most adorable blond puppy I'd ever seen! I was so surprised that I dropped the doggie dish, jumped to my feet, and squealed.

"Ohmigod! Ohmigod!" I cried. The puppy in Spence's arms began to wriggle, excited by my squeals, and then Spence laid her carefully in my arms and said, "Happy birthday, Amber."

For the next several minutes all I could do was cuddle and hug the squirming pup as she covered my face in kisses. Until that moment I hadn't realized how much I missed Jasper, my beloved cocker spaniel who'd passed away just six months earlier. The little bundle in my arms was clearly a golden retriever, and I'd always wanted one of those.

"How did you know?" I finally managed to ask Spence, my voice cracking with emotion. I'd wanted another dog so badly, but I'd felt guilty for wanting a new pup so soon, and I didn't think my parents would let me get a dog this close to my going away to college.

"I know how much you loved Jasper," Spence told me, stroking the pup's head. "So I asked your parents if it was okay, and they said yes right away. I think they really miss having a dog around, too."

I hugged the puppy tightly to me and felt a well of love for Spence that was so intense it almost hurt. "What're we going to do with her when we go to UCLA?" I asked him.

Spence chuckled. "Both our moms said they'd take care of her when we're out there," he said.

"Please let her stay with us, Amber?" Stacey pleaded.

I looked at Spence's little sister and my heart melted, but I also knew that a puppy was probably more responsibility than an eleven-year-old girl could handle, and I didn't think Mrs. Spencer would be much help. She probably wouldn't do more than throw some cheap kibble in a bowl and only occasionally let the poor pup out in the backyard. My parents, on the other hand, would take excellent care of her, of that I was sure. "You can come visit her at my parents' house anytime you'd like, Stacey."

Spence's little sister pouted a little, but then she nodded and said, "Okay."

The afternoon moved on and everyone wanted a turn holding my new pup. It was the most amazing birthday I'd ever had, and I couldn't stop thanking Spence. At some point I wandered into the kitchen to get the puppy some water and found Spence's mother putting the finishing touches on my birthday cake. Mrs. Spencer was not an attractive woman. Tall and imposing, she had broad shoulders, a thick neck, and shoulder-length, greasy, gray hair. She typically dressed in polyester pants and an oversize shirt, and today was no different.

"Oh, hi, Mrs. Spencer!" I said when I saw her. I realized I hadn't even spoken to her since I'd been brought there blindfolded. "That cake looks amazing."

"It came from a box. It's not rocket science," she said, her tone clipped and curt like always.

Mrs. Spencer made it so hard to like her. She was often short with people, and she complained far more than she complimented.

"I don't like yellow cake, but I had a coupon," she went on. "I wanted the Duncan Hines, but the stupid coupon was only good for Betty Crocker, which is tasteless unless you load on more icing, and that's how they get you. You gotta pay for *two* packages of icing. It's all a big racket."

I forced a smile and pretended to agree with her by nodding.

"What're you naming the puppy?" she said next.

The fact that she seemed to have taken a shine to my new dog was pretty surprising.

"I think I'm going to call her Bailey," I said, snuggling the pooch to my face to get a few more kisses.

Mrs. Spencer set down the knife she'd been spreading the icing with and held out her arms for the dog. I hesitated just a moment before reluctantly handing her over.

"I've been calling her Patty," she said to me, as if to correct me. "Spence brought her home three nights ago from the breeder, and we've been taking care of her."

I forced myself to smile. "Patty's a very cute name," I said carefully. "But I really like Bailey."

Mrs. Spencer frowned and abruptly changed the subject. "I don't know where he got the money for her," she said, making a motion with her chin toward the living room where Spence and Jamie appeared to be in a deep discussion about something.

Moving to the sink, I put the dog bowl under the faucet and filled it with cool water. Mrs. Spencer was always talking about money. How little she had. How much everybody else had.

"It was incredibly sweet of him," I said.

"I've volunteered to look after her while you two are off at college, but if Patty stays with us you'll have to send money here for food and vet bills," Mrs. Spencer said.

I stiffened. It was suddenly very clear to me why she'd volunteered to look after my puppy when Spence and I went off to school. She wanted the money and she wanted to get Bailey used to being called Patty. "I think Momma and Daddy will take care of her," I said firmly.

"You'll break Stacey's heart," Mrs. Spencer sniffed.

"I've already let Stacey know that she can come over any time to visit Bailey," I said, putting a little emphasis on the pup's name.

I then held out my arms expectantly. I wanted nothing more than to take Bailey away from mean old Mrs. Spencer.

Instead of handing me the dog, however, Spence's mom narrowed her eyes at me, then bent down and placed the puppy on the linoleum. Bailey promptly ran back into the living room without getting a chance to take some water.

I very nearly snapped at the bitter woman, but managed to hold my tongue and wave at the cake. "I've always liked yellow cake. I've even liked it without frosting." With that, I turned away from Mrs. Spencer and hurried off to get my puppy, but she had already disappeared from sight.

The Spencers' small living room was packed with people; it seemed that more of our friends had arrived in just the last few minutes, and I couldn't spot Bailey anywhere. I moved through the room, saying hi to everyone who'd just arrived and surreptitiously looking for Bailey, but I couldn't find her. And then I had a very worrying thought. If the front door had been open, maybe Bailey had gotten out.

Rushing to the door, I saw that it was open a little and through the crack I could see Spence and Jamie just outside on the front porch. As I watched, Jamie stepped close to Spence and handed him something that looked like a folded-up piece of paper.

"Don't let anybody find that on you, Spence. Not even Amber," he said.

My breath caught. What could they be talking about? I was about to pull open the door, when behind me there came a startled cry, and the room went quiet except for the voice of Pam Ritter, captain of the cheer squad. I turned to see Pam in the middle of the room and Bailey backing away from her.

"She just nipped me!" Pam cried. "Your stupid dog just bit my finger!"

Lily

"SHE WON'T BITE," COLE ASSURED ME AS I STIFFENED and stood up straight.

"Oh!" I said. "I know. I wasn't worried about that. I mean, goldens are so gentle. Once they get out of the teething phase, they won't hurt a fly."

"You've had one?" he asked.

"No. But I spent the summer at a horse sanctuary that also rescued dogs and cats. One of the dogs was saved from a puppy mill, and her pups were little terrors, biting anything that moved, but by the end of the summer all their teeth had come in and they turned into the gentlest, most loving dogs.

"Anyway, I spent a lot of time learning from one of the animal trainers there and she taught me how to work with the mama golden, who was super-sweet but had to be taught how to walk on a leash, sit, come, fetch, and all the things that most dogs are taught while they're still puppies."

"You worked with abused dogs?" Cole asked, his head slightly cocked. "Wasn't that hard?"

I shrugged. "Yeah, at times. I mean, seeing a new animal who'd been really abused come to the shelter was the worst. It was sad and it'd make me really angry, but then Rachel—that's the trainer—would work with them and within a week that scared, pathetic animal would have a whole new personality. Animals are so forgiving; it's really amazing."

"Sounds like it," Cole agreed. I could tell he wasn't just saying that.

"I want to study veterinary medicine with a specialty in behavioral science," I said. And then I realized I'd just blurted it out, and I blushed.

Cole smiled. "I want to go into the FBI."

That surprised me. "You do?"

He shrugged slightly. "Yeah, I think it'd be cool."

"Me, too," I told him.

There was a bit of an awkward silence that followed and Cole added, "Two years ago I got to go into a program at Quantico called FAIT."

"Fate?" I said. "Like, it was fate?"

He grinned. "No, *F-A-I-T*. Future Agents in Training. You gotta have a good GPA, show leadership skills, and pass some other tests to get in. It's a little like an internship, but they don't call it that. Anyway, it's a four-day–long series of classes that gives you hands-on experience learning about the FBI's mission, what the different divisions are, and we even got to work on solving cases."

"*Real* cases?" I asked. "Like, you got to work on solving real FBI cases?"

"Sometimes," he said. "And, yeah, I saw some stuff that would make most people puke, but it's what they deal with, so you gotta suck it up, you know?"

"Whoa," I said. "Impressive."

Another awkward silence followed and then Cole leaned forward to pat his dog and say, "Anyway, I wanted to show you something."

"Right," I said. "What?"

Cole pointed to a bar stool at the kitchen's island. "Take a seat. I'll be right back."

He moved through the kitchen toward the front of the house and I was left to pet Bailey, who was incredibly sweet. I didn't have long to wait; Cole returned with a thick, somewhat beat-up folder. Taking a seat next to me, he placed the folder on the counter, resting his hand on the surface as if he was suddenly hesitating about something.

"This is kind of intense," he said.

"Okay," I told him. I had no idea what was in the folder, but I was pretty damn curious.

Still, Cole didn't move his hand to open up the folder. Instead, he studied me. "I'm serious, Lily. What's in here could be overwhelming."

I felt myself get defensive. "Overwhelming? Cole, I'm not some delicate little flower, you know."

Cole held up his palms in surrender. "Sorry," he said. "I didn't mean it like that. What I meant was...given what I heard on that video, I think I have to show this to you, but it's pretty graphic, and I don't want it to set off another panic attack."

"Oh," I said, realizing he had a point. But what could

be in that folder that would bring on another panic attack? "Whatever it is, I'm braced, okay?"

Cole nervously drummed his fingers on the cover of the folder. "This is a murder file."

My eyes widened. "A *murder* file? Whose?"

"My uncle's."

My jaw dropped. *"How* did you get your hands on your uncle's murder file?"

"One of my landscaping clients is a detective with the Fredericksburg PD. He's a nice guy, and when I started asking him if he knew anything about the Ben Spencer case, he wanted to know why I wanted to know. I told him that Ben was my uncle, and that I was considering joining the FBI, and he said he could get me a copy of the file if I cut him a deal on his lawn—and if I promised never to tell anybody where I got it from."

"So, by showing it to me, you're breaking your pinkie swear, huh?"

Cole didn't smile. "Lily, that video of you under hypnosis really freaked me out. There're things that you said in that shrink's office that nobody but the police know about Amber, and I know that because I've read this file."

All playful humor left me. "What does it say about Amber?" I asked, my voice moving down to a whisper. "I mean, I thought it was Ben Spencer's murder file."

"It is. But the two deaths were definitely connected. The police just didn't know how. The lead detective on my uncle's case was a guy named Nick Paparella. He concludes in his final report that Amber Greeley killed my uncle in a jealous rage and then committed suicide four days later."

I winced as if what Cole had just said physically hurt me. "That's not what happened," I said. "I don't know how I know that, Cole, but I do. Amber didn't kill Spence."

Cole nodded as if he'd already concluded the same thing. "I don't know that anybody but Nick Paparella thought Amber killed Spence, Lily."

"Why do you say that?" I asked.

Cole pointed to the file. "I've been through this thing a dozen times. It's a compilation of crime scene photos and witness testimonies and a timeline of the prom. No one, and I mean *no one* ever remembers any trouble between Amber and Spence. Witness statement after witness statement says that they were crazy about each other. And there's even a photo of them in here dancing together during a slow song. You should see them, Lily. There's no way either of them was unhappy with the other. It's obvious from the picture that they're crazy about each other."

I tapped the file. "Can I?" I said. "See the file?"

Cole took a deep breath. "The reason I'm not sure about showing it to you is because there're also photos of Amber's body in here."

"There are?" I said, pulling my hand back.

"Yeah. Paparella put them in to show that Amber had felt so guilty about killing Spence that she committed suicide, but he also included the coroner's report, which ruled her death suspicious but undetermined."

"Undetermined?" I said. "What does that mean?"

"He couldn't rule suicide either totally in or totally out," Cole said. "The medical examiner stated that stabbing oneself to death was a highly unusual form of suicide, especially for a girl. He did say, though, that Amber could have made the angle of the wound if she was motivated enough. Paparella included a close-up photo of the knife sticking out of Amber's chest and another photo of her hand with the bloody imprint of the knife handle in her palm to make his case for suicide."

I glanced nervously at the file under Cole's palm. I wasn't so curious to see what was in it anymore. "Can you tell me why you wanted to show the file to me?"

"Yeah," he said. "Ever since I was a little kid, my mom has told me how much I act like my uncle. She'd point out stuff that I'd do or say, and tell me that her brother used to do it the exact same way. Then, when I was seven, my mom got me a pet guinea pig. I told her he was my new best friend and I named him Jamie."

I blinked. The name struck a chord with me, but I couldn't quite figure out why.

"My mom said that her brother's best friend had been named Jamie."

"Whoa," I said.

"Right? And then, when Jamie the guinea pig died, I asked my mom for a dog. I think I pestered her for nearly a year before she gave in and said okay, and then I wouldn't let up about what kind of dog I had to get."

My eyes dropped to the floor where Bailey was lying quietly at Cole's feet. "A golden?" I asked.

He nodded. "We went to the breeder and I got to pick her out. The second I held her I told my mom that I was going to call her Bailey."

Cole reached into the folder, withdrew a photo, and put

it on the counter. The photo was of a large blond dog—a golden retriever—lying next to a bed with a yellow comforter, with a trail of blood leaking down it. The angle didn't allow me to see what was on the bed, but it was obvious to me that it'd been taken inside Amber's bedroom.

"This is the dog that Spence gave Amber for her eighteenth birthday. She named her Bailey."

"Whoa," I said, reaching for the print.

I felt such a familiarity with the beautiful dog. It was like an instant connection, and I longed to wrap my arms around her. But of course she'd be long dead by now.

And then I also realized that Cole was speaking of things that were similar to the odd coincidences in my own life. I lifted my gaze to meet his. Could he be trying to say what I thought he was? My eyes settled on the amber bead at his throat. For a moment I was mesmerized by it. My breathing and heart rate ticked up, too.

"My mom is super-cool," Cole said. "I mean, she and my dad split when I was three, and he moved to Toronto where he's from, so she's been both a mom and a dad to me. She's always been there, but she also gives me a lot of freedom to do what I want, within reason, and we get along really good, but she's not like other moms. She's a little bit out there."

"What do you mean?" I asked, still focused on the bead at Cole's throat.

"Well, she's really into metaphysical stuff. I mean, she believes in ghosts and crystals and past lives and psychics and all that."

"Really? She does?" I asked, lifting my gaze.

"Yeah. Anyway, her favorite psychic is this guy she met

about two years ago named Kyle. He's supposedly been really accurate with all his readings for her. Like, he told her she was getting a raise when the clinic where she works froze all salaries due to budget cuts, but three days after she sat down with Kyle, Mom's boss called her into his office and gave her a raise because he said she was his most valuable nurse and he didn't want to lose her.

"And Kyle also told Mom that my dad was getting divorced again, when we thought his marriage to his second wife was solid. He got divorced last May."

"Wow," I said. "He's that specific?"

"He is," Cole said. "But that's not the freakiest part. The freakiest part is that the first time Kyle read for my mom, about two years ago, she had him over for a little psychic party she threw for a few of her friends. Kyle read for everybody at the party, and I tried to stay out of it, you know. It's not my thing."

"Sure," I said, careful to suppress a grin, because clearly, Cole was a bit intrigued by this man Kyle.

"Anyway, at the end of the night I was sitting right here, eating some leftover pizza from the party, when Kyle came out of the back room where he'd been doing the readings and he just, like, started looking at me all weird. My mom was here, too, and she asked him what was up, and Kyle pointed to me and said that I was the reincarnation of a guy who'd been murdered who had a connection to our family. He said it was why I had a future in law enforcement. In a past life, I'd died unjustly, and my reincarnated soul had to work through that karma by getting a badge."

"Whoa," I said in a breathy whisper.

"Yep," Cole agreed. "Anyway, the *really* weird part is that he said all that before I'd even told my mom that I wanted to join the FBI. And then, Kyle pointed to this"—Cole paused to reach up and touch the bead at his neck—"and said it was my lucky charm. He said it had a connection to the past and that it was an important totem. I'd made this *that* morning, Lily, and it wasn't until Kyle mentioned it that I even connected that the bead I'd used was made of *amber*."

I put a hand to my mouth, stunned. "He really said all that?"

Cole nodded. "Mom swears that she never told Kyle anything about my uncle. She never mentioned Ben in her session with him, and she said that I only came up when she asked him how I'd do in school."

"He could've looked you guys up on the Internet," I said, thinking that that's how I'd learned that Cole and Ben Spencer had been related. But then I remembered that the article I'd read was less than a year old. Kyle had said all these things to Cole two years ago.

"Lily, I did a search on us and my uncle the second Kyle left," he said. "There wasn't anything online about Ben's murder. He was killed before the Internet was a big thing, and no one has written or talked publicly about it in thirty years. There was nothing out there to connect us to Ben or Amber's murder, not even our last names."

"Is that why you got the file?" I asked.

Cole smoothed his palm over the folder. "Maybe," he said. "It was like, once Kyle put the idea into my head, I couldn't get it out, you know? I started asking Mom about Ben's murder, but she was only eleven when it happened, and she doesn't remember much. My grandma won't talk about Ben at all. You mention his name and she changes the subject, starts talking about the weather. In her house, his bedroom is a shrine. She hasn't changed a single thing in thirty years. Nobody's allowed in. She keeps the door locked at all times, but I remember, when I was little, being at her house and she'd leave the room. I'd go looking for her and I'd find her in there, sitting on the bed, holding the pillow and just staring out into space and crying quietly.

"Mom says that Gram never got over losing Ben. She told me that he was her favorite, and the day he died something in her died, too."

"That's heartbreaking," I said.

"It is," he agreed. "More than anything I think I want to know who really murdered Uncle Ben for Gram. I mean, I know the police told her Amber did it, but I just don't buy it. Mom doesn't, either, and I don't think Gram thinks she did, either. All these years, that's gotta eat away at you, and I want to give her some peace about it."

We fell silent for a moment and my thoughts tumbled over one another. "So what did you think about the part where Kyle told you that you were reincarnated?" I asked. It'd never occurred to me that Cole and I would share so many weird coincidences.

He shook his head. "It was the one thing I really wanted to shrug off, you know? Like, how crazy does that sound?"

"Pretty crazy," I said. "And I mean that from experience."

"Exactly," he said, pointing at me. "But there are all these things, all these weird little coincidences in my life that we've never been able to explain. And it goes way beyond a guinea pig named Jamie and a dog named Bailey. There're like a hundred other similarities between my Uncle Ben and me that are just too dead-on to be random.

"So when you showed me that video where you actually *became* Amber, I mean...Lily, it's like everything sort of clicked into place."

A wave of relief washed over me. "So, you think it's possible? This whole reincarnation thing?"

"Yeah," he said, as if it was a no-brainer. But then he grew quite serious and he said, "It explains why I haven't been able to get you out of my mind from the moment I met you."

My breath caught and the air between us felt charged with electricity. I hadn't been mistaken. There *was* a connection between us. Something special. Something intense. Something both familiar and brand-new. "Whoa," I whispered.

His hand lifted slowly off the folder and came up to cup my cheek. "I never really believed that I could be Ben," he said. "I mean, I've thought about what Kyle said to me for two years, and it always nagged at me, but I'd kinda dismissed it. I thought it was all new-age crap. But the other day when you called me Spence, you know what the first thing I thought was?"

"What?"

"I thought of what Kyle said. That I was Ben reincarnated. It just popped into my mind. And then you called me Spence again the next day, and I wondered how you could see through me to him. It didn't freak me out; it just felt...right."

My breathing had quickened as the energy between us

grew more intense, more charged, more electric. He leaned toward me, still cupping my cheek. My eyes closed, and then, there it was: the featherweight caress of his lips against my own. Up close he smelled of lightly scented soap and fresh-cut grass. My fingers sought his shirt, and through the fabric I found the ripple of taut muscles and the heat of his skin. Splaying my hands against his chest, I felt the thunder of his heartbeat, which sent my own into a faster rhythm.

Cole's lips settled more firmly against mine, and the sharp stubble of his chin prickled my skin. But mostly there was the kiss; I'd never felt lips so alternatively soft yet hungry, so gentle yet commanding, so sweet yet wanting. It made me tremble.

His hand moved to my hair, and he wound his fingers through my locks as his other arm reached around me to pull me off the bar stool and close against him. The intensity of our kiss began to mount as his lips parted mine, and I sank into that extraordinary moment of passion, wanting it to go on and on and never end.

Just when I was about to lose myself, my iPhone rang, and Cole and I sprang apart as if someone had just walked in on us. I fumbled to answer the phone. "Hello?!"

"Lily?" Mom replied, her voice concerned. "Are you okay?"

"Yes. What's up?"

"You sound out of breath. Are you having another panic attack?"

I forced a laugh. "No, really, Mom. Everything's cool. . . . I was . . . I was just running up some stairs."

"Where are you?"

"Uh…" I didn't think Mom would like to hear that I was at Cole's house unchaperoned. Mom was really cool, but she had her limits. "At the library."

"On a Friday afternoon after a half day of school?" she asked. Mom's got a pretty good lie detector.

"Yeah, but I'm leaving now," I said. Glancing up at the clock on the stove, I remembered I had to pick her up before we headed into Richmond to see Dr. Van Dean.

"Okay," she said, but I could tell she was still concerned. "Drive safe, sweetie, and don't speed or text while you're driving."

"I won't," I told her, smiling at Cole, who was looking curiously at me. And then I thought of something and I added, "Mom, wait. Can you hold on a sec?"

"Of course," she said.

Holding the phone to my chest, I said to Cole, "What're you doing this afternoon?"

"Not sure. Why? You leaving me already?"

I ignored that obviously flirtatious question and said, "My mom and I are driving to Richmond to meet this doctor who's an expert on reincarnation. He saw the video of me under hypnosis and he wants to talk to me about the dreams I've been having. I was wondering if you wanted to come, too."

Cole's brow shot up. "Hell yeah."

"Really?" I was surprised that he seemed so excited by the idea.

"Lily," he said to me, "meeting you and talking about this stuff is the coolest thing that's ever happened to me. I mean, I know it's freaky, but you gotta admit: if it's actually real, it's pretty awesome."

I felt a tension I hadn't been aware I'd been carrying leave my shoulders. Until Cole had said that, I'd been so anxious and scared about what was going on with me. The fact that he thought it was interesting and cool made me feel so much better about what most people thought was pure make-believe.

"Mom?" I said, putting the phone back to my ear. "I'll be there in fifteen minutes. And, just so you know, I'm bringing a friend. . . ."

Amber

"ARE YOU WAITING FOR A FRIEND?" I HEARD A VOICE SAY.

I stood away from the locker I'd been leaning against while I flipped through *Seventeen* magazine, and smiled at Mrs. Wishborne, one of the school secretaries who must've come in on a Saturday to get some extra work done.

"My boyfriend," I said, motioning to the closed door of the classroom.

She looked to the door and nodded, then carried on down the hall.

Spence was inside taking his SATs. This would be his third attempt at the test. Jamie's, too. Both of them had taken the test once last year, then again early this year, and neither had done very well. Spence had a hard time with tests in general, especially multiple choice. He was a decent enough student overall, but when it came to big exams like finals, the ACTs, and SATs he'd get so anxious that sometimes he'd bomb.

Jamie was an entirely different story. He was a very smart kid who just didn't apply himself. He'd shown up at the SAT in September half-asleep and never finished it.

I'd been working with Spence on the practice tests for the last three weeks, and I'd also offered to help Jamie study, but he'd only shown up at the first session, and I had no doubt he'd bomb on this try, too.

Still, I had high hopes for Spence. He'd been doing well enough on the practice tests for me to keep my fingers crossed about his chances of getting into UCLA. His application had already been sent in, and he'd talked to the coach, who was very interested in Spence joining the team, but even he'd warned him about maintaining his grades and doing well on this last attempt at the SATs. He'd told Spence outright that UCLA didn't make an academic allowance for incoming athletes. Spence would have to get in on his own merits before the coach could offer him a place on the team and, hopefully, some money.

That was another hurdle we were going to have to overcome. The coach had said that most of his scholarship budget had already been assigned to other incoming freshmen, and the best he could offer Spence if he got in was a partial scholarship for tuition only. We'd have to figure out how to get the money for room, board, and books on our own.

There was a scholarship fund from the Bennett foundation, and I'd helped Spence fill out the application, but he still had to interview with Mrs. Bennett and impress her, and I wasn't sure anyone could impress Mrs. Bennett. A good SAT score could only help his cause with her, but I didn't know that she'd be sympathetic to the star of the football team with the B average, no matter how great his financial need.

But we weren't entirely out of options yet. There was hope.

I began to pace the hallway, nervous about so much riding on Spence's performance today, when the door to the classroom opened and out came several students. From the pack, both Jamie and Spence appeared, and one look at their faces told me they thought they'd done well.

"Hey, Ambi," Spence said, stopping in front of me to give me a quick kiss.

"How'd it go?" I asked, trying to keep the anxious tone out of my voice.

"It was good," he said.

"Really?"

He took up my hand and started to lead me down the hallway. "Yeah. Those extra practice tests helped. I got through the whole test this time, at least."

I let out a relieved sigh. "Oh, thank God!" Then I turned to Jamie. "How'd you do?"

"Good," he said.

I eyed him curiously. Jamie was the kind of guy that had everything handed to him in life. He was good-looking enough to be a model, his parents spoiled him rotten, giving him a new car for his birthday, and he mostly floated smugly through school, charming his teachers into granting him better grades than he deserved.

Maybe it was because I was so in love with Spence, but I found Jamie to be lazy, callous, and often arrogant. The only reason he wasn't an A student was because he didn't apply himself. Ever. But I also knew that his parents put tremendous pressure on him to excel, which was why I had a small measure of sympathy for him.

As we walked down the hallway, however, I noticed the wicked smile he wore, and a look passed between him and Spence that sent a warning bell through my mind.

"What?" I asked Jamie.

"Nothing," he replied a little too quickly. "I did good. Spence did good. Everything's good."

I looked from Spence to Jamie, but their expressions had become very neutral all of a sudden. "Something's going on," I said.

Spence wrapped his arm across my shoulders and pulled me close to offer me another kiss. "Nothing's going on, babe," he said. "You guys hungry?"

I stopped in my tracks, pulling away from him. "Tell me," I demanded.

Spence sighed and Jamie rolled his eyes. That irritated me more than I could say.

"Ambi," Spence said, his tone soft and soothing. "There's nothing going on. But my brain is fried and I'm starving, so can we please go for some food before I have to beat up Jamie for that Snickers I know he has in his backpack?"

Jamie laughed and adopted a defensive pose. "Get your own damn bar, Hoss."

Spence made a darting move toward Jamie, who then took off down the hall with Spence giving chase. I scowled after them.

"Juveniles," I muttered, but I couldn't help smiling. And yet, it worried me that Spence had been so dodgy. What was that subtle exchange between him and Jamie? My mind flashed back a few weeks to that scene on the porch when Jamie had handed something to Spence and told him not to tell anyone, even me.

When I'd asked Spence about it, he'd said it was nothing, but then, after I'd pressed him about it, he'd finally admitted that Jamie had taken money out of his savings account to give Spence a small loan to help make ends meet. And I knew that things were very tight at the Spencer household of late. I'd felt so guilty about the fact that he'd spent money he didn't have buying Bailey that I hadn't asked him anything else about it.

But now I was wondering if what Spence had told me was the truth. Something was up between him and Jamie, something secretive and perhaps bad. I wondered if whatever it was that they were hiding was legal. Small tendrils of doubt were starting to fray the fabric of trust that our relationship was built on, and it was keeping me up at night. To my knowledge, Spence had never lied to me. In fact, I'd thought of him as the most honest person I knew. Lately, though, I couldn't shake the feeling that something had changed.

But if Spence wouldn't talk to me, then what were my options? I watched him and Jamie wrestle with each other down the hall. It was all good-natured fun, but it bothered me to see them pretending everything was all right when I knew that it wasn't.

I felt myself getting angry over it, and I made up my mind then and there to get to the bottom of it. Somehow, some way, I'd figure out what was really going on. If only for the sake of my own sanity.

Lily

"YOU MUST BE FEELING LIKE YOU'RE GOING A BIT insane," Dr. Van Dean said to me.

He was a short, nearly bald man with a perpetual smile. His squinty eyes observed me over the rim of his reading glasses.

"A little," I admitted.

"And I'm sure this feels a bit far-fetched to you as well," he added.

"It's just . . ." I said, lost for the best way to describe it.

I looked to Mom and Cole for help, but it was Dr. Van Dean who said, "Weird?"

"Yeah," I said. "Sorry," I added, with an apologetic smile.

"Don't be," Van Dean told me. "I spent much of my twenties and thirties living in India where the concept of reincarnation is taken for granted. A majority of the society believes in it, so I know what it's like to live in a culture that is both accepting of it, and one that is not. Ours is not. At least not yet."

"So you *really* believe in this?" Mom asked him.

Van Dean pointed to the rows of filing cabinets that lined nearly his entire office, which was large, but cluttered.

"In every single drawer are cases and cases and cases of reincarnation that we've actually been able to *verify*, Dr. Bennett. So, you might say that after twenty-five years of extensive investigation, I'm convinced by the overwhelming evidence that suggests it's very real."

"What kind of evidence?" Cole asked. I was a bit surprised he'd spoken. He'd been fairly quiet on the ride over, but maybe that was because my quick explanation to Mom about why Cole was coming along had made the drive a little awkward.

The doctor steepled his fingers. "What kind of evidence? Well, all sorts of things," he said. "We've been able to verify names, dates, manner of death, relationships, family histories, and even a few family secrets that were known only to elder family members.

"Basically, what my colleagues and I do in these cases of suspected reincarnation is conduct extensive interviews with the subject, who's almost never older than ten, and based on those interviews we begin to research through census data, interviews with extended family, court records, obituaries, newspaper clippings, and other resources whether or not the memories the child has of his or her former life match the life of someone who's deceased. The accuracy and detail some of those children convey would make your hair curl."

I turned my head to gaze at all the filing cabinets. There were dozens of them. I began to understand the scope of what Dr. Van Dean was researching.

"How many cases do you think you've got in those cabinets?" Cole asked.

"Close to twenty thousand," he said. "We ran out of room two years ago, and all subsequent cases are being digitally compiled. The files in this room are also being scanned and saved, and in the next year or so I might even be able to clear out some of the cabinets. But the cases never stop coming, and each one is fascinating."

The room fell silent, and Dr. Van Dean seemed to study me for a moment before he said, "Your case is most unusual, Lily."

I stiffened. "It is?"

"Yes," he said. "I don't typically entertain cases where there's been any hypnotherapy. It's too easy for the therapist to plant a suggestion in the mind of the patient and for the patient to then adopt that suggestion as truth. What's exceptional about your case is that, after watching your session with Dr. White several times, I'm convinced that he did not plant anything of Amber Greeley's life into your subconscious. The details you offer up are also quite extraordinary. You named dates, places, people, and events that were all relevant to Amber, but there was no easy way, and in one or two instances, no discernable way, for you to have discovered them.

"I believe, as Dr. White does, that you may, in fact, actually be the reincarnated soul of Amber Greeley, but why you've come back through the bloodline of a total stranger is the question that is quite puzzling to me."

"What do you mean?" I asked.

"Well, in about ninety-five percent of the cases I've studied, the reincarnated soul comes back as a family member.

Sometimes, there isn't a direct line. One soul might come back as his great-grandson's cousin, but there almost always seems to be a consistent link to the family tree. To my understanding, you are not in any way related to Amber Greeley, correct?"

I looked at Mom. She shook her head. "No," she said. "There's no familial connection that I know of."

"But your grandmother lives in Fredericksburg," Dr. Van Dean pressed. "And was there at the time of Amber Greeley's passing?"

"Yes," I said. "And she did know Amber's mom. Mrs. Greeley owns a hair salon and does my grandmother's hair. From what Mrs. Greeley told me, Grandmother was kind to her after Amber died, but I don't know if Amber ever actually met my grandmother."

"Interesting," Dr. Van Dean said, tapping his finger to his lips.

Then he pointed to Cole, whom he'd also interviewed at the start of our session, after I'd told him all the coincidences Cole and I had uncovered.

"You see, your story is consistent with a reincarnated soul coming back as the first available relative. The naming of your pets is a big clue. We often find children will name dolls or pets after people who were important to them in a previous life. Of course, I'd need to do a more thorough interview with you and your relatives to verify that you are the reincarnated soul of Ben Spencer, but it wouldn't surprise me at all. Your story contains all the markers: your uncle died tragically, and young; you named your pets after your uncle's best friend and his ex-girlfriend's dog; you have similar interests—he worked in landscaping; you work in landscaping—you both drove Mustangs and you bought yours without knowledge that it was the same make and model as the one your uncle drove; and perhaps even most telling was that you were drawn to that amber bead, which was the name of your uncle's girlfriend. Odd coincidences to be sure, but maybe not so odd after all.

"Cole, let me ask you," he added, leaning forward. "Do you have a birthmark?"

Next to me, Cole looked taken aback. "Yeah," he said. Tugging on the neck of his T-shirt, he exposed two red dots on his chest.

I gripped the arm of the chair in shock. The texture and color of Cole's birthmark was very similar to my own.

Dr. Van Dean nodded and pointed at Cole. "Your uncle died of two gunshot wounds to the chest, correct?"

"Yeah," Cole said, dumbstruck. He tucked his chin to eye the marks. "I never made that connection before."

"It's a consistent trait with reincarnated souls," he said. "When the death was sudden, about twenty-five percent of the subjects come back with a mark that bears a striking resemblance to a wound they received at the time of their death. One child I interviewed talked openly about his hanging, and at the back of his neck was a large birthmark that looked very much like the coils from a rope. It was extraordinary."

I rubbed at my own birthmark. This was a lot to take in. "And what about my dreams?" I asked him.

"Ah, yes," he said. "It's quite common, Lily, for reincarnated souls to be plagued with nightmares, especially about the moment of their passing. From what you described to me, the dreams are not part of your subconscious creation, but an actual memory from your previous life as Amber, with perhaps a few dreamlike qualities."

I looked over at Mom. Her eyes were wide and she was shaking her head, as though she really couldn't believe this was real.

"They're causing her insomnia, Dr. Van Dean," she said. "And I'm worried about her."

He nodded as if he totally understood. "My guess, Dr. Bennett, is that moving from Richmond to Fredericksburg was a trigger for the part of Lily that still retains some of Amber's memories. I know you're concerned, but we've found that in those cases where the memories of the reincarnated soul are causing disruption in the current life of the soul, that there's a reason for it. A message, shall we say, for the new soul that the old soul wishes to impart."

"Message?" I said. "What kind of message?"

Dr. Van Dean shrugged. "It could be anything, really. Perhaps Amber simply wants you to know that she didn't murder her boyfriend. That seemed to be what she was focused on when she spoke to Dr. White yesterday. And maybe now that she's made that clear to you, your nightmares will subside."

"But they haven't," I said earnestly. "I had one last night, only it was even more intense than the others."

Out of the corner of my eye I saw Mom lean forward and look at me.

Dr. Van Dean sighed and shook his head. "I'm so sorry, Lily. I know it must be quite troubling. In a few of the cases similar to yours—where the previous spirit is still actively involved in the life of the current spirit—what I've found helps is some type of ritual that honors the life of the previous soul. I know that sounds strange, but what might help Amber to let go of you is to perhaps visit her gravesite. Pay her homage. Thank her for her presence, but let her know that you're moving on in this life solely as Lily Bennett."

"That's it?" Mom said. "She visits Amber's grave and that'll be the end of the nightmares?"

"Sound too simplistic?" the doctor asked her.

"A little," Mom said.

Van Dean laughed softly. "Never underestimate the power of ritual, Dr. Bennett. Paying homage to a spirit is a very powerful thing, and it could be the key to freeing Lily of these nightmares."

"But what if that doesn't work?" I said. "What if I go visit Amber's grave, and the nightmares keep happening?"

Dr. Van Dean became serious. "Then I believe that Amber wants more than to simply be acknowledged. If that becomes the case, then it's quite likely she has a stronger message for you, and we'll have to figure out what it is she's trying to say."

"It almost sounds like you're talking about a ghost," Cole said. "I mean, it's like those movies where some evil spirit starts haunting some poor kid and then the body counts rise."

Dr. Van Dean chuckled again. "It's nothing quite so dramatic or violent, Cole, but I see your point. So let me be clear: Amber isn't a ghost. No more than Ben Spencer is a ghost. At best, they're simply vestiges of a previous personality."

Pointing to Cole's chest he said, "Within you, you could

be harboring the memories, hopes, dreams, and desires of Ben Spencer, but something about the process of rebirth has stripped away access to almost all of it—save for a few remnants of seemingly small and trivial things that don't affect you or your life very much. In Lily's case, the vestige of Amber's personality is more committed, more present, and, given the intensity of her nightmares, more urgent. There may be a message there, Lily, which you'll need to unlock from Amber. Treating her as a separate individual, rather than as a part of yourself, might help. Try the ritual first, and see if it brings you some relief. If it doesn't, then we can set up some sessions together and attempt to tease out the message."

"When?" I asked. I had a feeling that the gravesite ritual wasn't going to be enough, and I desperately wanted an end to the nightmares. A few sessions with Dr. Van Dean seemed reasonable, and I welcomed any help I could get.

The doctor, however, grimaced before answering. "Unfortunately, I'm leaving for Nepal tomorrow morning, and I'll be gone for the next two weeks. I'll be back at the end of the month and we can schedule something then."

"Two weeks?" I repeated. How the hell was I going to make it two more weeks if Amber kept giving me nightmares?

"Should we go back to Dr. White and have him try to hypnotize Lily again?" Mom asked.

"Of course you could," Van Dean said. "But I don't recommend it. You see, now that Lily knows and is expecting Amber to show up in a hypnotic state, whatever happens is likely to be tainted by her subconscious."

My brow furrowed. What did that mean?

Van Dean must've read my confusion, because he explained.

"The subconscious is an extremely complex environment, Lily. It's the well of our creativity as humans, and the source of our imagination, but it also provides the highway for our connection to the divine. What we've discovered in researching past lives is that the former souls come in through the subconscious, but sometimes they can pick up a little litter along the way. At times, there's a mix of both the creative and inventive parts of our subconscious, and the more pure communications from previous souls. The more you tap into that highway, the more likely you are to pollute the information coming from the source—in this case, whatever Amber might have to say. And while I believe that your first hypnotic session was relatively litter-free, if you will, any subsequent session would likely be a blend of both your imagination and any attempt that Amber may have to communicate with you."

"This is all so cool," I heard Cole whisper. And while I appreciated that he thought the situation was fascinating, I was the one struggling with nightmares every single night.

I sighed tiredly and glanced at Mom. She looked concerned. "Do you have any other suggestions for my daughter?"

"Yes," he said, leaning forward to rest his hands on the desk. "First, Lily, I want you to know that much of what's happening to you right now with the appearance of Amber may be caused by the stresses you've been facing in your own life. Your parents' divorce, the uncertainty of a new school environment and trying to make friends there, living with your grandmother and all the pressures that come with the Bennett name in a town like Fredericksburg. So, I would advise you to seek counseling solely based on the changes you've been facing of late. I'd like you to go back to see Dr. White, or whomever you're comfortable with, to talk only about the challenges in your life right now. I don't know that you'll want to bring up Amber Greeley to anyone but me or Dr. White, however, because I'm not sure that another therapist would have the pragmatic understanding of how that is affecting you without jumping to other conclusions."

In other words, he didn't want me to mention that I might be the reincarnated soul of Amber Greeley to anyone else who might think I was cuckoo for Cocoa Puffs.

"That also goes for extended family and friends," he added gently.

I nodded. I could just imagine my grandmother's reaction to this, not to mention the freak-out my dad would have if he knew.

"Weekly counseling might ease your anxiety, Lily," Dr. Van Dean said. "And in turn, that might cause Amber to relax as well. As I said, she seems to be most insistent in making herself known right now. True, your move to Fredericksburg could have been the trigger, but I suspect it's also because, at the end of her life, there was a great deal of anxiety and upheaval. She may be reaching out to you because she feels that anxiety mirrored in you."

"Okay," I said. "That makes sense."

"Excellent." Dr. Van Dean rose to his feet, and the rest of

us stood up, too. He surprised me then by taking my hand and saying, "As I suggested, start off by visiting Amber Greeley's grave. Take her some flowers. Show her that you honor her, and perhaps that will be the end of the disruptions she's bringing to your sleep. If not, come back to me in two weeks, and in the meantime, think about seeing a therapist to talk about the challenges currently affecting you."

Turning to Cole, he added, "And as for you, young man, I would very much like to talk to you again, too. Would you consider coming back to discuss your uncle?"

"Sure," Cole said, and I could see that he was excited by the idea.

It so surprised me how cool he was with this whole concept of reincarnation. Tanner would've laughed at the idea, and then he likely would've openly challenged Dr. Van Dean. My ex was like that: always ready to challenge authority and people who had ideas in contrast to his own. It occurred to me that he'd been an arrogant prick and a bully, and I suddenly wondered what the hell I'd been thinking while I'd been dating him. How could I have been heartbroken over an asshole like Tanner?

The drive home was a lot less awkward as my mom decided to try for a normal conversation.

"What does your mom do, Cole?" she asked.

"She's an RN at Robinwoods Clinic."

Mom turned slightly to look back at Cole. "Your mom's not Stacey Drepeau, is she?"

"Yeah," Cole said. "You know her?"

"I not only know her, I worked with her two days ago!

We have to spend a few hours at an off-site facility each week, and Wednesday was my day at the clinic."

"Cool," Cole said.

Mom nodded. "It was a pleasure working with her. I mean, I'm sure I don't have to tell you she's pretty great. A lot of the nurses get impatient with the residents, but not your mom. She's efficient, cool under pressure, and she knows her stuff. You should be proud of her."

In the side mirror I saw Cole push his chest out a little. "Yeah, she's cool," he said.

He and Mom then talked about Fredericksburg and the high school while I sat mostly silent, lost in thought.

"Hey," Mom said as we approached our exit off the highway. "You okay, sweetheart?"

"Yeah," I said. "I was just thinking about what Dr. Van Dean said. You know, about finding Amber's gravesite and taking her flowers."

"It's sweet in a way, don't you think?" she asked me.

I grinned sideways. "Yeah. If it wasn't so creepy. And if I actually knew where she was buried."

"I know where her grave is," Cole said.

I turned to look back at him. "You do?"

"My mom used to go visit her at the cemetery," he said. "She goes to my uncle's gravesite, too, every year on his birthday. Amber's in the same cemetery, and a couple of times she took me with her."

"Your mom visited Amber's grave?" I asked.

"Yeah. They were tight, I guess, and Mom never believed that Amber did it."

I studied Cole for a moment. "Are you gonna tell your mom about all this?"

He blew out a breath. "Haven't decided yet. But I won't if you don't want me to."

I felt a rush of gratitude and something warmer flood into me. Was Cole really as amazing as he seemed to be? "Thanks," I said to him. "Can I think about it?"

"Sure," he said.

"You guys hungry?" Mom asked. "We could stop for dinner before we drop you off, Cole."

"That'd be awesome," he said. "Thanks, Dr. Bennett."

Mom took us to a steakhouse with white tablecloths but an open, casual feel. Over rib-eye steaks and fully loaded baked potatoes we discussed going to Amber's gravesite. I had to admit that I was a little nervous about the idea. What would I say? What could you say to your dead former self to bring peace to her?

"I think some flowers and maybe a little prayer would be all you'd need to do, Lily," Mom suggested.

"I just want to get it over with," I said. "I want the dreams to stop, and I want to get Amber out of my head."

"We could go tonight," Cole suggested, an adventurist's glint in his eye.

Mom smirked. "I'm guessing you like a good horror movie now and then, too, right, Cole?"

He grinned and held up a hand. "Guilty as charged, Dr. Bennett."

"I'm not going to any graveyard at night, even if it means having another nightmare," I said, shuddering at the prospect. When I was seven, a babysitter let me stay up and watch *Paranormal Activity*. I'd been terrified of anything that might go bump in the night ever since.

"Well, if you want to go tomorrow, Lily, I won't be able to go with you," Mom said. "I have to be back at the hospital at midnight tonight for a thirty-six-hour shift."

"I'll go with you," Cole said.

I turned to him hopefully. "You will?"

"Definitely," he said. "You want to go in the morning? I've got a couple of lawns to mow starting at ten. We could go around nine if you want."

I nodded eagerly. "Thanks, Cole. I'll get some flowers from my grandmother's house and meet you at the gate."

"Don't let her catch you stealing her flowers," Mom warned.

"You think I should go to a flower shop?" I asked.

Mom chuckled. "No. Get them from Maureen's garden. Just don't get caught."

Amber

SPENCE WAS TRYING NOT TO GET CAUGHT SNEAKING me into his house after dark. It was just after nine, and his mom and Stacey were no doubt soon on their way home from the movies, but Spence and I wanted to spend some time alone with each other after celebrating the night with friends.

"You're sure she won't see my car down the street?" I whispered as Spence led me through the back door and into the darkened house.

"She'll be coming from the other direction," he said, holding my hand as he led me expertly through the house, weaving his way around the furniture to his bedroom on the first floor. "When she and Spunky come in, I'll come out to say good night, and she'll never know you're here."

I giggled. We were being so wicked, and I loved it. "What if she hears us?" I pressed. I was nervous about his mom barging in and finding us together.

"I'll turn on the TV," he said as we reached the door to his room. Taking me in his arms, he kissed me and I melted against him.

"I'm so proud of you," I said when his lips left mine. "I can't believe this is happening!"

Spence grinned down at me. I'd never seen him so happy. Three weeks earlier, his SAT results had come back, and we'd all been stunned but elated that he'd scored in the ninetieth percentile. Then this morning, he'd gotten a call from the coach at UCLA who said that an official acceptance letter was on its way, but he wanted Spence to know that he was making a spot for him on the football team and awarding him a partial scholarship.

The previous week Spence had also met with Mrs. Bennett, and he'd obviously found a way to charm and impress her, because she'd told him that if he made it into UCLA, she'd give him enough to cover the rest of his tuition as well as room and board. All he'd need was money for books and incidentals, and I knew that Spence had been working extra hard to save up enough to cover that.

"It's really happening," he told me. "We're going to California, Ambi!"

I hugged him fiercely, so relieved and excited. And then I looked up into his beautiful face and without saying a word Spence knew what I wanted next. He took my hand and turned back to the door, opening it to lead me into his bedroom.

The room was dimly lit from the streetlamp outside, but almost immediately we knew something was wrong. "What the hell?!" he said, stopping in his tracks as he looked at the floor. He reached for the light switch and what was wrong became clear.

The room was in shambles: drawers to Spence's dresser, nightstand, and desk had been pulled out and the contents scattered on the floor. His bedcovers had been yanked off, and his mattress lay askew of the box spring. Right next to his bed, a section of the wood floor had been pulled up to reveal a hole.

I took it all in, dully noting that the lone window in the room was wide open, allowing the night's breeze to billow the curtains. But Spence was entirely focused on the hole in the floor. "No!" he yelled. "No, no, no, no, *no!*"

Letting go of my hand, he jumped forward and fell to his knees next to the hole. He reached in, felt around, and lifted out a small strongbox. Flipping open the lid, he stared at the inside in shock. It was empty. He raised both hands to cover his face and rocked back and forth on his knees.

I was still stunned by the scene, but his actions jarred me to my senses and I moved to his side. I realized as I looked down that the section of the floorboards that had been pulled up was actually a small trapdoor that I'd never noticed before. The thief must've stumbled upon it purely by chance when he'd been tossing apart the bed, and I knew by Spence's reaction that the trapdoor must've hidden his most valuable possessions.

I put an arm across his shoulders; he seemed so distraught. "Spence?" I asked. "Honey, what was in there?"

He shook his head. I bit my lip, my own eyes welling. "Spence?" I asked again.

"Everything," he said, his voice catching with emotion. "Everything was in there, Ambi."

I pulled him close and tried to console him, but for a long time, all Spence could do was cry bitter, heartbroken tears.

Lily

I SAT ON THE FLOOR AND WIPED THE TEARS STREAM-
ing down my face. Mom had left for work at eleven P.M., and
I'd fallen asleep the moment my head hit the pillow, only
to be woken up three hours later by that same recurring
nightmare. But this time, as I'd entered the field, I'd spotted Ben Spencer right away, and then I'd felt an arm snake
around me, and the knife had plunged into my chest and
the pain was so real, so terrible that it'd stolen my breath.
I'd woken up gasping, and tumbled out of bed to collapse
on the floor, my hands pressed hard against the birthmark
over my sternum.

At last, the pain subsided and my breathing slowed, but
the tears kept coming. I was so tired. So exhausted. I wanted
the assault on my sleep to stop. "Please, Amber," I whispered
into the dark stillness. "Please, stop it."

Of course there was no reply, and I ended up crawling

back to bed and curling up into a ball. In spite of how nervous I was about falling asleep again, somehow I managed, and, thankfully, I wasn't awakened by the nightmare again.

My alarm went off at seven thirty, and I sighed with relief when I realized I'd gotten at least a few hours' sleep. After getting ready and eating a hurried breakfast, I headed out the front door to make my way over to my grandmother's gardens. Glancing nervously at the house, I chose a section that was partially hidden by a row of hedges and ventured to a small cluster of flowering plants, where I began to carefully snip a few buds. Grandmother had quite an assortment of flowers, and I was drawn to making a mostly white and lavender bouquet.

"What the devil are you doing, child?!" an angry voice snapped.

I straightened immediately, but froze in place after that, totally lost for words.

"Lily!" Grandmother commanded. "Turn around and tell me what you think you're doing."

I obeyed and came face-to-face with my grandmother, still in her silk robe and slippers.

"I...these...I..." I stammered. "I just wanted a few flowers for Mom," I said, thinking up the lie and running with it. "She's been working so hard, and I thought these would help brighten up the kitchen."

My grandmother's lips compressed into a thin line. She studied me distrustfully, but then seemed to accept my answer. "If you wanted flowers from my garden, you should have asked one of the gardeners."

"I know," I said quickly. "I'm sorry, Grandmother. I didn't want to bother anybody, and I just needed a few stems."

"Yes, well, the damage is done now. Go put them in water and join me for breakfast."

"I can't," I said, and then realized that sounded a little too harsh. "I mean, I already ate."

"Then join me while I eat breakfast," she said impatiently.

I hopped from foot to foot. "I'm really sorry, Grandmother, but I'm meeting somebody from my school in, like, ten minutes."

"Meeting someone from your school?" she repeated, as if she couldn't fathom that. "Who?"

"Uh..." My mind blanked. I knew I needed to offer grandmother a girl's name, but for the life of me, the only name that popped into my head was Cole's. Probably because none of the girls at school had bothered to talk to me yet.

"You don't know him," I said, and immediately regretted it.

"Try me," she said.

I sighed, resigned. "His name is Cole."

"Cole who?"

"Cole Drepeau. He's really nice. He helped me on my first day of class when I got lost."

It might've been my imagination, but I swore I saw my grandmother stiffen at the mention of Cole's last name. "You will have nothing to do with Cole Drepeau, Lily," she said. "Do you hear me?"

I blinked. "You know who he is?"

"Of course I know who he is! He's trash. His whole

family is trash, and I will not have my granddaughter associating with the likes of them!"

Her outrage caught me completely off guard. Was she serious? What the hell had Cole or his family ever done to her? I opened my mouth to argue, but at that moment Cecilia, my grandmother's personal maid, hurried up to her and said, "Mrs. Bennett, your son is at the front door!"

I dropped the stems I'd been holding.

"What?" my grandmother said. "What do you mean my son is at the front door?"

"Dr. Bennett, ma'am. He's at the front door." My heart began to pound. Was Dad looking for me? "I know you don't want to see him," Cecilia continued. "But he refuses to leave. He says he won't go until he talks to you."

I stiffened. So he wasn't here for me. He was here for Grandmother. Whom he wasn't speaking to. And why *hadn't* he asked for me? I was his freaking daughter!

Meanwhile, the displeased expression on Grandmother's face had turned into a wicked sneer.

"Show him to the foyer, Cecilia. Make him sit on the bench by the door. He's to come no farther into my house than that bench. Tell him I'll see him after I've freshened up my appearance."

"Would you like me to press a dress for you?" Cecilia asked.

"Heavens no. Bring me two poached eggs and some cinnamon raisin toast. I'll take my breakfast in the salon. Then I'll read the paper. And perhaps then I'll be ready to receive my son."

I couldn't help but smirk and wish I had the power to

keep my father waiting for an audience with me. *Go, Grandmother!* I thought.

For her part, Cecilia looked a bit puzzled, but she bowed slightly to my grandmother and hurried away. The formidable woman then turned to me and said, "You should get back to the guesthouse, Lily. Put those in water and wait for me to send for you. No reason you should have a run-in with your father today."

"What's he doing here, anyway?" I said, still shocked that he'd come to her home.

"Oh, I think I know," she said with a crocodile smile. "I'm recruiting all the women in his life—including that atrocious, greedy little tramp Jenny—to my side. I'm sure he's fit to be tied about the lovely chat she and I had the other day regarding the child she's carrying. That's why he's here, of course. Your father never could stand it when I gained the upper hand. He's come here to demand I back off." She laughed lightly, as if she enjoyed upsetting him. "Ah, well, he'll come around. Eventually. Or when he figures out that she with the most money, wins."

With a final chuckle and a nod, she turned away from me and strolled back toward her mansion.

I was left dumbstruck and wondering what to do. In my back pocket my phone buzzed, and I retrieved it to see that Cole had just sent me a short text.

Hey! It's Cole. U ready?

I glanced toward my grandmother's, then back toward the guesthouse. If I didn't go through with the ritual, I might never sleep again, and all I wanted was a good night's sleep. Just one.

Making up my mind, I tapped out a reply, bent to retrieve the blooms, then rushed toward the walk leading to the drive. Avoiding looking at my dad's car, I ran toward the front gate, and stepped through the pedestrian door. Cole was parked by the side of the road. He smiled and offered me a salute as I walked up to his car. After I got in and buckled up, he said, "You good?"

"Peachy," I told him.

I wasn't, but hell if I was going to stick around and watch my dad and grandmother duke it out. And no way was I going to hang out at the guesthouse and wait to be summoned. I was sure both Mom and I were going to catch grief for it later, but right now I didn't care.

"Let's roll," I told Cole.

We arrived at the cemetery about fifteen minutes later. It wasn't a big place, but there were plenty of headstones. Cole parked about midway into the grounds, along a road that never seemed to straighten out as it wove through the many graves. Once he'd parked, we got out and he motioned me over to the left side of the lane. We then picked our way through the gravesites, careful not to disturb any of the flowers and mementos placed there by loved ones.

Cole stopped in front of a brass grave marker and stood there solemnly. For a moment I thought he'd brought me to Amber's final resting place. When I took in the marker, however, I felt a well of sadness so intense that I sank to my knees. It read simply:

HERE LIES BEN SPENCER

BELOVED SON AND BROTHER

AUGUST 5TH, 1968–MAY 23RD, 1987

"Hey," Cole said, immediately at my side. "Lily, what happened?"

I shook my head and squeezed my eyes closed, trying to push away the wave of grief that'd come out of nowhere. Taking a deep breath, I let it out as slowly as I could and swallowed hard a few times. When I thought I had a grip, I opened my eyes and tried to smile to reassure Cole that I was okay.

"Sorry about that," I said, getting to my feet.

He helped me up. "Was it a panic attack?"

"No, nothing like that." I chanced a glance at the marker again and had to bite my lip to keep myself from crying. "I don't know what it is. I just saw his grave and I felt so sad."

Cole gently squeezed my arm. "It's Amber," he said. "It's gotta be her."

"Oh, wow," I said, realizing he had to be right. "Of course it is. She catches me off guard all the time, and I never think it's coming from her until after I'm really upset."

Cole motioned to his left with his chin. "She's over there."

The sight of her gravestone made me super-nervous. "Wow," I said. It suddenly became very real. "Okay. Let's do this."

Cole walked close to me as we made our way to Amber's grave. When we got there, I was stunned. The gravestone was chipped, cracked, and pitted, and there were big black splotches on the white stone that looked like paint. Clearly, the headstone had been vandalized over the years.

"Who would do this?" I asked, bending down to take a closer look.

"Huh," Cole said. "It looks worse than the last time I saw it."

"Why?" I said, unable to help myself as I reached out to touch the gravestone. I felt another wave of hurt come over me, but not nearly as intense. Then a burning, fierce anger formed in the pit of my stomach, and I wanted to punch the person or persons who'd done this to poor Amber's grave.

"Don't know," Cole said. "But this isn't the original gravestone. I think it's, like, the third one. Maybe the fourth. Her mom keeps replacing it, and some asshole keeps wrecking it. You'd think Mrs. Greeley would buy a brass plaque like my uncle has, but she keeps paying for new white marble headstones."

"That's so sad," I said, thinking of the lovely woman who'd been so kind to me. "Why would someone do this?" I repeated.

Cole shrugged slightly, but I knew the answer, and I suspected he did, too. Someone blamed Amber for Spence's death.

I put the flowers on her grave and tried to think of what to say. "Amber," I whispered. "I'm sorry that life didn't turn out the way you wanted it to. I'm sorry that Ben was killed and that you were blamed for it. I don't blame you. I know you were innocent. And I don't know who killed you, but I'm sorry that it happened."

Next to me, Cole squatted down and lowered his head, as if in respect for my words.

I cleared my throat and struggled with what to say next. "The thing of it is, Amber, I'm really, really tired. Your nightmares aren't letting me get any sleep. And they're freaking me out. I want you to know that I'm grateful to you for showing up in my life, but you need to let me go, Amber. You need to let me live as Lily Bennett. You need to let me sleep through the night. Okay?"

I waited then, in silence, not for an answer, but for the feeling that Amber had left me. That what I'd said had convinced her to move on. But I felt no different than I had before I'd come to her gravesite.

"Did anything happen?" Cole whispered after a long pause.

"I don't know," I told him. "Maybe." The weariness I'd been struggling against came back with a vengeance, and I suddenly felt dizzy with fatigue. "We should go," I said softly.

As I got to my feet, I stumbled and Cole caught me. "Hey," he said. "You sure you're okay?"

I leaned against him. "I'm so tired," I said. Then I thought of my grandmother this morning and the expectation that I'd come to her when summoned. I groaned at the idea of explaining my absence and spending the afternoon with her. I knew I couldn't take it.

"What?" Cole asked me.

"All I want to do is go back to bed, but I can't go home. My grandmother's on the warpath."

Cole grinned. "You can come over to my house and sleep."

I rolled my eyes at him. That was a line if ever I'd heard one.

He laughed. "Not like that," he said. "You can take a nap on the couch. My mom's at work, and I've got a couple of lawns to cut. You can have the house to yourself."

I looked gratefully at him. "You'd really let me do that?"

"Sure," he said. "Besides, it's the only way to test if Amber heard you or not, right? If you get a few hours of sleep without having a nightmare, then coming here to talk to her was the right thing to do."

We began to walk back toward Cole's car. "You have no idea how much I appreciate it," I told him. "Thanks."

Cole left me at his place with a blanket, pillow, and Bailey curled up on a rug next to the couch. He told me to text him if I needed him, gave me a quick tour of the house, and offered full run of anything in the pantry or fridge. Again I was struck by his thoughtful kindness. Tanner had never once been so considerate. I wondered if I shouldn't respond to Sophie's text with a *thank you for helping me dodge a bullet*, because the more I thought about my heartbreak over losing Tanner, the less I actually felt it.

After Cole headed off to cut his lawns, I walked around his house for a bit, not trying to be nosy, but curious about the place he called home.

His mom had amazing taste. The living room was open and cozy, with light-mint-green walls, white overstuffed furniture, and dark wood accents. There were punches of color from bright pink-and-yellow throw pillows, and a bold fuchsia-colored vase on the mantel, but mostly the tones were cool and soothing.

Cole's room, which I only peeked into, was painted a slate blue, with red-and-navy plaid curtains, an azure comforter, and light brown wood accents. His choice of décor didn't surprise me, because it was pretty typical for a guy's room, but the place was neat as a pin, and that did surprise me a little.

It wasn't long after settling on the couch that my lids got heavy and I drifted off to sleep, hopeful that I wouldn't be awakened by any more nightmares.

That hope was short-lived. Cole found me around eleven thirty, bent at the waist, gasping for air. The dream had come again with a vengeance, only this time, there'd been something more. Something that hadn't been in any of the dreams before.

Cole brought me some water as I wiped my cheeks and tried to steady my nerves. I fought back against the first hints of a panic attack and managed to keep it together—but just barely.

"Was it the dream?" he asked, sitting down on an ottoman across from me.

"Yeah," I said.

"Damn," he said. "So, I guess the gravesite thing didn't work, huh?"

I took an unsteady sip of water. "Not so much."

Hanging my head, I tried not to cry, but it was too overwhelming. The nightmare was unrelenting and my nerves were coming undone. How was I going to make it another two weeks to talk to Dr. Van Dean again if I was already this much of a mess?

"What can I do?" Cole asked gently.

I shook my head. "There's nothing more we can do," I said miserably. "She won't let go. For whatever reason, Amber wants to torture me with this dream and she won't let up. This time she combined both nightmares and gave me a whiff of something. . . ."

"A whiff? What whiff?"

"I don't know. There was a smell, like something in the air. I can't remember exactly what it was, but something smelled off."

"Off how?"

I rubbed my tired eyes. In my mind, I tried to recall it, but the room was filled with the scent of fresh-cut grass, and I realized that Cole's clothes were spattered with clippings from the lawns he'd mown.

But then it struck me. The reason that I'd become aware of something off about the scent I'd smelled in the dream. It had been like a scent found only indoors had been outside. I said as much to Cole, and he scratched his head.

"That's weird," he said.

"Right?"

"And you're sure that's new?"

"I'm sure. I don't ever remember smelling anything in the nightmare before."

"Huh," he said, and I could see that he was thinking about the significance.

"I have no idea what it could mean," I said. "It was just

so weird, and it's the last thing I remember before that arm came around my chest and the knife went into my heart."

Cole winced. "God, Lily," he said, looking at me with haunted eyes. "Is it really like that every time?"

"Lately," I said.

He shook his head. "That sucks."

"It does. But what's worse is not knowing why Amber is doing this to me."

Cole was silent for a moment before he said, "Maybe it's like Van Dean said. Maybe she's got a message for you, and you need to figure out what she's trying to say."

I looked up at him. "What could she possibly want to tell me? I mean, we already know she didn't kill Ben. What more is there to say?"

Cole's face became quite serious. "Maybe she wants you to know who did. Maybe she wants you to know who killed both of them."

There was a shift in my mind, something nearly indescribable, almost like a release of pressure when I hadn't even realized there'd been pressure there, and I also suddenly felt less anxious than I had a mere moment before. The relief was incredible.

"Ohmigod," I whispered. "Ohmigod, Cole! That's *exactly* what she's been trying to tell me!"

His eyes widened a little. "It's just a guess, Lily."

I shook my head. "No! It's true! I mean, I don't know how I know it's true, but the second you said that, she . . . pulled back a little. I can't describe it other than . . . It's like the minute you said that, she eased up on the pressure that's been making me feel so anxious."

Cole bit his lip and turned his head toward the hallway leading to his bedroom. I had a feeling I knew what he was going to say next.

"I have my uncle's file," he said. "We could dig around a little."

"You mean, like, you and me investigate the case?"

He nodded.

I laughed. Was he serious? "Cole, shouldn't we leave that to the police? We could go to that detective who gave you the file and tell him that we know Amber didn't murder Ben and get him to reopen the case."

Cole stared down at his feet. "He won't do it, Lily," he said. "I already told him my mom and I didn't think Amber did it, but he said he had enough on his plate without reopening closed cases. I tried to put some pressure on him a few months ago by calling a reporter for the newspaper, and getting him to publish a story about how there were a lot of unanswered questions around my uncle's murder, but nothing happened. It seems like nobody's willing to investigate it."

My limbs tingled with a shot of adrenaline. The idea of looking into Amber's and Ben's deaths was like doing something forbidden: tempting but irrational. And yet, deep down I just *knew* that it was *exactly* what Amber wanted.

"How would we do it?"

A smile quirked the edges of Cole's lips. "We look at the file, at the evidence collected and the interviews the police did, and see if something in there points us in a direction. Then, we go talk to some people who knew Amber and Ben, and see if they have any theories or remember something that maybe isn't in the file."

A foreboding chill went up my spine. "Cole?"

"Yeah?"

"What if we find out who killed them?"

"We go to the police," he said simply. "But, Lily, we probably won't figure it out. We're just gonna look through the file and talk to a few people. See if we can dig up some clues big enough to convince Fredericksburg PD it's worth looking into."

I swallowed hard. "What if we end up talking to the killer?"

Cole blew out a breath and ran a hand through his hair. "We'll talk to everybody in broad daylight," he said. "We stick together, and we don't make any accusations or let on that we might suspect anybody. And if somebody confesses, we get the hell out and get our asses over to the police."

"What if they chase us?"

Cole bounced his eyebrows. "My car's really, really fast."

I looked at him doubtfully. "Is it faster than a bullet? I mean, Cole, what's to stop the killer from trying to shoot us like he did Ben?"

Cole was quiet a long time. "Maybe nothing," he said at last. "But if we never let on that we suspect anybody, then maybe it'll be okay. Like I said, we're just asking a few questions. We're not detectives working the case. But if you don't want to start poking around, it's okay. We can leave it alone."

I shifted in my seat. Part of me wanted nothing to do with Amber and Ben's murder file. But part of me was a little thrilled by the prospect of looking into their deaths and discovering something the police didn't know. I definitely didn't want to end up like Amber and Ben, though.

And yet . . .

What ultimately made up my mind was that, intuitively, I didn't think the nightmares were going to stop until Cole and I managed to get the police to reopen the case. I suspected that the reason Amber was showing up so strongly in my life was because Dr. White had made her aware, in that session with him, that she was the one everyone suspected as having murdered Spence.

Amber wanted her name cleared. I felt it somewhere deep inside me. Truthfully, if the tables had been turned, *I'd* want my name cleared, too.

"Okay," I said.

"You're in?" he asked.

"Yeah. Where do we start?"

Amber

"HEY, DON'T START WITH ME, SPENCE!" I HEARD
Jamie yell from outside. "I came over here to clear the air,
not get into it with you."

"Dammit, Jamie!" Spence replied, just as loudly. "I told
you we were gonna get caught!"

Nervously, I moved to the front window at Spence's
house to peek through the curtains. Jamie had come over
just a few moments before, and Spence hadn't even let him
through the door. Instead he'd put a hand on Jamie's shoulder and barked, "We need to talk." He'd then practically
shoved Jamie out onto the porch, and followed him outside,
shutting the door firmly in his wake.

As I peered through the curtains, I saw Spence standing threateningly close to his best friend while he jammed
him in the chest with a finger. He was as mad as I'd ever
seen him.

"Hey, take it down a notch, dude!" Jamie protested,

knocking Spence's hand away. "Come on, man! I've got as much to lose as you do!"

"Oh, *you've* got as much to lose? You, Jamie? *You?!*"

"Hoss, I didn't say anything. And I didn't go through your shit! If somebody got into your room and messed around with your stuff, it wasn't me!"

"See, I'd believe that, except that you're the only one who knew where to look!" Spence roared.

I wrung my hands together. Even though Spence hadn't told me anything, I knew what'd happened. I'd pieced it together over the past week, and it'd killed me to know what my boyfriend had done—the lies he'd told and the fraud he'd committed. But I hadn't said anything because I was desperate not to leave him behind. Living in this house any longer than he had to would kill him. The responsibility... the pressure... the constant criticism—it was too much for anyone, even someone as strong as Spence.

I knew that if I left him here, we wouldn't survive as a couple. And I knew that the dark places Spence's mind would sometimes go when he was really stressed-out would become his every day. It'd kill him. I was certain of it.

So when he refused to call the police about the break-in at his house, and he hadn't even told his mom that his room—and only his room—had been burglarized, I knew Spence had something to hide. There'd been something in that strongbox that he didn't want anyone, even me, to know he had, and whatever it was had been taken.

In the moments following the discovery of the robbery, after Spence had collected himself, he'd only denied my repeated requests to call the police, and instead he'd hurried through the house looking to see what else had been stolen. But the other rooms were untouched.

When he came back to his bedroom he'd looked stricken, and perhaps even panicked. He'd then begun to go through the mess, and that's when we realized that nothing else in Spence's room had been stolen, either. Not his grandfather's watch. Not the color TV I'd given him for Christmas, or the expensive gold chain I'd given him for his birthday. Nothing but whatever had been in that strongbox.

Around nine thirty that night, after we'd put the room back together, and while I was still trying to convince him to call the police, we'd heard Stacey and Mrs. Spencer come through the back door. Spence had put a finger to his lips and walked me over to the window to help me sneak out. "Please, don't tell *anyone* about this, okay?"

"Spence," I'd said softly. "*What* was in there? What don't you want me to know?"

He'd shaken his head, his lips pressed tight. "Just a few bucks, Amber, nothing else very special."

But I'd known better.

"How much?" I'd asked. If it was money, then we could find a way to replace it.

Spence had shaken his head, and he'd looked away as if ashamed. "Close to two grand," he'd whispered. "Everything I had saved for UCLA."

"Oh my God," I'd said.

Spence had looked back at me then and he'd forced a smile and stroked my hair. "It'll be okay," he'd said. "It's just money. I can always take on more lawns this summer."

I'd looked into his eyes and I'd seen the lie there, and it'd broken my heart. I had no doubt that Spence had managed to put away that much money. He saved every tip he got, and the money from any extra lawn he could fit in on his weekly schedule went straight to his college savings, rather than to the household. But he wasn't telling me what else had been stolen—what had him so anxious and upset.

It'd been an awful ten days since. Spence had been edgy, distracted, and quick to temper. It was as if he knew something terrible was coming, and, sure enough, that very morning he'd been called to the principal's office.

Their meeting had been over an hour long, and Spence had finally confessed to me what it'd been about without admitting any guilt. Someone had sent an anonymous tip to the principal that Spence's high SAT score was bogus. They'd sent the same anonymous tip to UCLA, and the administration there had contacted the principal to tell him that Spence would need to retake the exam that weekend, and earn a similar score, or his admittance and scholarship could be rescinded.

As we were trying to figure out what to do, Jamie had knocked on Spence's door, and now their argument was unfolding out on the front lawn.

"This is all your fault," Spence spat at his best friend. "I never should've let you talk me into it!"

"I never told you to get most of the answers right," Jamie snapped in return. "Christ, Hoss! What were you thinking?"

"Maybe I'm thinking that Yale should get the same anonymous tip that UCLA did!" Spence spat, his hands curling into fists.

Jamie's entire posture changed. He stood up tall, squaring

his shoulders, and leaned in angrily toward Spence. "You tell *anyone*, Spence, and I'll kill you. You hear me? You got yourself caught. And if you're looking for who's really to blame, how come it never occurred to you that it might be your girlfriend, huh? Little Miss Perfect probably made that call herself! You want to know who grabbed your test answers from your little hidey-hole? Ask Amber."

I gasped as much at the accusation as for what happened next. Spence punched Jamie so hard he went flying, and landed on his back in the grass. Stacey came up next to me, her eyes wide with worry.

"What's going on?" she whispered, trying to peer through the curtains herself.

I grabbed her by the shoulders and pulled her away from the window. "Nothing," I said. "Nothing, honey. But I need you to sit right here for a minute while I go outside, okay?"

"But—"

"Stay!" I ordered, then ran to the door and hurried out on the porch. Jamie was in his car, his cheek swollen and red, glaring hard at the both of us as he squealed away from the curb and flipped us the bird.

I rushed over to Spence, who was holding a hand over his left eye. "Oh, God, are you okay?"

Spence shrugged me off as I tried to reach for his arm. "I'm fine," he said.

My own temper flared. "Why?" I demanded. "*Why?*"

He considered me angrily from his one good eye. "He did it," he said simply. "He's the only one that knew about that hiding place. You saw my room, Amber. Nothing else was stolen but my cash."

"Why would Jamie, of all people, be after your money?" I yelled.

Spence glared down the street in the direction that Jamie's car had gone. "I don't know," he admitted. "But he was the only one who knew about the hiding place, and he was the only one who didn't show up to celebrate with us after I got the call from the coach at UCLA."

I shook my head in disbelief. "Didn't I hear him tell you that he couldn't make it because his dad was getting that award and he had to go to the ceremony?"

Spence snorted. "He weaseled out of that before they even served dessert," he said. "Told his parents he had a stomach thing and left the award ceremony early. He was bragging about how gullible they are after class today."

"So, because he doesn't have a convenient alibi *he's* the burglar?"

"What's going on?" I heard Stacey call from behind me. Whirling around, I saw her standing in the doorway looking frightened and upset.

Spence turned slightly away from her so that she couldn't see the mark on his face from where I assumed Jamie had punched him. "Nothing, Spunky," he said. "Go back inside and start in on your homework. I'll be upstairs in a minute to help you."

Stacey hesitated in the doorway, but I nodded encouragingly to her and eventually she did as her brother had asked.

I looked at Spence, who was now carefully touching the swollen area around his eye. A small trickle of blood also leaked from his nostril and he wiped at it, frowning when he saw the red on his fingers.

"What can I do?" I asked him.

Spence's shoulders drooped, and he stared at the ground. "There's nothing you can do, Ambi," he said gently. "What's done is done."

"It's really that bad then, huh?" I couldn't believe that it'd all come to this. Just ten days earlier our lives had been perfect, and now everything was a mess.

I wanted Spence to tell me that everything would be okay, that we'd figure it all out, but he didn't. Instead he said, "I gotta get cleaned up." Then he moved past me into the house and shut the door.

Lily

COLE GOT UP AND SAID, "HANG ON; LET ME GET cleaned up a little."

He went down the hall and I heard a door shut. A moment later I heard the shower turn on. I tried not to imagine him in there, because I really was becoming crazy-attracted to him and shower thoughts would definitely be bad for my concentration. He came back out with slick wet hair, fresh clothes, and the thick file. I tried not to notice how amazing he smelled, or how good he looked with slick, wet hair. Setting the folder down, he said, "You're the only other person besides Detective Hasslett that knows I have this."

"I won't tell anybody," I promised.

"Cool," he said, his hand still hovering over the cover. "Are you really ready to take a look?"

I stared at the folder. I couldn't imagine what awful images it might hold, but then I thought of my nightmare—of Ben lying dead and bloody in the field. How much worse than that could it be?

"I'm ready," I said.

Cole opened the file and began with the first few pages, talking me through them. "The prom was on May twenty-third, nineteen eighty-seven. Ben and Amber went with a group of their friends. Right around ten o'clock, Amber and Spence left the dance. What's weird is that one of the teachers who was chaperoning said he remembered seeing Ben leave around nine thirty, and then he remembered seeing Amber leave about twenty minutes later."

My brow furrowed. "They didn't leave together?"

"No," Cole said. "And that was the last anybody saw of Ben until around ten thirty when a guy walking his dog came across his body."

Cole turned a page and revealed a crime scene photo of Ben, lying in the field almost *exactly* as he'd appeared in my dreams.

It stole my breath.

Cole closed the cover and offered me an apologetic expression. "You okay?"

I sat there, a bit dumbstruck. "Yeah," I said after a moment. "It's just so crazy-eerie. That photo could've been pulled right out of my nightmare."

"Do you want to stop?"

"No," I told him. "I'm okay. You can go on."

Cole opened the file again and I was able to look at the photo a little more distantly. He flipped to another image, this one taken from farther back, and it showed Amber, in a Tiffany-blue dress with bloodstains, being supported by several people. She looked utterly destroyed. The photo had captured her in a moment of anguish, her mouth open, cheeks wet, hair a mess. She sagged between two boys in tuxes, while others were looking on in shock.

I reached out to touch her image. "Poor thing," I whispered. I felt such compassion for her.

Cole nodded. "This is the photo that gets to me," he said. "You take one look at that face, and I don't know how you can think she had anything to do with Ben's death."

We studied the image for another moment in silence and then Cole continued. "The police did about forty interviews between that night and when Amber died," he said, moving on to a stack of papers held together with a paper clip. "Mostly other students. They're all the same. Nobody saw anything, nobody heard anything, nobody remembered anything. Most of the kids from the prom were alerted to what happened by the strobe lights from the fire truck that arrived at the scene. It flashed inside the school gym where the prom was being held and kids went out to see what was going on. Amber was already there. She'd pushed her way through to Ben and had to be pulled off by paramedics."

As Cole spoke, I felt like I was seeing it all just as it unfolded. That awful moment when Amber first realized that Ben was gone, hitting her like a shock wave. The grief was overpowering, and I felt my eyes burn with tears. I blinked them away and cleared my throat quietly, trying to come back to the reality of Cole's house.

Luckily, he didn't notice my reaction.

"Paparella stopped interviewing people when Amber

died. She left a note at the scene. . . ." Cole paused to pull out a piece of paper, which was a copy of a handwritten note in big, curly cursive. There were splotches on it—fingerprints standing out in dark relief. It was obvious that the police had dusted the letter for prints.

He handed it to me, and I studied it. Immediately, I felt goose pimples rise on my arms. Amber's handwriting was very similar to my own; we both wrote in large, loopy letters, but hers—at least on the note—seemed a little messy and uneven. Some of the text looked shaky, as though Amber had struggled with her nerves while she was writing the note, which, given the context, was completely understandable.

I read the letter out loud. "'Dear Momma and Daddy, I'm so sorry for all this. Don't blame Spence. It wasn't his fault. It was me. All me. I just want to be with him. Please take care of Bailey. I'll love you forever. Amber.'"

"Whoa," I said when I'd finished. "Now I see how Paparella believed she'd killed Ben."

"Yeah, and also why he concluded she'd committed suicide even though the ME's report was inconclusive. Paparella confirmed, though, that the suicide note was Amber's handwriting, and the paper only had her prints on it, so he overrode the autopsy report, called the note a suicide confession, and closed the file, pinning Ben's murder on Amber."

I noticed that Cole had surreptitiously shut the folder again. I knew he was hiding Amber's crime scene photo from me.

"How bad is the photo of her body?" I asked, touching the top of the folder.

"Bad," he said.

My mouth went dry. "Don't show me," I whispered.

"Okay," he said, and pushed the closed folder away from us.

I handed him back the paper with Amber's apparent suicide note. Playing devil's advocate, I said, "If Amber didn't kill herself or Ben, then why would she write this note and leave it for her parents to find?"

"I don't know . . . Maybe she somehow knew it was coming?" Cole said.

My eyes widened. "She knew she was going to be murdered?"

"I know, it sounds crazy, but if someone had told us a month ago that we might be reincarnated . . ."

"Okay, good point." I frowned. "But she's clearly taking the blame here. See? She says, 'Don't blame Spence. It wasn't his fault. It was me. All me.'"

"I don't get it, either," Cole said. "But that's part of the reason we need to dig into this. We have to find out what really happened."

"Okay," I said. "So now what?"

"Now we investigate." He stood up with an excited glint in his eye.

"That internship with the FBI really put the bug in you, huh?" I said, getting up, too.

"Hey, don't knock the FAIT, Lily," he said. "It taught me mad skills."

"Okay, Mr. Mad Skills, so where do we start?"

"With Ben and Amber's friends," he said. "Somebody in their inner circle had to know something."

"You know who their friends were?"

"I know where to look," he replied, pointing across the room to a low bookshelf. "Their yearbooks."

I squinted at the shelf and the three large leather-bound books there: one blue, one white, one black. "Those are their yearbooks?" I asked.

"Uh, no. Those are mine. But my gram still has Ben's yearbooks at her house. I looked through them once."

"Was it weird?" I asked, wondering if he'd felt any overwhelming bond to Ben.

"Kinda. He wasn't that different from me. I don't know. I didn't have any déjà vu or anything, but there was this... connection I guess. You know?"

I smiled. "I do."

He smiled, too, and motioned with his chin. "Come on. Grams works on Saturdays, so we can sneak in and out without her knowing, then we can grab something to eat, look over the yearbooks, and decide who to talk to first."

I hesitated to follow him to the door. "We're sneaking in?"

"Yeah. I don't want her to know that I'm taking them."

"Uh... why?"

"My grandma is a little weird about her stuff," he explained. "Especially Ben's stuff. And, honestly, she's a little weird in general. Don't get me wrong—I love her, but she's not like most grandmas who want their grandkids around a lot. She keeps to herself mostly. I think it's because of my uncle. Mom says she's never been the same since Ben died."

"That's so sad," I said, thinking of my mom's mom, who'd died three years ago from cancer. She'd lived in Connecticut and would've given me the world if I'd asked for it. And then I realized I hadn't even thought of my dad's mom. Which reminded me that she'd be expecting me to show up whenever she got around to summoning me. I'd have to give Mom a heads-up. I wasn't going to give up my Saturday afternoon for her any more than I was going to give up my dreams of becoming a veterinarian and behavioral scientist for her.

I followed Cole to his car, and as we pulled out of the drive, I texted Mom. She called my phone almost right away.

"Lily?" she said. "How was it at Amber's gravesite?"

I bit my lip. What to tell her? I decided to fib a little. "It was good, Mom. I think it helped."

"Oh, that's great, honey!" Mom said, her relief shining through her words. "I'm so happy. I want you to take a nap today, all right? You've got quite a bit of sleep to catch up on."

"I really want to," I said, choosing my words carefully, "but Grandmother wants me to spend the afternoon with her. And, Mom, I'm *so* tired. All I want to do is hang out in my room and try to get some sleep."

There was a pause then, "I'll take care of it, sweetheart. You rest. If your grandmother sends for you, don't answer the door. Just stay in bed. I'll be home tomorrow morning, but check in with me between now and then, you hear?"

I sighed with relief. "I will."

"There's lasagna in the fridge," Mom added. "Don't forget to eat, okay, lovey?"

"I won't," I promised.

We clicked off, and I sat back in satisfaction. That'd been easier than I thought.

"Everything cool?" Cole asked.

"Perfect," I said. At that moment my phone pinged, and I lifted it to see an incoming text from Sophie:

> Tanner and I broke up. He's an asshole, and I miss you. I've been crying all morning. You're my best friend, Lily. Please, please forgive me and come home.

I read the text with a hammering heart, and then I promptly burst into tears.

Amber

"OH, BRITT," I SAID, HUGGING MY BEST FRIEND AND rubbing her back as she cried onto my shoulder. "I'm so sorry he broke your heart."

"Why, Amber?" she wailed. "Why?"

Britt and her boyfriend had split up the day before. The timing couldn't have been worse. Spence was at school taking his SATs for a fourth time, and I'd wanted to be there to support him, but Britt had called and she was so upset that I'd been a little worried about her hurting herself. I had spent the night at her house and we'd stayed up until two A.M. talking about what an ass Grady—her ex—was. I'd thought she was past the tears, but the second I'd mentioned going to meet Spence, the waterworks had started all over again.

"Who's going to take me to prom?" she sobbed.

"You'll come with us," I told her.

She shook her head into my shoulder. "I'll look like a loser hanging out alone!"

"No way!" I said. "You won't look like a loser. Momma can do your hair and we'll find you an amazing dress, and we'll show Grady what an idiot he was for letting you go."

Britt continued to sob, and all I could do was hug her and tell her that it'd be okay. I'd tried to get her to eat something, but she'd refused all food, and as she leaned against me I could feel the sharpness of her frame against mine. What if this sent her on another one of those starvation sprees? Britt couldn't afford to lose any more weight.

At last the tears subsided a little and we made our way downstairs. "Where're your parents?" I asked as I sat her at the table. I went to the cabinets and rummaged around for something tempting enough to make her eat.

"Dad's probably at the golf course, and Mom's at aerobics."

Britt's parents were almost never around. Her two older brothers were off to college, and her mom and dad acted like she was gone, too. They often went away on vacation leaving her behind for weeks at a time, and not once had they come to any of our school events or to see her perform in school plays.

Britt had an incredible voice, and had been the lead in the school musical every single year we'd been in high school. We all thought she'd move to Hollywood and try to make it big some day. I was rooting for her. I found a box of Pop-Tarts in the back of the pantry and toasted two—one for her, one for me. When I set the plate in front of her, she simply stared at it moodily.

"I'm not hungry," she said, before getting up to retrieve a Tab from the fridge.

I made a face. That stuff was so gross; I didn't know how she could stomach it. I nibbled on the other pastry and said, "How about when Spence gets done with his test we go to a movie? *The Secret of My Success* looks good."

Before she could answer there was a knock on the door. Britt looked panicked. Maybe she thought it was Grady and she didn't want him to see her all disheveled.

"I'll get it," I said.

When I opened the door I found Spence there, looking anxious. "Hey," he said. "How's she doing?"

"It's just Spence!" I shouted back to Britt. Stepping out onto the porch, I motioned for him to follow me to the chairs. Keeping my voice low, I said, "I'm really worried about her. She hasn't had anything to eat since yesterday at lunch, and you saw what she had then."

"Couple of carrot sticks and a Tab," he said.

"Yeah. This whole thing with Grady has her in a tailspin."

"I didn't know she was all that into him," Spence said.

"She wasn't, but he was her date to prom, and the fact that he broke up with her has crushed her confidence."

Spence scratched his temple. "What can we do?"

I wound my arm through his and squeezed. "We'll take her to prom and let her hang with us. Maybe you could dance with her a few times?"

"You sure?" he asked.

We both knew that Britt had a major crush on him. She'd never said anything about it to either of us, and she wasn't a threat to me, so it didn't upset me. I was crazy about him, too, so I understood. For his part, Spence pretended not to notice the way Britt would sneak looks at him or laugh at everything he said or occasionally touch him in a flirtatious way. It was super-obvious to everybody, but we loved her like a sister, so we put up with it.

"It's fine," I told him. "I just want her to stop being miserable."

"Okay, then," he said, puffing up his chest. "I'll be the only guy there with two dates. I'll become a legend."

"Thanks, honey," I said with a laugh. "How'd the test go?"

He shrugged. "It went. I did okay, I think."

I regretted what I said next the second it came out of my mouth. "But not like last time, right? Not *that* good."

Spence didn't reply, and suddenly the space around us was filled with tension. He still hadn't admitted to me that he'd cheated on his SATs, and by now I was convinced that's exactly what he'd done. I tried to change the subject.

"I was thinking we could take Britt to that new Michael J. Fox movie to help take her mind off things."

When he didn't reply, I lifted my head from his shoulder to look at him. He was staring off into space, his mouth pressed into a thin line.

"I can't," he said at last. "There's something I gotta do today."

"What?" I asked as he carefully got up and moved away from me.

"It's nothing big," he said. "Just something I need to take care of."

I sat there, stunned. Spence was starting to dismiss me so easily these days. It hurt more than I could say. "More secrets?" I said meanly.

He looked away from me again, toward his car. "I gotta go. Tell Britt to hang in there. I'll call you later."

With that, he was gone and I was left to wonder what the hell was happening to us.

Lily

COLE PULLED OVER AND PUT A HAND ON MY SHOUL-
der. "Hey," he said. "Lily, what happened?"

I shook my head and covered my eyes with my hand,
beyond embarrassed. The trouble was that I couldn't stop
crying. I missed Sophie so much, and part of me wanted
to call her immediately to comfort her, but then I remembered how heartbroken I'd been *because* of her and it was all
so conflicting.

"Hey," he said. "Come on. Tell me what's wrong?"

I gulped back a sob and held out my phone to him. He
saw the screen and his brow furrowed. And then it rose, as
if he'd suddenly put it together. "Your best friend just split
up with your ex?"

I swallowed back another sob and nodded vigorously,
wiping at my cheeks and trying so hard to pull myself
together.

Cole handed me the phone, then twisted in his seat to

reach into the back. He came up with a small box of Kleenex. "Here," he said, offering it to me.

I took a tissue and hid my face while I dabbed at my eyes. "I don't even know why I'm crying."

"Maybe it's because, as long as she was dating your ex, you could be mad at her and not miss her, but now that she's split with him, it's not making you as angry and it means you can miss her for real now."

I stared at him, a bit surprised. "Wow," I said. "If it doesn't work out for you with the FBI, maybe you should give psychology a try."

He grinned. "It's not that hard to figure out, Lil. She's been your best friend for how long?"

"Eleven years."

He nodded knowingly. "Do you know Chris Borgus?"

I furrowed my brow. "No. Should I?"

"I'll make the intros next week. He's been my best friend since we were in sixth grade. If he broke the bro code, I think it'd be really hard, but I'd still be his best friend. I mean, Lily, eleven years is a lot of history to try and forget. No way can you just shrug that off like it's no big deal."

I took a deep breath and let it out slowly. "I really do miss her, Cole."

"Then call her."

I turned my head to look out the window. "I don't know if I'm ready to do that yet."

"Okay, so text her."

I rolled my eyes. "It's not that simple."

"Sure it is," he said. "I mean, what's the harm? Yeah,

what she did was really shitty, but she seems sorry. I don't know; if it were me, and we'd been friends for eleven years, I'd probably forgive her."

I heard what Cole was saying, and it made a lot of sense, but I think I was still a little too hurt to just forgive and forget. Tucking the phone away, I said, "Maybe later."

Thankfully, Cole let it go, and we got back under way. He stopped just a minute or two later, across the street from the same house that'd brought on a panic attack—his grandmother's place. I started to feel anxious just looking at it.

"I can go in alone if you want to stay here," Cole offered.

"Nah," I said, not wanting to look like even more of a wimp. "I'm cool."

Cole got out and I followed after him, looking over my shoulder to see if anybody was watching us. He didn't seem at all nervous; he just headed up the drive like he owned the place, and undid the latch on the gate that let us into the backyard. When we reached the back porch he moved aside a planter and retrieved a silver key.

"Ta-da!" he said.

"What if she comes home while we're in there?"

"She won't," he said. "She works a ten-to-four shift on the weekends at CVS. And even if she did come back, we could always sneak out the front door. Come on, we're cool."

We entered the house and I immediately took note of the gloomy interior. Every shade in the place was drawn, and the hum of the air conditioner could be heard from the kitchen to the left. Cole pointed to the doorway leading to the family room.

"How about I wait by the door?" I suggested. I couldn't help it; I was super-nervous about trespassing.

Cole gave me a thumbs-up and went off to retrieve the yearbooks. I waited in the kitchen and looked around. The place was very simple, but clean. Honey-colored cabinets and off-white Formica counters. The kitchen looked dated, like something out of the eighties, when Amber was my age, and I suddenly remembered that Cole's grandmother had known my former self. Still, as I gazed around the kitchen, I couldn't say that it looked familiar, but maybe there was something about the general layout that tugged at my memories. Or Amber's memories.

I closed my eyes for a moment and tried to picture the house. I was sort of surprised to realize that I knew that if I walked out of the kitchen and through the living room, there'd be a set of stairs to the left that led up to Mrs. Spencer's room, and little Stacey's. Spence's room would be at the front of the house, off a short hall leading to the bathroom.

So weird.

"Got 'em," Cole said, and I jumped, opening my eyes to see him in the doorway with three leather-bound books very similar in color and style to the ones on his own bookshelf.

"Thank God," I said, turning to the door and rushing back outside. I quickstepped to the gate and was about to open it when I heard a car pull up the drive on the other side. Behind me, Cole was busy locking the door.

"*Cole!*" I whispered. I pointed to the gate, and mouthed, *Someone's here!*

Cole's eyes widened, and he rushed to lock the door and

shove the key back under the flowerpot. Darting down the steps, he grabbed my hand and pulled me to the side of the house, where we flattened ourselves against the aluminum siding.

From that angle we had a view of the car in the driveway through a crack in the gate.

"It's my gram," he whispered. "What the hell is she doing home?"

My heart was pounding against my rib cage. "What do we do?" I said softly.

"Follow me," he said. Grabbing my hand, he pulled me to the back of the yard and over to a small shed. We ducked behind it, and not a moment later, we heard the squeak of the back gate opening, and then the clang as it closed. Footsteps told us that Mrs. Spencer had moved up the stairs to the door, and then we heard it open and close.

I looked at Cole and he mouthed, *Let's go!* and just like that we were off and running for the gate. Keeping low, we hustled through it and dashed to the left down the driveway. We didn't stop running until we'd made it to Cole's car.

Cole handed me the yearbooks as he struggled to retrieve his keys from his pocket. I made it around the side and into the passenger seat by the time he pulled open his door.

And that's when a sharp, clear voice rang out from across the street. "Cole!"

He froze, but I crouched down as far as I could, tucking the yearbooks on the floor mat by my feet.

To my surprise, Cole adopted an easy smile, shut the door, and turned around to face his grandmother.

"Hey, Grammy!" he said, moving toward where she stood in the doorway of her house. "I came over to see if your grass needed a mow."

Cole's grandmother was fairly tall. She had salt-and-pepper curly hair, glasses, and a little bit of a gut. To my relief, she hadn't seemed to notice me ducking down in the car. Still, she put her hands on her hips and snapped, "You just mowed it Wednesday."

Cole rubbed the back of his neck lazily and said, "Yeah, but I'm gonna have to put you back on a Saturday rotation now that school's started. I'm gonna have a lot of homework this year. Less time to mow lawns after school."

"I don't like you here when I'm not around," she said tersely.

"Okay," he said. "Sorry, Gram. What're you doing home, anyway? You sick?"

She held up a large prescription bottle. "Forgot my blood-pressure pills."

An awkward sort of silence followed and Cole said, "Okay, Grams, I'll let you go. If I can't make a Wednesday, then I'll have one of my guys take care of you."

"I don't like strangers, Cole," she snapped again. She didn't seem to like much of anything.

"I'll get Tyler to do it," Cole said easily. "You've met him."

All she did was frown.

"Okay, Gram," Cole said, backing up toward the car again. "Don't work too hard today."

She went back inside and shut the door without so much as a good-bye. The second the door was closed, Cole pivoted and rushed to get into the car, inserting his key into the ignition and getting us the hell out of there.

"You can sit up now," he said when we'd reached the end of the street. I couldn't help noticing that he was grinning.

"Do you think she saw me?" I asked, inching my way up from my crouched position.

He shook his head. "She would've said something if she had."

"She seemed mad."

He laughed. "She's always like that. You can't take it personally."

I marveled at how easily he shrugged it off. My own grandmother's terse and domineering personality set me right on edge, but Cole rolled with it.

"Do you think she'll notice that the yearbooks are gone?" I asked.

"I doubt it," he replied, but then his smile faded and he looked a little nervous. "At least I hope she doesn't. I'll catch hell for it."

I stared at the bound volumes still at my feet. "Maybe we should take them back? I mean, she was heading to work again, right? Maybe we can put them back before she notices."

Cole shifted in his seat. "We'll take 'em back after lunch," he promised. "I want to look through them and get a list of people to talk to."

That brought up another uncomfortable topic. "How're we going to get these people to talk to us, Cole? Won't they think it's a little weird that two teens are investigating Ben and Amber's murder?"

"We can tell them that we're researching a school project," he said, quick enough for me to believe he'd already thought of this approach. "I'll tell them that Ben was my uncle, and I'm doing a biography on him for my English class."

"Huh," I said. "That's not bad."

Cole flashed me a Cheshire-cat smile and bounced his brows. "I've got mad skills, remember?"

That made me laugh, which helped stem the flow of all that adrenaline pumping through my veins. Then I realized that I hadn't had a panic attack in a few days. Not even with the recent developments.

Cole drove us to a place called Jersey Mike's for lunch and after we sat down, subs in hand, we each took up one of Ben's yearbooks.

"Whoa," I said, running my hand over the inside cover, where Amber had quoted a love poem to Ben.

"Find something?" Cole asked, setting aside his sandwich to lean forward and look at the yearbook.

I pointed to the smooth, almost elegant black cursive text in the upper left hand corner, which was very different from her suicide note and was even closer to mirroring my own handwriting. "This is a quote from a love poem written by a woman named Christina Rossetti called 'I Loved You First,'" I said, stunned by what I was seeing. "I did a paper on her in my English Lit class last year and this is by far my favorite poem of hers. Rossetti was amazing, but she's not super-well-known, so it's a little freaky that Amber knew about her, too."

Cole squinted at the text, and I swiveled the book so that

he could read it. "One more connection for you to Amber," he said.

"Yeah," I agreed, marveling at the newest coincidence. "So what're we looking for again?"

Cole took a bite of his sub and chewed it before answering me. "See if you can find any photos of my uncle or Amber with other people, or maybe there's something in the notes from their friends who signed the yearbook."

I flipped to some of the signatures in the yearbook's beginning page and frowned. "Nobody is signing here with their last name. Everybody's just putting their first names in."

Cole leaned over as I pointed to a few of the personal notes. "Damn," he muttered. "Okay, we'll see if you can cross-reference any of the first-name signatures to kids Spence or Amber were photographed with."

"How is this going to help us again?" I asked, thumbing a little more through the pages.

"Some of their friends could still live in the area and we could interview them to see if they knew of anything weird going on with Ben and Amber."

"Got it," I said.

As I turned the pages of the yearbook, I quickly became fascinated. The kids were dressed so differently. Lots of upturned collars, huge earrings, rubber bracelets, and wild patterns. I couldn't get over how pronounced the fashions seemed to be. Everything was flashy, big, and dramatic. And I didn't see a single hoodie or pair of sweatpants. The guys all wore jeans. Almost nobody wore shorts or T-shirts. And the hair! I never saw so much frizz, feathering, or high bangs. And a few of the kids had Mohawks. Everybody seemed to be trying so hard to stand out, which was the complete opposite of how it was in school now. I kind of marveled at the boldness of those kids. They didn't seem to be walking through the hallways with their chins down, hurrying to their next class. Instead they appeared to swagger down the corridors, brimming with confidence.

We studied the yearbooks in silence for a while, and then I thought of looking in the back to the index to find the pages that Ben and Amber would be on. I quickly discovered that Ben was the captain of the football and track teams. There were photos of him in uniform, on the field, and racing around the track.

Amber wasn't a jock, though—she was a brain. She was recognized her junior year for having the highest GPA, and she also scored the highest for the entire class on her SATs. She was the junior class vice president, and led the debate team to regionals.

Still, most of the photos of her were on Spence's arm, but I did find two shots of her with two other girls: Sara Radcliff and Britta Cummings. The caption under the photo read, *Best friends forever.* It dawned on me that these were the very girls that I'd mentioned to Dr. White when I was hypnotized and speaking as Amber.

"Here," I said, swiveling the yearbook around so that Cole could see. "These two might know something."

Cole made a note of the girls' names on his iPhone. "We can look them up on the web after we get these back to Grams's."

"Did anyone stand out in the sophomore yearbook?" I asked.

Cole nodded. "This guy," he said, pointing to a photo of a tall, thin boy with braces. He and Ben were wearing suits with shoulder pads, long chains around their necks, and fedoras tipped low. They posed with their arms crossed and major attitude on their faces, rapper style.

"Who is it?" I asked.

"Bill Metcalf," he said. "They did a skit for the school talent show. Also there's this guy," he said, thumbing through the yearbook to the last few pages. "Grady Weaver. There's a photo of him and Ben at a track meet high-fiving each other."

"Anybody else?"

Cole frowned. "It's really hard to tell," he said. "All of the other photos of Ben are either team shots, action shots at a football game, or with his arm around Amber."

"It's the same in this one, too," I said, tapping the junior yearbook. Then a thought occurred to me. "What about their senior year? Didn't you grab that yearbook?"

Cole frowned. "Ben and Amber were dead by the time it came out," he said. "We get our yearbooks here the last week of school—mid-June. I figure it was the same back in the eighties, too."

"Wouldn't Ben have ordered one, though?" I asked. "I mean, I know he wasn't around to collect it, but maybe it got sent to your grandmother's?"

"If it was, I've never seen it," Cole said.

"Bummer," I muttered. "There could've been some good clues in that yearbook." Then I thought of something else. "Would your mom know any of the kids that Ben used to hang out with?"

Cole took a pull from his Dr Pepper. "Maybe," he said. "Sometimes, it's hard for her to talk about Ben. She said that his death on top of her dad's death was a lot for her to deal with."

I blinked. "Right. He was killed in a car crash?" I said, remembering what Dr. White had told me.

Cole nodded. "Yeah. About a year and a half before Ben was murdered. Mom says he wasn't much of a dad, but he was the only one she had."

"Why wasn't he much of a dad?"

Cole shrugged. "I guess he drank a lot. Supposedly, he was heading home from a bar when he crashed his car about two miles away from their house. Ben got to the scene of the crash before anybody else did. It was bad. The car was on fire, and his dad was trapped inside."

"Ohmigod," I gasped. "I didn't know Ben was there. That's awful!"

Cole nodded. "Ben was the one that broke the news to my mom. She says that he became the head of the house after that. He worked after school to help my grandma pay the bills and stuff."

I felt bad for thinking poorly about Cole's grandmother. She'd suffered two unimaginable blows nearly back to back. No wonder she was harsh.

"Your poor grandmother," I said.

"Yep," he agreed. "She's had a rough life."

"Your mom had it rough, too," I said.

"She did. But she worked really hard in school and ended up getting a scholarship to UVA. Now she's an RN, and she just finished her master's last year."

It was easy to see the pride that Cole had for his mother. I liked that about him. I liked a lot about him.

"What about your dad?" I asked, curious.

Cole played with the straw in his drink. "He was from Canada, and when they got divorced he went back. He lives in Toronto now with my stepbrother and -sister."

There didn't seem to be any bitterness in Cole's voice. Was he really as okay with his absent father as he seemed to be? "Do you get to see him?"

"Every summer for the month of July, and every winter break. It's not much, but we make it work."

"That's nice," I said.

I wondered if I'd ever get to a place of peace with my dad. I was still feeling bitter about the fact that he'd come to my grandmother's house that morning to confront her about the discussion between her and his girlfriend, and he hadn't even bothered to ask for me.

"Should we talk to your mom about Ben's friends?" I asked.

Cole glanced at his phone. "It couldn't hurt," he said. "As long as we're careful not to upset her. You'd think after all these years she wouldn't miss my uncle so much, but when we visit his grave on his birthday, she gets pretty upset."

"I'll let you do the talking," I said.

He grinned and then tapped out a text. Within a minute he had a reply. "She says she can take a break if we want to meet her at work."

I gathered up the wrapper and empty cup from lunch to take to the trash and said, "Let's go."

Amber

"BAILEY, LET GO!" STACEY YELLED, PULLING ME from my thoughts. I moved over to where she was struggling to free her little canvas purse with the wood handle from Bailey's mouth. My dog thought it was a fun game of tug-of-war and jerked Stacey nearly off her feet.

"Whoa!" I said, grabbing Bailey by the collar to get her attention. She let go of Stacey's purse immediately.

"She ripped it!" Stacey cried.

Mentally, I berated myself. I should've been keeping a closer eye on Bailey, especially knowing that Stacey liked to keep snacks in her purse. I'd been so distracted worrying about Spence that a lot was starting to slip my mind and my notice.

"Oh, Stace," I said squatting down in front of her and taking a look at the two-inch tear in the fabric along the handle. "Please don't worry. My mom can mend that no problem."

Stacey's eyes were watering, and I hoped she didn't start crying. I couldn't take it when Spence's baby sister got upset. The guilt was twofold because I'd promised to watch her while Spence mowed his Tuesday-night lawns, and his mom was on the other side of town cleaning some big house that always took her hours to finish. Stacey was only eleven and had spent too many afternoons home alone for my taste.

"I promise we can fix it," I said gently. "And I know Bailey's really sorry."

Stacey swallowed hard and glared at Bailey.

"Tell you what," I said. "If my mom can't mend that good as new, then I'll buy you a new one."

Stacey wiped at her cheeks and tried to put on a brave front. "It's okay," she said. "You don't have to. I know you're saving for college."

My heart melted with love for Spence's little sister. True, I had been saving for college, but it wasn't my college I'd been saving for. Spence had gotten word that his SAT scores were much improved from his first two tries, but weren't anywhere near what he'd scored a few months back, and the coach and UCLA, suspecting strongly that Spence had cheated, had pulled the scholarship. UCLA hadn't denied Spence admission, thank God, but now he had no way to pay for school, and the coach had told Spence that the best he could do for him was allow him a shot as a walk-on.

Because of the break-in, Spence now had no more than a few hundred dollars to his name. Even if he worked all summer, he still wouldn't have enough for the tuition at UCLA, let alone books, room and board, and other living expenses. I'd promised him all of my savings, which was only eight hundred dollars. Not much, but it was a start, and I hoped that with the two of us working overtime this summer, we'd come up with enough for the first semester.

And yet, when I looked down at Stacey's freckled face, I couldn't resist trying to make her feel better with a treat. "Come on," I said. "The shop where I got you this one should be open for another hour if you're up for the long walk."

"Really?!" she said, jumping with excitement. "Really, Amber?"

I took Bailey's leash from her hand and said, "Yes, sweetie. Let's get you something pretty."

Stacey and I stayed at the specialty shop until closing—mostly because she couldn't decide which pattern she liked. The store had dozens and dozens of wooden-handle Bermuda bags, and I even caught myself fawning over a blue-yellow-and-peach plaid purse with a light wood handle. At last, Stacey picked one that was mint green with little hot pink hearts, and it suited her. I parted with the twelve dollars a bit guiltily and we headed back to her house, which was a mile and a half away.

As we approached, I saw an unfamiliar car parked in front of the Spencers' house.

"Who's that?" Stacey said, pointing to the porch.

In the dim light I could just make out Spence and a man with his back to us, standing close to each other. The hair on the back of my neck rose. There was something tense about the way they were facing off.

Gripping Stacey's hand and tightening my hold on

Bailey's leash, I quickened my step toward the house. All of a sudden the man gripped Spence by his shirt and shoved him hard up against the house. I was so surprised I stopped in my tracks. "Oh my God, isn't that—?"

"Why's he doing that?!" Stacey yelled as she squeezed my hand. "Amber! Don't let him hurt Spence!"

"Hey!" I shouted to get their attention and began trotting down the street with Bailey and Stacey. "Hey!"

But neither of them paid me any attention. Instead, Spence shoved back against the man, who was his equal in height, but not nearly as muscular. "Get off me, Bishop!" Spence yelled. I stopped again as Spence shoved hard and the man let go. We were three houses away.

"You tell *anyone*, you little shit-ass punk, and I will *end* you!" his assailant roared.

With that he turned and rushed down the stairs, over to his car, and drove away, all before we could reach the front steps to Spence's house. For his part, Spence simply stared angrily at the departing car, his face red, hands balled into fists.

"Spence!"

He either didn't hear me, or he was intent on ignoring me, because he continued to stare down the street, working his jaw, and clenching and unclenching his fists.

"Benny?" Stacey whimpered. "Are you okay?"

The call from his sister seemed to break the spell, and he finally glanced over, as if noticing us for the first time.

"Yeah, I'm fine, Spunky." Turning to me, he said, "Can you get her inside?"

I opened my mouth to reply, but no words came out. There was a look in his eyes that I'd never seen before. It scared me so much it left me speechless.

"Come on, sweetie," I said, taking up Stacey's hand again. "Let's get you some dinner."

It was ten minutes later when I realized that Spence had left the porch and taken off for parts unknown.

Lily

COLE, HIS MOTHER, AND I SAT ON THE PORCH OF the coffee shop across the street from the clinic where Mrs. Drepeau worked.

"Oh, I knew I should've taken the day off," she said, leaning back in her seat and cupping her iced coffee in her hands. "It's too nice a day to be working."

Stacey Spencer Drepeau didn't strike any familiar chords with me. Maybe it was because she was now a middle-aged woman, and the Stacey that Amber had known had been a little girl. I tried to picture the pretty mom with chestnut hair, light brown eyes, and a smattering of freckles across her nose as that little girl, but I couldn't. There was something about her that was ageless and wise, and to imagine that in an eleven-year-old wasn't something I could do.

"Thanks for the coffee," I said, holding my own iced drink aloft. She'd been nice to treat us.

She smiled warmly at me. "My pleasure," she said. "So, what's up?"

We hadn't mentioned anything about why we'd come to see her, and as promised, I let Cole do the talking.

"We got an assignment in English this week," he explained. "We have to research and do a presentation on an ancestor we admire. I'm doing mine on Uncle Ben."

Mrs. Drepeau winced, but then her expression softened. "That's nice, Cole," she said, reaching out to squeeze his arm. "I know I tell you this all the time, but you two are a lot alike."

Cole and I exchanged an amused glance. He took out his phone and said, "Can I record you and ask you questions?"

"Sure." His mother sat up a little and leaned forward. She didn't speak until Cole's phone was recording, and then she began to tell us about Spence. "Your uncle was the greatest guy. He was smart, funny, warm, and kind. He looked out for us, you know? Your grandma and me. Even before Dad died, Ben worked cutting lawns—just like you—and gave Mom the money so we could keep a roof over our heads. He was so responsible for someone so young," she added wistfully. "Did you know that after your grandfather was killed in that car crash, we found out there was nothing? No savings or anything. So when Ben turned eighteen, he got himself a life insurance policy. I don't know what we would've done without it when he was murdered. Your grandma and I would've been out on the street for sure because she couldn't even function after Benny died. She didn't work for three years afterward. She was so heartbroken she could barely get out of bed. It was very, very hard."

Mrs. Drepeau dropped her chin and I could see how much her brother's passing still affected her.

"Mom?" Cole asked.

She looked up again. "Sorry," she said. "I miss him."

Cole glanced at me, and I could see that he was beginning to regret bringing up the topic of Ben to his mom. "We don't have to talk about him," Cole said.

She shook her head. "No, honey, I'm fine. Besides, it's your assignment, and I think it'd be good for the other kids to hear what an amazing young man your uncle was."

"You're sure?"

She smiled gamely at him. "Positive."

"Okay...uh...how about friends? Did he have any close friends?"

She laughed. "Oh my God, did he! The whole football team was always trooping through our house. And the track team. And the cheerleaders. And the girlfriends of all the players. On weekend nights, it was like a frat house!"

"Anyone specific?" Cole pressed.

Mrs. Drepeau pursed her lips. "Well, yes, honey, but if you want names I'm not sure I'd be able to give you those. It was a long time ago, and a lot of the details of those years got blocked out of my memory. The therapist I went to when your dad and I were divorcing said that I'd very likely had a good case of PTSD back then. Lots of names, dates, places, events, and stuff got muddled together."

Cole frowned. "Okay, well, what about Amber?"

Mrs. Drepeau seemed surprised that he'd brought her up. "What about her?"

"Well...did you like her?" he asked.

She smiled sadly. "I loved her, Cole. I loved her deeply. We all did."

"And you don't think she killed Uncle Ben, right?"

Mrs. Drepeau inhaled a long breath and turned away. "No," she said. "No, I don't."

I leaned in and rested my elbows on the table. "You don't?" I asked. I needed to believe she knew Amber couldn't have done it.

She turned back to me with watery eyes. "No, honey. I don't believe that Amber Greeley did anything to harm my brother. And I'm not convinced that she committed suicide, either."

I had a sudden urge to hug her, but held myself in check, knowing it'd be weird. Still, I was grateful for her answer.

"Do you have any theories about who could've murdered Ben?" Cole asked.

"Yes, in fact."

"You do?" Cole and I said together, shocked.

That made her laugh. "I do," she said. "But the police weren't about to take my word for it."

"What do you mean?" Cole asked.

"Well," she began, "a few weeks before my brother was murdered, a man came to our house and threatened him. I have no idea over what, but he shoved my brother and told him that he would kill him. Amber was with me that night, and I always suspected she knew who the man was."

"But you didn't know him?" Cole pressed.

"No. But my brother called him Bishop. That always stuck with me. I didn't know if Spence was referring to the man's name, either first or last, or if it was perhaps a title. I just heard him call the man Bishop, and then a few weeks later both Ben and Amber were dead."

"And you told the police?" I asked as something tickled at the back of my mind. That name. Where had I seen it?

"I did," Mrs. Drepeau said. "Well, at least I did indirectly. I told my mother, and she went to the police station. She came back hours later to tell me that a detective had promised to follow up, but as far as I know, he never did. Once Amber died and her suicide note basically confessed to the crime, the police closed the case."

"How come you never told me this?" Cole asked.

Mrs. Drepeau took a long sip of her drink before answering. "Because you never asked, and I didn't want to stir up the past. It's also something that I've never been able to reconcile, honey. I mean, this man showing up and threatening my brother and then possibly killing him—what was my brother mixed up in? I've always believed that Spence was, like, this larger-than-life character. He's been my hero my whole life, and I don't really want to find out otherwise."

Cole's mom glanced at her watch. "Oh, God! Look at the time! Honey, I've got to get back to work. If you want to ask me more questions later at dinner, that'd be okay."

We said good-bye to Mrs. Drepeau and watched in silence as she raced back across the street. When she disappeared through the doors of the clinic, Cole turned to me and said, "Well, that's a crazy twist."

Suddenly, I remembered where I'd seen the name Bishop. "Can you give me your keys?" I asked, jumping to my feet with excitement. "I need to get something from your car."

Cole eyed me curiously, but handed over the keys. I

raced off the porch of the coffee shop and was back a minute later with Spence's junior year yearbook. Flipping frantically through the pages I stopped on one where Amber and eleven other students were posing with a teacher. The caption read, *Mr. Bishop congratulates the top three GPA students from each class!* Swiveling the book around I held my finger next to Mr. Bishop's name.

"Do you think it could be the same guy your mom saw threatening Ben?"

Cole studied the photo. "She did say that she thought Amber knew the guy," Cole said. "Is he in any other photos?"

I pulled the yearbook back around and skimmed through the index, then went to the corresponding pages.

"He taught algebra," I said. "Freshmen class math." Flipping to the next photo I gasped. "Cole," I whispered, turning the page back to him.

He leaned over and studied the photo, which was captioned, *Mr. Bishop administers the SAT exams on an early Saturday morning.*

"That's my uncle," he whispered.

Seated in the first row was Ben Spencer. "They knew each other," I told him.

Cole sat back and looked at me like he could hardly believe it was that easy. "I think we just found our starting point."

"What're you thinking?"

Cole got to his feet and motioned for me to follow him. "First, I want to go back home and check the murder file. Mom said that she told the police about this guy Bishop, but I don't remember any mention of him in those pages. At the

FBI seminar they taught us that no tip goes undocumented, no matter what the source."

"You think it was swept under the rug?"

"If the detective wanted to make his case stick—that Amber killed Ben? Maybe."

We arrived at the car and, after getting under way, I said, "You know what's really weird to me?"

"Besides us investigating our own murders?" Cole said with a wink.

That gave me pause. "Yeah, besides that. What I think is strange is that Ben was shot and Amber was stabbed."

Cole glanced at me. "Why is that strange?"

"If we think that the same person murdered them both, then why didn't he just shoot Amber or stab Ben? Why change the method?"

"Huh," Cole said, tapping the steering wheel thoughtfully. "That's a good point. Maybe it's because he wanted to frame Amber, and shooting her would've made it look like a murder."

"True," I said. "But how did he know that she'd leave a suicide note?"

Cole shrugged. "I don't know," he said. "The only thing I can figure is that she might've known she'd end up murdered. Maybe she and Ben were both in on whatever it was that got him killed, so she knew she was in danger?"

I shook my head. "That night, though? I mean, isn't the timing a little too perfect?"

Cole nodded. "It is, but it's not the only weird thing that doesn't seem to have an explanation. I read in the file that the night Amber died, her neighbors said they heard Amber's dog, Bailey, barking like crazy, and they told the detective that they only heard Bailey bark like that when somebody was at the door, but when they looked out the window of their living room, they didn't see anybody on the Greeleys' porch."

"What about the back door?" I asked.

"Nope," Cole said. "Paparella asked them that same question, and Greeley's neighbor—I forget the guy's name—said he thought of that and went to check his back window, which had a view into the Greeleys' backyard. He didn't see anybody there, either, so he assumed that maybe Bailey had heard an animal outside or something."

"That *could've* been the explanation, Cole," I said.

"True," he admitted, "except for one thing. There's a photo of Bailey from the crime scene. She's got some of Amber's blood on her paws, probably from when she went to check on her. But there's also a spot of blood on Bailey's right side that I swear looks like a handprint."

"A handprint?"

"Yeah," Cole said. "Paparella even had the photographer take a close-up of it."

I felt my temper flare. "You mean like someone hit Amber's dog?"

"No," Cole said. "I think it might've been the opposite. I think somebody was trying to comfort Bailey. It looked like they were patting her."

"Whoa," I said.

Cole continued. "Paparella concluded at the end of the report that the bloody handprint probably came from Amber. He said it was the last thing she did before she died."

I looked at Cole. "But you think otherwise."

"I read the autopsy report. Amber had blood on her hands—one was covered in it; the other had some blood splatter. Know what the medical examiner didn't find on either hand?"

I blinked, trying to think where he was going with that, and then it hit me. "He didn't find dog hair," I said.

Cole pointed at me. "Ding, ding, ding, we have a winner. At FAIT we learned that blood is super-sticky. If Amber had given Bailey a pat before she died, she should've had dog hair all over her palm."

"Golden retrievers do shed like crazy," I said, seeing his logic.

"Yep, and I know from experience."

"So the killer got into Amber's house, murdered her, and when Bailey went crazy, he calmed the dog down?"

"That's a possibility," Cole said.

"Without being seen, though?"

"Once the dog calmed down, the neighbors stopped looking out at the Greeleys' house. The killer could've sneaked through the back door without anybody noticing."

"Do you think that Bailey's reaction means that she felt comfortable around the murderer?" I asked.

"Like, did Bailey know the killer and that's why she allowed him to pet her even though Amber was dying on the bed?"

"Yeah," I said.

Cole took a deep breath while he seemed to consider that. "It's really hard to say, Lily. My Bailey is friendly with everybody. Mom jokes a lot that if we were ever robbed,

Bailey would show them where the valuables are. She loves everyone."

"It's the breed," I agreed. "Goldens are true teddy bears. Still, that handprint is pretty significant, right?"

"It is. And it's always bugged me," Cole said with a shudder.

I knew how he felt. How could someone be so sick as to kill Amber, and then pet her dog?

By that time we'd arrived back at Cole's house. He retrieved the murder file from his room, and laid it out on the kitchen table, where he went through each page, looking for any reference to Mr. Bishop.

Meanwhile, I used his iPad to search for the mysterious suspect, starting with a list of teachers at the school. It was too much to hope that he was still employed at Chamberlain High, but I did find an Internet reference for a David Bishop who'd once worked at the high school and was now living in Bumpass, Virginia. Pulling up a map, I saw that it was a little over thirty-five miles away.

"It's not here," Cole said.

"What?" I asked, looking up from the iPad.

"There's no reference to Bishop and no mention of my gram talking to Paparella about it. The bastard covered up the lead."

I turned the tablet toward Cole. "I found a David Bishop who used to work at Chamberlain. He lives in Bumpass now."

"We could be there in less than an hour," Cole said, getting to his feet and pulling out his keys.

I blinked. "Wait, Cole, you want to go over there and what? Talk to him?"

Cole looked a little worked up. I could tell the thing with Paparella was upsetting him. "Yeah," he said. "Maybe."

"Are you crazy? What if he's the killer?"

"What if he is, Lily?" Cole said. "By the looks of that picture of him in the yearbook, he'll be an old man by now. Plus, he won't know who we are or where we live. We'll give him fake names, and talk about Ben and Amber and see how he reacts. If he gets upset or says something suspicious, we'll call Mike."

"Who's Mike?"

Cole pointed to the file. "Mike Hasslett, the detective who gave me the file."

"Can't we just go to him now and tell him what your mom said and have him go talk to Bishop?"

Cole gripped the back of the kitchen chair. "You gotta know Mike," he said. "He's a nice guy, but really lazy."

"What about one of the other detectives?" I pressed.

Cole laughed. "One of the other . . . oh, yeah. You're from Richmond, where they have a full-scale police department. There're only four detectives on staff in Fredericksburg, and they have to cover everything from car accidents to drugs to murders. They're way understaffed, Lily. I know from experience that they don't like to investigate anything they don't really have to."

"What do you mean?"

"One of my mom's ex-boyfriends broke in here a couple of years ago and stole a bunch of our stuff to get even with her for breaking up with him, and the detective who showed up, some old geezer named Cromely, didn't do anything more than file a report and try to talk Mom out of pressing charges 'cause it was more work for him. He wanted to let the guy off with a warning." When I stared at him in stunned silence, he added, "Glad you moved to such a safe community with a top-notch police force, right?"

That made me crack a smile. "They do sound pathetic," I said.

"Yep."

"Cole, all kidding aside, what you're talking about is dangerous."

"It's only dangerous if Bishop murdered Ben and Amber. If not, then it's just talking to a guy who used to teach at our school. Besides, we could both outrun a guy in his seventies, right?"

I wrung my hands together, undecided.

Cole bounced the keys in his hand and said, "I'm gonna go. I can drop you off at home if you want, but I'm heading over there."

I glared at him. Why was he so stubborn? But I couldn't very well let him go on his own. If it was a risky mission for both of us, it was definitely riskier for one of us. With a heavy sigh, I grabbed my purse and said, "Fine. I'll go. But if he pulls a gun, I'm throwing you in front of the line of fire and running."

"I can live with that," he said with a grin.

"Not if he has good aim."

But Cole's playful grin only widened, so I rolled my eyes and headed toward the door.

We arrived in Bumpass—a gorgeous and obviously expensive community surrounding Lake Anna—in well under an hour. On our way to the address I'd found for Bishop, we drove past huge homes dotting the lakefront.

Finally, we stopped in front of a long drive, which wound up a hill to a picturesque house perched at the top. The house was like something out of a magazine, with a series of gables along the front, a huge wraparound porch, and gingerbread accents all over.

There was something very familiar about it. If I didn't know better, I'd swear I'd seen the house before.

"Wow," Cole said as he leaned toward me to look up at the place. "That's a big house for a former teacher."

"It is," I agreed. I wondered how he'd been able to afford it. "Maybe he did something else after he left Chamberlain High. Something that made him a buttload of money."

Cole frowned skeptically, but then pointed down the road. "There's a sign for a public boat launch," he said. "Let's park there and see if there's a beach we can walk to get a better look at the house from the back."

Cole drove to the boat launch and, sure enough, there was a small parking lot, which was nearly full of cars, but we found a slot and got out.

"There," I said, pointing to the right, where a trail led to the beach. "That might go all the way back to Bishop's house."

"Let's do this," Cole said.

He walked around to my side, and I was surprised when he took my hand. I hadn't thought there was any romance going on between us that afternoon, so it was a really sweet surprise.

We walked in silence, and I was glad to see the beach

was mostly empty. It was also very narrow in places, and I wondered if we might've been trespassing at times. Although the beach was continuous, I didn't know if the beachfronts were public or private. There weren't any signs to indicate one way or the other, and Cole walked like he belonged there. His confidence gave me courage.

At last we made it to the beach in front of Bishop's place. We came upon it suddenly as it was around a small peninsula, and Cole saw it first. He stopped and pointed toward the hill.

"There," he said.

I glanced up, spotting first the miniature windmill, which stood sentinel halfway up the hill. The staircase leading to the house was built in a zigzag pattern, and there was a large trilevel deck at the top.

And then it hit me like a ton of bricks. "Ohmigod!" I said, feeling my knees go a bit weak. "Ohmigod!"

"Lily?" Cole said. "What's the matter?"

My breath was coming in short pants, and I felt the beginnings of a panic attack. I closed my eyes and tried to slow my breathing down, but my heart was hammering away in my chest so hard that it hurt.

I sank to the sand on my knees while sweat trickled down from my temples. Cole kept asking me what was happening, but I couldn't speak. All I could do was grip his hand for dear life.

He put his other hand on my shoulder and began to speak in soft tones.

"Hey," he said. "Lily, it's okay. You're okay. Hang on. Just keep breathing and hang on to me."

Every one of my limbs was trembling, and I bent at the

waist, feeling like I was going to melt into the ground. This was by far the worst panic attack I'd ever had. It was like a tsunami of fear and anxiety washing over me. I was drowning in it.

"Breathe, Lily," Cole said. I focused on his words. "It's okay. I've got you."

His free hand gripped my arm to steady me. Tears leaked out of my eyes, and when I opened them I got so dizzy that I had to close them again.

Please! I thought. *Please don't let me pass out!*

"Lily," Cole whispered. He was very close to my ear and there was something urgent about his whisper. "Listen, I'm gonna pick you up and carry you, okay?"

Feebly, I shook my head. If I moved, I'd black out.

"I have to," Cole said, easing his hand from mine and placing it across my back.

I was about to shake my head again when I heard, "You there! You kids all right?"

My eyes flew open as Cole carefully pulled me close and picked me up. I caught a glimpse of an old man making his way down a long staircase. A staircase I'd seen in an old photo album at my grandmother's house. There'd been photos of my dad as a young boy in those photos. They'd even been captioned. *The Lake House.* And, if there was any doubt about who'd owned it, I remembered one photo in particular of a boat parked at the dock with the windmill in the background. The boat had been named *Maureen's Folly* after my grandmother.

"We're fine," Cole said, hugging me close. "She forgot her inhaler."

I put my head against Cole's chest and gripped his shirt. The effort to keep air in my lungs was quickly exhausting me.

"Should I call someone?" the old man asked. He sounded closer.

"No, sir," he said. "She'll be okay. Just gotta get her home. Thanks!"

I felt the rocking motion of Cole carrying me across the soft sand. It wasn't helping me fight back the wave of dizziness.

I closed my eyes again and tried to think my way out of the panic attack. I focused on the smell of Cole's freshly laundered shirt. The feel of his arms supporting me. The pillow his muscular chest was lending my head, and the beat of his heart.

Like a tonic, the method began to work. I felt less dizzy, and I could keep air in my lungs for longer each time I breathed in. Finally, he stopped and eased to the ground with me still held in his arms. By then I was almost back to breathing normally. Cautiously, I opened my eyes.

"Hey there," he said when I looked up at him. "How you doin'?"

I swallowed, which was hard because my mouth was very dry. "I think I can stand," I told him.

"Good to know," he said. "But how about we hang out here for another minute?"

I managed a small smile and a mock eye roll. "Okay. If we must."

He chuckled. "So what happened back there?"

"That house," I said. "The one Bishop is living in..."

"Yeah?"

"My grandparents used to own it."

Cole's brow furrowed. "Your . . . what?"

I wiped the sweat from my brow and leaned against Cole's chest again, exhausted by the panic attack. "Bishop's house. I recognize it from an old photo album my grandmother has."

Cole looked over his shoulder toward where we'd just come from. "Bishop bought the house from your grandparents?"

I rubbed my temples. I'd asked Grandmother about the house in the photos. She'd said that it'd been taken over by a friend of the family. I remembered how she'd paused when she'd said "taken over," as though it was something done grudgingly. I distinctly remembered the note of bitterness in her tone, only I'd chalked it up to her general demeanor. Now I wasn't quite so sure.

"I don't think they sold it to him," I said. "I think my grandparents gave it to him."

Cole looked confused. "Why would they give a house that's gotta be worth a million dollars to some schoolteacher from Chamberlain High?"

I shook my head. "I have no idea," I said, easing my way out of Cole's arms to get shakily to my feet. "But I think we need to find out."

Amber

I STOOD IN THE HALLWAY SHAKING FROM HEAD TO toe. I'd gotten out of my last class a little early by faking a headache and asking to go see the nurse, and I'd come to this classroom to confront Mr. Bishop and find out the truth.

I'd never had him as a teacher, but I'd heard he was mean. The freshmen always complained about what a prick he was and how hard his math class could be. His reputation made me even more nervous about confronting him, but it was the only way I could get to the truth.

Spence wasn't talking about what was going on with him, but whatever it was, it was tearing him apart. He was moody and distant, wasn't eating much at lunch, and he'd stopped working out with his friends after school. All he did was come to class, say very little, then go home to mow lawns until dark. We hadn't spent any real time together lately because he was always either exhausted or busy working.

For the first time in our relationship, we were struggling, and it was killing me.

And then there was the lasting tension between him and Jamie, who'd been his best friend since elementary school. All of it had me worried enough to confront Bishop and find out why he'd threatened Spence. I couldn't prove it was Mr. Bishop on that porch when Stacey and I had come back from shopping, but I was ninety percent sure it'd been him.

At last the bell sounded and the classroom door burst open. Kids came pouring out, and I stuck close to the wall to wait for the room to clear. Finally it appeared empty, save for one figure earnestly erasing the chalkboard.

Gathering my courage, I stepped into the room and said, "Mr. Bishop?"

The figure turned. I blinked. The man standing in front of me was much younger than Mr. Bishop and looked nothing like him.

"He's on permanent leave," the man said. "Did you have a math problem you need help with?"

I was so surprised that for a long moment all I could do was stand there with my mouth open. "He's on...permanent leave?" I asked.

The man moved to the corner of the teacher's desk and perched sideways on it. "Yes. I'm Mr. Clawson. I'll be taking over through the end of the year."

"Why?" I asked. "I mean...what happened to Mr. Bishop?"

Mr. Clawson shrugged. "Hey, somebody offers me a job, I don't ask too many questions. Anyway, I didn't get the feeling he was coming back next year. I'll probably take over for him permanently."

I hugged the large binder I was carrying to my chest. "Oh," I said, totally at a loss. *Now* how was I going to get to the bottom of this? Belatedly, I realized Mr. Clawson was staring expectantly at me. "Um . . . thanks," I said, and fled the room.

Making my way through the mass of students hurrying to get their things and escape from school for the day, I finally reached my own locker and, with a heavy heart, saw that Spence wasn't there.

He always waited for me after school to drive me home. With a sigh, I put my head against the door of my locker and fought back tears. I wanted to tell somebody what I suspected was going on and I immediately thought of Mr. White, but if I went to him, I knew he'd start digging and he wouldn't stop until Spence got his acceptance to UCLA revoked.

I still held hope that Spence and I would go away to school together. He'd gone to meet with Mrs. Bennett yesterday, and afterward he'd told me that he was pretty sure she was going to grant him the scholarship even though she'd heard all the rumors about how he'd cheated on his SATs. I knew with her help we could come up with the rest on our own, and it was such a relief when he told me that. I thought he'd be happy about it and all the tension and anxiety he carried would finally go away, but if anything, since talking to Mrs. Bennett, Spence seemed even more on edge.

"Amber!" I heard behind me. I whirled around, startled out of my own moody thoughts, to find Bill Metcalf there with a panicked look on his face. "You gotta come with me!" he said, reaching for my arm.

"What?" I said in alarm. "Bill, why? What's happening?"

"Spence and Jamie!" he said, tugging me at a run down the hall. "They're fighting!"

We raced to the end of the hall and found a crowd of kids blocking the doorway. Far behind us came the urgent calls from Mr. Stewart, the gym teacher, but nobody was letting him through. Bill pushed and shoved and forced our way through the kids and out into the open, and there, rolling around in the dirt, were Spence and Jamie, each of them bloody and going for broke as they rained blows down on each other and tried to gain the upper hand.

I pulled out of Bill's grasp and threw my binder at them. *"Stop it!"* I screamed. *"Stop it right now!"*

The binder hit Spence in the forehead, and with a grunt he let go of Jamie, rolling away from him. Bill lunged forward, grabbed Jamie around the waist from behind, and pulled him away from Spence. Meanwhile, I put myself between the pair while Spence got to his feet, breathing hard and looking mad enough to murder someone.

"Stop it!" I shouted again, getting up in his face and grabbing hold of his torn and dirty shirt, then looking back over my shoulder at Jamie, who seemed every bit as angry as Spence. "What the hell's the matter with you two?!"

Around us there was total silence except for the repeated calls from Mr. Stewart somewhere down the hallway, demanding to be let through.

Stewart was a small, slight man, and mostly a joke.

Nobody respected him, and I knew the assembled crowd would be very slow to part for him. If he found Jamie and Spence fighting, he'd suspend both of them, which would threaten their graduation.

Neither of them answered me, and Spence sent one more blistering look at Jamie before he began to turn away. That's when Jamie lunged forward again, almost pulling free from Bill's restraining arms.

"You *ever* come near any of us again, and I'll fucking kill you, Spence!" he shouted.

With that, Jamie did manage to pry himself free from Bill's grasp, and stormed off.

I watched him go, and tears filled my eyes. Jamie was Spence's best friend, the closest person to him besides me. What would the end of their friendship do to Spence, who was already in a very dark place? I didn't have time to think on it. Mr. Stewart's shouts were getting closer, and I turned back to my boyfriend.

"You have to go," I said.

He bent down, picked up my binder, and handed it to me without a word. Then, averting his eyes, he turned and jogged away. I watched him for a long time, well after the crowd began to disperse, his form getting smaller and smaller, as he kept up that steady pace through the parking lot. With every step I knew that, in more than one way, he was getting farther and farther away from me.

Lily

WE SAT IN THE PARKING LOT OF MRS. GREELEY'S hair salon, trying to work up our nerve.

"Are you sure you want to do this?" Cole asked me for the fifth time.

I knew why he was hesitant; it was one thing to confront an old schoolteacher about any misdeeds he'd been involved in thirty years earlier. It was a whole other thing to confront the mother of a dead teen—a girl who was falsely blamed for the murder of her boyfriend.

Plus, I really liked Gina. She'd been so nice to me the other night. I hated to upset her. Not to mention the fact that if I really was the reincarnation of Amber Greeley, in a sense, Gina was my mother, and the last thing I'd want to do was hurt her by bringing up what had to be the worst weeks of her life.

But the only other option besides talking to Gina was

to confront my grandmother, and I wasn't brave enough for that. At least not yet.

"No, I'm not sure," I said, answering Cole. "But I think we have to try and talk to her. She might know something about Bishop."

Cole took a deep breath and then nodded. "Okay. Let's do this."

We'd already agreed to let me do the talking. After entering the salon, the same girl with blue-tipped hair who'd let me in a few nights before greeted us.

"Hey," she said, sizing us up. I couldn't help but notice that her gaze lingered on Cole. "Gina's just finishing up with a client. She told me to let you guys into the break room."

We'd called on the way down from Bumpass, and I'd mentioned only that I had something very urgent and personal to talk to Gina about, and that I was bringing a friend. She'd told me she could spare twenty minutes at two, so we'd raced to get to the salon on time. We'd made it with five minutes to spare.

The break room wasn't much—just a small walled-off room with a soda machine and a mini refrigerator, plus a round table with four seats. I stood near the table, but Cole moved off to buy two Dr Peppers for us.

"Thanks," I said when he handed me one. The act reminded me of a time when Tanner and I had been waiting to see his aunt, who was sick in the hospital, and he'd bought me a Coke, but only after asking me to pay for it. Tanner had been a tightass even though he had his own trust fund.

I thought about Sophie's text again, and the urge to reach

out to her was pretty strong, but what would I say? What words could mend all the hurt between us?

"Hey there," I heard as I twirled my phone in my hands. Looking up I saw Gina moving aside the curtain that separated the break room from the rest of the salon.

"Hi, Gina," I said shyly.

"Hi, Mrs. Greeley," Cole said.

She paused when she saw him and I swear a little color drained from her face. Walking to him she said, "You must be Cole Drepeau."

"Yes, ma'am," he said, taking her extended hand when she offered it.

"My Lord..." she said, gazing at him. "You look so much like your uncle. For a second there, it was like seeing a ghost."

He blushed, which I found adorable, and she motioned for us to sit down. "So!" she said. "What brings you two by?"

Cole looked at me and I cleared my throat nervously. "Gina, I...I want to talk to you about Amber."

Her eyes narrowed ever so subtly. The mention of her daughter and the appearance of Spence's nephew was no doubt making her wary.

"What about Amber?" she said.

"Cole and I have been doing some research for a school project, and we think we might have discovered something important."

"About my daughter?"

"Yes, and no," I said. "See, we don't think that Amber had anything to do with Ben Spencer's murder." Mrs. Greeley's gaze darted to Cole, he nodded, and she turned back to me with less suspicion and more curiosity. "We think," I continued, "that there might have been a teacher involved."

"What?" she said, her eyes widening. "Why do you think that?"

"Something my mom said," Cole told her. "She remembers seeing a man on her front porch threatening my uncle a couple of weeks before he was murdered. She heard the name Bishop and says the police were told about it, but they never followed up on the lead. It turns out that a guy named David Bishop used to teach at Chamberlain High. And we know from this"—Cole paused to pull up the yearbook we'd brought with us from the car, and turn to the pages we'd marked—"that both Amber and Ben knew him."

Gina seemed very rattled by the appearance of the yearbooks and the images captured inside. "Have you gone to the police?" she asked.

"No," I said. "Not yet."

She brushed her bangs away from her eyes. "That's probably wise," she said, but her mouth had drawn into a thin line. "This teacher named Bishop isn't much to go on, and I doubt those sons of bitches would reopen the case. They blamed Amber for Ben's murder, and never once believed me when I insisted my daughter didn't commit suicide. Still, it could just be a coincidence."

"We don't think it is," I said. "We think he had something to do with both their murders. And we also think my grandmother might in some way be involved, too."

"What?" she said, clearly shocked by my accusations. "Why?"

I looked at Cole for reassurance, and he nodded. "Because we found out where Bishop lives now."

"Where he lives now?" she repeated. "What does that have to do with Amber's and Spence's murders?"

"Bishop lives in a house that used to belong to my grandmother," I confessed. "It's on a lake in Bumpass."

Gina's mouth fell open. "You're telling me this teacher moved to *that* lake house?"

"You know about it?"

Gina got up and stepped a little away from us to fold her arms across her chest, as if she were suddenly very cold. "I know about the house," she said. "I thought your grandparents sold it."

"I asked my grandmother about it when I was looking at an old photo album of hers a few years ago. She said it'd been taken over by a friend of the family, but she'd said it in a way that made me think she wasn't so happy about it."

Gina was visibly trembling now, and when at last she turned back to us and moved to the table again to sit down, she was quite pale. "Who have you told about this?"

"Nobody," Cole said.

She put a hand on Cole's arm and squeezed it. "Don't," she said. "Do you hear me?"

"What?" I asked. "Gina, this man could've murdered your daughter. And if my grandmother was involved... I mean, she's my grandmother, but if she had *anything* to do with Amber's death, then I know my mom and I can't live with her, or, honestly, let her get away with it."

It dawned on me in that moment that I felt no real love for my grandmother. There'd always been something about her that was off. Her manipulations. Her conniving ways. How she bullied everyone around her. All of it left me wanting nothing to do with her. And then I had to wonder why? What would Grandmother possibly have against the teenaged daughter of her hairstylist? What had Amber or Spence done to Maureen Bennett? What was the connection between them other than Gina Greeley?

I glanced over at Gina, who I was surprised was shaking her head sadly at me, as though I wasn't really getting it.

"Lily, I'm going to tell you something that you have to promise me you will never, ever repeat. Do you promise? Both of you?"

"I do," I said.

"Me, too," Cole added.

Taking a big breath, Gina said, "Your grandmother is an incredibly powerful woman. She runs this town. Always has. Always will. That has never been something anyone from here has ever questioned, but after my daughter died there were rumors that I've always refused to believe. People can be vicious and cruel, and I thought it was just the town gossip, but the rumor going around was that Maureen Bennett shut down the investigation into Ben Spencer's murder the moment my daughter was found dead. The day after Amber died, one of my closest friends swore to me that she saw Maureen having a long lunch with the detective assigned to the case—"

"Detective Paparella?" Cole said.

Gina sat back in surprise. "Yes. You've heard his name before?"

Cole realized he might've revealed too much and he said, "My mom told me about him."

"Ah," Gina said. "He died almost a decade ago. Horrible man. I never wanted to believe that the rumors about Maureen swaying the investigation were true. Especially since I couldn't understand what would motivate her to do something like that. She knew Amber was my daughter, of course. Amber worked here on Saturdays, but their interactions, although sometimes tense, weren't anything that I felt mattered a great deal to Maureen. And yet, something about that rumor has always bothered me.

"Maureen never did explain why she deeded me this property, or sent her men and supplies to help fix it up. I suppose that, in those moments when I really thought about her uncharacteristic generosity, I recognized the taint of something else with it. It wasn't anything Maureen said or did, but there was a look in her eye when she found me unable to get out of bed. It was more than sympathy. It was . . . I don't know. The fleeting look of a guilty conscience, perhaps?

"But, one thing's for sure, once I got back to being busy with the salon and my growing client list, I had less time to pressure Paparella about reopening my daughter's case. I'm wondering now if all this"—Gina paused to gesture toward the walls—"was simply a distraction."

Cole and I looked around the room, then at each other, then back to Gina. It was a lot to think about and it left a sick feeling in the pit of my stomach.

"Anyway," Gina said next, "the point is that, as long as Maureen Bennett still has breath in her body, the investigation into Ben and Amber's death will remain closed. No member of the Fredericksburg PD will touch it, and I know that for certain now. Maureen loved that lake house. She never would've given it up if it hadn't been to her advantage."

"But what could that be?" I asked. "I mean, *why* would she want the murder investigation shut down?"

"I have no idea," Gina said sadly. "Like I said, Amber had met Maureen on a number of occasions here at the salon, and I knew that neither liked the other. My daughter was always polite to your grandmother, but the undertone of defiance was there. Amber was very protective of me, and, back then, Maureen liked to bully me and make snide comments about my appearance, parenting skills, and the way I ran my business. Amber chafed at all of that. I knew that Maureen picked up on Amber's defiance, and that sometimes caused her to treat Amber like a lowly servant. She'd send Amber on ridiculous errands just to throw her weight around. I put up with all of it because Maureen supplied me with referrals and because Amber never complained." Gina sighed and put a hand to the side of her face. "I failed my daughter in that way. I certainly did."

"Did Amber ever mention this Mr. Bishop?" Cole asked.

Gina shook her head. "No. But in the final weeks before she died, she was very worried that Spence was caught up in something that had gotten out of hand. She told me one afternoon that Spence had gotten into a fistfight with a friend of his, which wasn't like him at all."

I leaned forward. We hadn't heard about that. "Who?"

Gina shrugged. "Amber never told me. When it came to Spence she was very guarded. He and his family always seemed to be caught up in some sort of crisis, and Amber's father and I worried about her getting sucked into things no teenage girl should have to handle. Amber knew we would react protectively and that we worried, so she was always light on the details. I did know that the boy in question was one of his friends from the football team, but which one I don't know. Still, I do remember that Amber was very upset by the fact that the two friends were no longer speaking to each other. I could tell she was especially worried about Spence at the time. He'd been behaving oddly, and she confessed to me that she was afraid he'd gotten himself into some kind of personal trouble and was in over his head."

"Do you think this teammate would know what trouble Spence was into?" I asked.

"The young man from the fight?"

I nodded.

"Maybe," she said. "Amber and I were very close, but she kept a lot from me. When I pressed her about what trouble Spence might be in, she wouldn't tell me. Instead, she backpedaled and said she was probably just being dramatic. I simply figured it had something to do with the Spencers' financial situation, which had always been precarious. When Spence was murdered, however, I wondered if the trouble he'd gotten himself into had been the reason he was killed. In the days after he died, Amber totally shut down. She didn't eat or sleep or talk, and I kept thinking she'd open up to me once the grief had subsided a bit. Of course, she never got the chance to get past the grief."

Gina's eyes misted and she dropped her chin to take a moment to compose herself. After clearing her throat she continued. "I realized after Amber died that she'd hidden a great deal from us. I never knew that she and Spence were intimate with each other, or that she was seeing a counselor at school to talk about her problems. With me, she was always putting on a happy face. She was in love with Spence, and she was looking forward to her future as a psychiatrist." Gina's expression turned both prideful and melancholy. "She got accepted into one of the top schools for psychiatry, you know. UCLA. She and Spence were all set to move to California together."

"Uncle Ben was going to UCLA?" Cole asked, genuinely surprised.

"Yes," Gina said. "Didn't you know that?" Cole shook his head. "Ah, well, your uncle had gotten a scholarship to play football there, but at the last minute the funding got pulled. Amber said the coach had overextended his budget, but Spence had another scholarship lined up and he'd still be going. It was a relief to us, because that out-of-state tuition was very expensive, even back then."

Gina looked down at her hands again. "None of that matters now, though. The kids never made it there."

We all fell sadly silent and that's when the curtain parted and the girl with blue tint poked her head in. "Gina? Your two thirty is here."

Gina got up from the table, and put a hand on her lower back, as if it ached a little, then she moved to the doorway. Pausing to turn back to us, she said, "Remember what I told you kids. I know you're anxious to have the case reopened, but I wouldn't push any further with this. Nothing good will come of it, and your grandmother, Lily, could turn on you. Don't forget how powerful she is in this town. We all know that she's already turned on her son. She can make your life, and your mother's, very difficult if she wants to."

With that, she was gone, and Cole and I were left to sit and think about what she'd said.

"What do we do?" I finally asked him.

"Do you want to stop?" he asked me in turn.

"No," I admitted. "I mean it, Cole: if my grandmother had anything to do with Ben and Amber's death, I won't be able to live under her roof. And my mom won't, either."

"She got your mom that job at the hospital though, right?" Cole said carefully.

I sighed. "She did. But there have to be other hospitals Mom can do her residency at. If I told her that I thought Grandmother had something to do with Amber's death, she'd pack us up and move. She would."

"Okay, so let's keep digging," Cole said. "And let's agree that if we get enough clues together to reopen the case, I'll send an email to one of the special agents I met at FAIT and see if I can convince him to look into it."

"You want to get the FBI involved?" I said uneasily. That was hard-core.

"It's probably the only way to bring some justice to Ben and Amber, and avoid having your grandmother getting involved and shutting down an investigation. The feds might also be able to protect our moms from retaliation. I mean, I'll bet your grandmother wouldn't hesitate to get involved with a Fredericksburg PD case if she thought it might lead to trouble for her, but I doubt she'd be willing to gamble with an obstruction charge from the FBI."

I sat with that for a minute. If Grandmother really had been involved in the murders of Ben and Amber, then I honestly wasn't going to shed a tear if she was taken off to jail. I'd gotten to know Amber and Spence in the past twenty-four hours, and they felt more like friends than strangers. If she'd been responsible, then I knew she'd have to be brought to justice.

And yet . . . she was family. Her blood ran though my veins, and instinctively, I felt a little protective of that kinship.

"Lily?" Cole asked me. "You look like you want to back out."

"No," I said, finally arriving at a decision I thought I could live with. "No. I'm not. If she's responsible, Cole, then my grandmother needs to be brought to justice."

He laid a hand on my shoulder and said, "Let's keep digging and decide once we've put all the clues together. If everything points to Maureen Bennett, then I'll let you decide if I make that call to the FBI. Fair?"

I pressed my palm against the back of his hand. "That's only fair to me," I whispered.

His flesh and blood had been murdered, and it might have been because of something *my* flesh and blood had done. I didn't know if I could've made him the same offer if our situations were reversed.

"Yeah, but I'm okay with it," he said. "My mom and I have to live in this town, Lily, and Gina's right—your grandmother totally runs this place. This whole thing could backfire on us and my uncle has been dead for thirty years. Plus, I feel like I know Spence well enough to think that he wouldn't want anything bad to happen to us because we were trying to solve his murder. I doubt he'd think it was worth it."

I lifted my chin and looked at him. Really looked at him. He was such a wise person for someone so young.

"Let's keep going," I said. "We can both decide if and when we find anything that breaks the case open."

"Deal," he said. He let go of my shoulder to reach into his backpack and pull out his tablet. He typed something quickly and hit ENTER.

"I found Grady Weaver," he said. "Maybe that's the best friend Mrs. Greeley said he got in a fight with."

"Do you think he'll talk to us about Ben?"

"Only one way to find out," Cole said, putting the yearbooks and his tablet back in his backpack and motioning me to follow him out. We waved to Gina on our way through the front door, hopped in his car, and took off.

Fifteen minutes later, we were sitting in front of a nice, two-story, A-frame house with teak-colored shingles and a cabin-in-the-woods feel. There were no signs of life on the property, even though the windows were large enough to give a view of the living room.

I rubbed my palms on my shorts. I was nervous. "We're really doing this?" I whispered.

Cole grinned at me. "You don't like talking to strangers much, huh?"

I grinned back. "I talked to you that first day, didn't I?"

"Thank God," Cole said, patting his heart. "I never would've gotten over it if you hadn't."

I laughed, and just like that a lot of my nervousness vanished. "Okay, let's do this."

We got out of the car and walked along the front path. Leaning close to Cole, I said, "You can do the talking."

He chuckled. "Can I? Gee, thanks."

I nudged him with my shoulder, and he smiled. Just as we were about to walk up the three steps to the door, we heard from behind us, "Can I help you?"

We both froze. Cole turned around first. "Hi," he said. "Mr. Weaver?"

A good-looking middle-aged man with a square jaw, olive skin, and dark hair graying at the temples, stood in the drive with a garden hose.

"You guys collecting for the school?" he asked.

"No, sir," Cole said.

"Well, good, 'cause I don't have anything to give you. So, what do you want?"

Cole cleared his throat. "My name is Cole Drepeau, sir. I think you knew my uncle, Ben Spencer?"

At the mention of the name, Mr. Weaver's eyes widened. "Spence was your uncle?" he said. "You're little Stacey's kid?"

"Yes, sir," he said.

Weaver came forward to us and stuck out his hand. "Man!" he said as he pumped Cole's hand up and down. "You look just like him. And you're as big as him."

Cole seemed to stand up a little straighter under the man's scrutiny, and I could tell he was pleased.

"So what brings you by?" Weaver asked, finally noticing me and offering me his hand, too.

"I'm doing a school paper on my uncle," Cole said. "And I wanted to talk to some of his friends and see what he was like."

Weaver considered Cole for a minute. I didn't think he believed him. "A school paper?" he said. "Didn't you guys just start classes?"

"Last week," I said. "We were given an assignment in our English class to do a research paper on someone from our family tree who had an impact on the family in some significant way."

Weaver pointed back and forth between us. "You two in the same class?"

"Yes, sir," I said.

"Who'd you pick?" he said to me.

"My grandfather." Weaver studied me and there was doubt in his eyes so I added, "Dr. William James Bennett."

Weaver's brow shot up in surprise. "You're a Bennett?"

I held up my hand. "Guilty."

"Huh." Weaver's expression became neutral. Turning back to Cole, he said, "Your uncle was a great guy. One of my best friends. He'd help anybody out of a bind, and give you the shirt off his back. Spence was one of the best people I ever knew."

Cole beamed with pride. "Thanks," he said. "There's just this rumor going around that's sort of bugging me, though."

Weaver cocked his head. "The UCLA thing?"

Cole blinked. "Uh, yeah," he said, pretending like he knew exactly what Weaver was talking about. "Can you clear that up for me?"

Mr. Weaver shrugged. "Spence loved Amber," he said. "Like, *loved* her. She said she was going to UCLA, and he decided he was going with her. Problem was, he had a hard time with exams, especially when there was a lot of pressure to do well. He managed okay in school, I mean, his grades were pretty good, given his anxiety around finals, but he bombed his first two attempts at the SAT. He wouldn't have been able to get in the door at UCLA.

"Then, one day, he takes the test and bam! He scores really high. Those were the scores he submitted, and all of a sudden he's in and has a scholarship to boot. But a month or so later, we heard that the school was questioning the scores. Spence had to retake the test, and he actually did okay—good enough to get in at UCLA at least—but nothing like his earlier scores. UCLA suspected he'd cheated, but they couldn't prove it, so they pulled his scholarship but still let him attend if he could pay for it. Trouble for him was, he didn't have the money to go, but then all of a sudden I heard that he did. Somebody came up with the cash for him. At least that's what I heard. I always wondered if it was Amber's parents who came through, or maybe some other mysterious benefactor. Spence was loved by a lot of people, so it was possible."

My heart was hammering in my chest. The photo of Ben sitting in the front row of the classroom, about to take his SATs with Mr. Bishop, flashed over and over in my mind.

A quick glance at Cole told me he was likely thinking of it, too. "Did my uncle have any problems with any of the teachers?" he asked.

Mr. Weaver scratched his head. "Problem? No way. Like I said, everybody loved him."

"We heard that he had an issue with Mr. Bishop," I said boldly, if only to possibly trigger Weaver's memory.

"Bishop?" he said. "Who was that?"

"He taught freshmen algebra," I said.

Weaver shrugged. "Never heard of him. But I was advanced math, and back when I went to Chamberlain, high school started in tenth grade. It changed to start in the ninth grade when I was a junior, so if Bishop taught only freshmen, I'd never have had him."

"We also heard that Spence beat up one of his friends," Cole said carefully. It was maybe one question too many about Ben's character. Weaver's eyes narrowed.

"Yeah, I wouldn't know anything about that." It was clear to me that now Weaver was lying. "Listen, I gotta get back to watering the plants. Good luck to you guys with the paper, okay?"

On our way back to the car, I said, "So, do we both think that Bishop somehow helped Ben score really high on the SATs?"

"Has to be," Cole said as he opened the car door. "But why would that be worth killing him over?"

I thought about it as I walked around and slid into the passenger seat. "Maybe because Spence was going to come clean?"

Cole sat down behind the wheel and nodded. "Okay, so how was your grandmother involved?"

I laid my head back against the seat. "I have no idea. But we know that he took the SATs with Bishop. The photo in the yearbook proves it." And then another thought occurred to me. "Ohmigod! Cole! We forgot to take the yearbooks back to your grandmother's!"

Cole glanced at the clock on the dash. "Shit! If we hurry, we can get them back before she comes home from her shift."

"I'm not going inside with you this time," I said. "'No more trespassing for me."

"Glad to know you're going straight," he said lightly.

I rolled my eyes. "Just drive."

Cole eased down the street and stopped several houses away. "Dammit," he muttered. His grandmother's car was parked in the driveway.

"I thought you said her shift ended at four." I sat hunched down, nervously clutching the yearbooks.

"Sometimes they rotate her onto an earlier shift," he said, tapping the steering wheel with his fingers.

"What do we do?" I asked.

Cole picked up his phone and looked at the display. "If she was gonna notice, she would've already. They came from my uncle's room, and I don't think she goes in there much. She even keeps the door locked."

"She keeps the door locked? How'd you get in to get the yearbooks?" I asked.

Cole shrugged like it was an easy thing and pulled out his wallet from his back pocket. Taking out his school ID, he said, "All you have to do is slide this between the door frame and the latch, and—presto—you're past security."

I let out a small laugh. "If it's that easy to get past, I wonder why she bothers to lock the door."

Cole glanced sideways at me. "She doesn't know I can get in there," he admitted. "Like I said, Grams is a little weird about Ben's room. It's her shrine. Ben was her favorite by far. Sometimes she still talks about him in the present tense—like he's still here. She just couldn't get over losing him. She tells me all the time that he was the only one that used to take care of her. I guess he stood up for her against my granddad and stuff. Spence would make sure she didn't get hit."

I sucked in a breath. "Your granddad beat up your grandmother?"

Cole nodded solemnly. "He was a real asshole."

"Why didn't she leave him?" I asked, looking back toward the house. I felt such sympathy for Mrs. Spencer.

Cole shrugged. "Don't know. I asked Mom that same question, and she said that her dad bullied Gram for their entire marriage. She believed she wouldn't make it on her own if she left him. Not with two kids in tow."

"Wow," I said. "That had to have been rough."

"It's why I cut her a lot of slack when she's not really nice to us."

I thought about my own grandmother, who had every indulgence and luxury. She'd come from money, married money, and had never wanted for anything. And she was equally bitter and mean, only she had no excuses.

"So, what do we do about the yearbooks?" I asked, putting them back on the floor by my feet.

"She works Sundays, too. We can come back here tomorrow and sneak them in."

"We're hanging out again tomorrow?" I asked.

Cole's cheeks were tinted with red. "Uh . . . I kinda hoped so. Unless you've got other stuff to do."

"No, I'm good for tomorrow, too," I said, feeling heat in my own face.

"Cool," Cole said.

"Cool," I agreed.

"Okay, then," Cole said.

"Right. Okay, then."

There was an awkward silence before Cole pulled away from the curb and turned the car around. "Let's figure out who we should talk to next."

"What about that other friend of Ben's?" I said.

I was kind of enjoying spending the day playing amateur sleuth with Cole. It was both nerve-racking and exhilarating, plus it didn't hurt that he was freaking gorgeous.

"What? Why are you looking at me like that?" Cole asked, glancing over at me while he drove.

I realized I'd been grinning. "Nothing," I said quickly. "I guess I'm just having a good time hanging out with you."

He grinned, too. "Yeah?"

"Yeah."

"Good," he said. "Maybe it'll become a habit."

Cole slid the car over into the lot at a grocery store and parked.

"We going shopping?" I asked curiously.

Before answering, he pulled out his tablet from his backpack. "Naw. I wanted to look up that other friend of Ben's, like you said. Bill something..."

I waited patiently while Cole tapped at his tablet. "Dammit," he muttered after a minute.

"What?"

"Bill Metcalf—the guy in the photo with Ben—moved to LA. He's a TV producer at Warner Brothers."

"Wow," I said. That was pretty impressive.

"Yeah," Cole replied, still tapping at the tablet.

"What if we tried calling him?"

Cole stopped tapping to eye me skeptically. "He's got no contact info here. If he's up in the food chain at Warner Brothers, I doubt we'd be able to get through."

I frowned. "So where does that leave us?"

Cole motioned to the yearbooks at my feet. "We could try looking up some of the other football players on the team. Maybe one of them was close to Ben and knew what was going on."

But I had a better idea. "Why don't we try working this through Amber's friends?" I said. "I know that I used to tell Sophie everything that was going on with Tanner and..." My voice trailed off as I considered that that might not have been a good idea in hindsight.

Cole's expression turned sympathetic. "You should really think about calling her."

"I know. I will," I said sadly. "But let's focus back on Amber. Maybe she told her two best friends about what was going on with Ben." After reaching for the yearbooks, I turned to the page I'd marked and opened it up. "Sara Radcliff and Britta Cummings."

Cole began tapping again at his tablet. A minute later he said, "Bingo. Sara Radcliff lives eighteen miles north of here."

"Wow," I said flatly. "You're really good at looking people up on the internet."

"Mad skills, remember?" Cole said with a wink.

I laughed. "Yeah, yeah. Okay. Let's go see her."

Cole began to back out of the space. "Who's going to take the lead this time?"

"You again," I said.

He cocked an eyebrow at me. "She might open up better if you asked her questions."

"Yeah, but why would I be asking her about Amber?"

Cole thought on that for a bit. "Maybe Amber was your mom's cousin?" he said. "And you're doing a report on her for school?"

I felt very nervous about that approach. "If she knew Amber well enough to know her family, and starts asking me questions about relatives, the lie is going to unravel. What about if we say something like we're working for the school paper, and we decided to cover Chamberlain High's most controversial event—the murder of Ben Spencer by Amber Greeley? We can dig around in Sara's memories all we want if that's our cover story. She won't think it's suspicious that we're asking personal questions about them."

Cole pointed a finger gun at me. "I like that," he said. "I like that a lot."

"Okay, then that's the story we'll stick with, and we'll hope that she can tell us something new."

Amber

"SO WHAT'S THE STORY WITH YOU AND SPENCE?" Sara asked me as we changed into pajamas.

I felt myself stiffen. "Story? There's no story."

Sara shook her head at me. "Come on, Amber. You guys are barely smooching in the hallway anymore. What gives?"

I pulled on my fuzzy slippers and refused to look at her. I loved Sara, but as graduation was approaching, she was turning into someone I barely recognized. All she did was spend a lot of her time wasting it. She seemed to have no ambition beyond where she could get her next buzz. The choices she made were starting to really worry and upset me, but I'd been setting aside both my opinion and irritation in favor of our friendship. I tried to remind her about how much potential she had, how much I believed in her, but, lately, it was falling on deaf ears.

"Nothing gives," I said lightly, in answer to her question.

Then I pointed to the clock on the wall. "Come on, if we want to watch the movie before my parents get home, we'll have to start it now."

My parents had just gotten a brand-new VHS player and Daddy had taken me to the video store earlier to rent *Grease*—one of my favorite films. Sara and I had planned a pajama party to watch it as my parents were going to be out late. Spence was hanging out with his friends that night, too.

Well, most of his friends. He and Jamie still weren't speaking since their fight the week before. And no matter how much I asked about it, Spence wouldn't tell me what'd sparked the fight or the one before that on his porch. And I didn't think the first fight was a continuation of the previous thing. There was something else that'd been added to their feud, but whatever it was, Spence wouldn't tell me. He'd become even more distant with me in the ensuing days, and I was terrified he was about to break up with me.

The doorbell rang just as Sara and I were getting settled on the couch. I opened the door to find Britta standing there, triumphantly holding up two six-packs of beer.

"Ta-da!" she said, dancing into the living room.

"Oh my God!" Sara squealed. "You got it?"

"Told ya I'd come through," she said, handing off the package to Sara, who promptly popped open one of the cans.

Sara took a big swig. "Oh, man, that's good!" she said.

I made a disgusted face. I didn't like beer, and I didn't know how Sara could stand the bitter, awful taste. She offered me one of the cans, and I shook my head. "No thanks."

Britt gave Sara a look that said, *Told ya so.* It irritated me.

"I've got rum," Britt said, her eyes glistening with

mischief. Opening her jean jacket, she pulled out a fifth from one of the inside pockets. "Diet Coke in the fridge?"

"Yeah, but don't go crazy, Britt. My parents are coming home soon."

"I thought they were out till, like, eleven?" Sara said. I wanted to punch her.

"Sometimes they come home early."

"God, Amber, will you lighten up?" Britt said. "You're always Little Miss Perfect. It's annoying."

My chest tightened, my face got hot, and my eyes immediately misted. I turned away from Britt and Sara so they wouldn't see. I knew I was pretty anal, but I'd been that way since I could remember, and it hurt my feelings to hear one of my best friends say something so mean. Still, I didn't say anything in reply. I was barely holding it together these days anyway, and if I lost it in front of these two they'd bug me until I confessed all my fears and worries about Spence and me.

The truth was that I didn't know where we stood anymore. I couldn't get Spence to give me a straight answer about the scholarship from Mrs. Bennett. He kept insisting that she was still coming through with the money, but he never met my eyes when he said it. There wasn't an easy way for me to find out, either. I certainly couldn't ask Mrs. Bennett.

Or maybe I could? Maybe when she came in for her next hair appointment I could casually thank her for helping Spence out, and if she told me she wasn't, then I'd know.

I had no idea what we'd do if she didn't give him the money. I'd dropped off the financial aid package that his mother needed to fill out months ago, but so far, she hadn't done it, and Spence refused to pressure her about it because his mom had issues. Emotional. Mental. The works.

"Hi, Bailey!" I heard Britt say. I softened a little toward her when I saw her plop down to her knees and snuggle with my dog. I was going to miss Bailey so much! But it was only for a couple of years. Mom and Dad promised me that they'd get her to California for my junior and senior year— provided I found available housing that was dog-friendly. By then, Spence and I could be living together. If we were still together, that is.

"So, what's going on?" Britt said, getting up to saunter over to the love seat with her rum and Diet Coke. I wondered if those were the only calories she'd had all day.

"Not much," I said, flipping on the TV and reaching for the video, still in its plastic holder. "We were just about to watch *Grease*."

Sara made a *pffing* sound. I noticed she'd already downed the first beer and was working on the second. Turning to Britt, she said, "Little Miss P won't tell me what's going on with her and Spence."

"What's going on with her and Spence?"

"Well, according to Spence's mom, they're gonna break up."

The room went completely silent except for the TV as both Britt and I looked at Sara in shock. How dare she say something like that!

"What the hell are you talking about?" I demanded.

Sara waved her beer can at me. "Don't yell at me," she said. "Yell at Mrs. Spencer."

"What did she say?" I snapped.

"Well," Sara said, as though she was amused by the proclamation, "you know Mrs. S cleans our house, right?"

I did know that. It was a fact that Sara often mentioned around Spence. It had never seemed to bother him, mostly because he was proud of the fact that his mom was working.

"What about it?" I snapped again.

"Well! According to my mother, Mrs. S said that Spence had no intention of flying off to California next fall. He was going to stay at home and take care of her. She said he was thinking about community college for a year before transferring to UVA."

Heat filled my chest like molten lava slipping into a well. "That's a lie, Sara," I said quietly, my tone laced with warning. Out of the corner of my eye, I saw Britt sitting on the love seat across from us with big eyes. Her mouth hung open. I ignored her and gave Sara all of my angry attention. "If you repeat that lie, then you and I will never be friends again. Do you understand?"

Sara finally seemed to get that no one in the room thought she was funny. "I was just letting you know," she said. "I mean, God, Amber! If Spence is about to break up with you, shouldn't I tell you that?"

"He's not," I growled. "And you're not my friend if you keep saying that."

Sara's eyes watered. "I'm sorry," she said. But the tension in the room wasn't ebbing.

Britta got up and came over to squeeze in between us. Handing me her cup, she said, "Drink."

"I'm not—"

"I don't care," she cut me off. "You need to chill out. So drink."

I took the cup from her, my hands trembling, and much to my own surprise, downed the contents.

Lily

"CAN I GET YOU TWO SOMETHING TO DRINK?" SARA
Radcliff asked Cole and me.

"No, thank you," we said together.

She smiled kindly and pointed us to the sofa in her gorgeous living room. When we'd first pulled up to the house,
I'd wondered if we'd gotten the address right. The home was
a very modern-looking structure, with lots of sharp angles
and huge windows. It looked like a house of the future. And
it was big.

Sara had answered the door herself, and she was very
pretty—very elegant. She had long blond hair set in stylish
waves, her skin was flawless and her makeup simple, but also
flawless. She wore a pair of lightweight gray silk pants that
billowed when she walked, and a cream shell underneath a
thin powder-pink sweater that draped across her shoulders.
We'd introduced ourselves by first name only, and told her
that we were from Chamberlain High, working on our first

senior-year story for the paper on Amber and Ben. She'd seemed a bit surprised by the topic, but had readily agreed to talk to us.

Once we were all seated, she said, "First of all, you should know that Amber was a good person."

I felt some of the nervous tension in my shoulders relax. "We keep hearing that," I said. "Can you tell us about her?"

Sara glanced over my left shoulder, and I turned slightly to see that one of the bookshelves in her living room held a series of framed photographs. I couldn't see the images up close, but I suspected there was one of Amber among them.

"She was my best friend," she said. "Since we were very little. And she was my best friend when nobody else could stand me. I was a holy terror when I was younger, but Amber either took pity on me or saw something in me. She used to always say to me, 'Sara, you're smarter than you think. You could be anything you want to be. Why are you settling for mediocrity?'" Sara paused to press her index finger against her upper lip and dip her chin, as if it pained her to remember that. "No adult had ever said anything that wise to me. She was always my best cheerleader, and she believed in me. Somehow, she saw through the tough, rebellious act I was putting up for everybody else. She knew I had potential that I didn't even know about. Amber was . . . amazing."

A little pang hit me mid-chest. Sophie used to say similarly validating things to me. Listening to the way Sara spoke of Amber made me wonder if I'd ever talk like that about Sophie. Would I regret never speaking to her again? Looking at the glint of tears in Sara's eyes, I knew that somehow, some way, I'd have to find a way to forgive Sophie, because I didn't ever want to look that sad when speaking about my best friend.

"After she died," Sara said, brushing away one stray tear, "well, I went into a tailspin. I drank myself out of school my freshman year of college. Drugs followed. I nearly died twice. But one day when I was in rehab, I had a dream about Amber. She came to me looking so pretty, wearing her prom dress, and she said those same words to me again. She asked me why I was settling for mediocrity. I didn't have an answer for her, but I felt such sadness. Such hopelessness. She told me to get help. To go back to school. To start building things. And then she said, 'I'm gonna see you again, girl. And when I do, I want you to have done something with your life.'"

I felt a chill travel up my spine and my arms tingled with goose pimples. Something about the story of Sara's dream tugged at the back of my mind. Almost like I remembered having that exact dream, but I knew I hadn't, and I wondered at what Amber had said to Sara in her dream. That she'd see her again. *Was* Amber seeing Sara again through my eyes? The goose bumps on my arms got bigger.

"The next morning," Sara continued, "when I woke up, I knew what I had to do. So I got clean, went back to school, got my associate's in architecture, then my master's, and finally my PhD."

"You're an architect?" Cole asked with admiration.

She smiled. "I am. I'm also a professor at UVA, and I own my own firm, but only because I did exactly what Amber told me to do, and it saved my life and built this one. And that's really what you need to keep in mind when you're writing about her. That she was a good person who saw the potential in everybody."

"So you don't believe shc could've killed Ben Spencer, right?" I asked, knowing we'd found another ally.

Sara surprised me. "Oh, I didn't say that. I do believe Amber killed Spence. But I couldn't really blame her. I mean, I knew how much she loved him, and how deep a betrayal he'd committed against her. It'd make anybody crack."

Cole and I both sat forward. "Ben betrayed her?" I said, shocked by the statement. "Did he cheat on her or something?"

Sara sighed sadly. "No, I don't think so, Lily. It was much bigger than that. I don't know what happened between them other than he lied to her about going away with her to UCLA in the fall. He strung her along to the bitter end, making her believe that he had every intention of going with her to California. The night of prom, I suspect he finally confessed that he'd be staying home, and he broke it off with her. I think she just snapped."

I sat there, stunned, and my heart felt like it was breaking. Amber's best friend believed she was capable of murder. It hurt as deep as when I'd found out that Sophie and Tanner were dating. It felt like a terrible betrayal.

Cole said, "See, we've been digging into the murder a little, and we don't think Amber was responsible."

It was Sara's turn to sit forward. Eyeing him curiously, she said, "Why do you say that?"

"There's a rumor going around that a teacher might've murdered them both. Some guy named David Bishop."

Sara's brow furrowed. "Bishop?" she said, and then tapped her cheek with her finger. "Huh."

"Did you know him?" I asked hopefully.

"No," she said quickly. Maybe a little too quickly. "I didn't. But I had heard that one of the freshmen math teachers had been fired. I think his name was Mr. Bishop." She seemed to think on it some more and said, "But what would he have to do with Ben or Amber?"

Cole and I exchanged a look, and I nodded to him to tell her. "We think it had something to do with the SATs," he said. "And someone said that maybe the Bennetts were involved."

"Oh, that!" she said with what sounded to me like a forced laugh. "Yeah, I heard a little about that, too. Did Britt tell you about it? She knew more about it than I did."

"Britta Cummings?" I said, remembering the name from the yearbook.

"It's Schroder now," Sara said. "Britta Schroder. She married a plastic surgeon. If you guys don't know that then I guess you haven't talked to her?"

"Not yet," I said. "She was next on our list."

Sara nodded. "She lives in Ashland now. Her and her husband have a couple of kids from what I hear." She seemed about to say something more, but hesitated.

"What?" Cole asked her.

"I'd be careful with anything that Britta tells you about Amber," she said. "She was very jealous of her, because Britt was in love with Spence. She and Amber got into it at prom. And, while they were arguing in the ladies' room, Spence left the dance. Amber went looking for him a little later, but neither of them was seen for at least forty-five minutes after that. By then, Spence was dead."

Something clicked in my mind and I said, "Was Britta there with you during that time?"

Sara turned to me as if I'd just touched on something that'd bothered her for a long, long time. "No," she said. "Her date walked out on her, and she took off, too. I remember seeing him before we heard about Spence, but I don't remember that Britt ever came back to the dance."

Cole nudged my knee with his, and I nudged a little back. We had ourselves yet another suspect in the pool.

We left Sara's house and got back in the car.

"How far away is Ashland from here?" I asked him, anxious to go talk to Britta.

Cole glanced at the clock. It was nearly five thirty in the afternoon. "Depending on traffic, it'll take us at least an hour," he said.

I frowned. "Crap. They'll probably be eating dinner by then."

"Might not be a good plan to interrupt their dinner," Cole agreed. "Plus, it's Saturday night. They could be going out or something, too."

"So what do we do?" I asked.

"We can go see Britta tomorrow," he said. "You up for that?"

"I am. I'll have to figure out what to tell Mom. Her thirty-six-hour shift ends at six A.M. tomorrow, but she'll head straight to bed, so I can probably just leave her a note that I'm hanging out with you and that'll be okay."

Cole glanced again at the clock on the dash. "Do you want to get a snack before I take you home?"

I was a little hungry, and it was an excuse to hang out with Cole a bit longer. "I'm always up for a snack."

He started the car and backed out of Sara Radcliff's driveway. "Taco Bell or ice cream?" he asked.

"Ice cream," I decided.

We got a couple of cones and ate them leaning against Cole's car, talking about stuff that had nothing to do with Amber or Spence, which, honestly, was a relief. At least for a little while. Cole asked me about living in Richmond and my old school, and I asked him about certain teachers and classes I had at Chamberlain High. Once we'd polished off the cones, he motioned to the car and said, "Can we make one more quick pit stop before I get you home?"

"What's the pit stop?"

"I want to check the murder file again," he said. "There were all those witness statements taken the night of the murder and no mention that Britta had left the dance early, or that Amber and Britta had gotten into a fight. If Sara knew about the fight, probably some other people did, too, so I just want to check the file to make sure I didn't miss something."

"Sure. Let's do it."

We got to Cole's house and he pulled into the back of the drive. "What time does your mom get home?" I asked him.

"On Saturdays she usually gets home around seven thirty. She likes to hang out with some of the other nurses at a pub near the clinic and unwind. I'll end up making her dinner before I get to my poker game."

I glanced at him as we walked to the back door together. "Poker game?"

He made a face like he was sorry he'd let that out of the bag. "Yeah, just me and a couple of friends. You know, guy stuff."

"Cool," I said. He kept surprising me, and I liked the image of him sitting around with his buddies, playing poker. There was just something sexy about guys being guys.

Cole seemed to think I was put off by the confession, though. "Lily, I'd invite you over but we're not all that civilized on poker night."

I put a hand on his arm. "Cole," I said. "It's cool. Have fun at your poker game. Really."

His expression relaxed. "But I'll see you tomorrow, right?" he asked, pausing at the door.

"Definitely," I said coyly.

Cole leaned toward me, and our gazes locked. He was going to kiss me again, and I nearly moaned with anticipation. The last kiss we'd shared had been surreal. I was eager to feel his lips against mine again.

But an inch from me, Cole paused. His gaze traveled up and behind me, and then he pulled back and said, "What the hell?!"

I turned to look back. The window into what appeared to be the laundry room was broken and there were little bits of glass on the ground. The latch had been pushed up enough for someone to crawl through.

Suddenly, I felt Cole's arm snake around my middle. "Get behind me," he said.

I went from alarmed to petrified in under two seconds. "You're not going in there, are you?" I whispered.

"Yeah, so stay here," he said.

I grabbed his shirt. "Don't be an idiot! We should call the police! What if they're still in there? What if there's two of them?"

"Stay here," he said again, and gently eased out of my grasp to try the handle on the door. It opened easily, and I remembered that he'd locked it when we'd left the house earlier.

"Cole!" I whispered. "Don't!"

But he slipped through the entry on his own. Meanwhile, I stood there shivering in fear, and straining my ears to hear anything that might indicate he'd come upon the intruder. Or intruders. Nothing.

I dug out my cell and started to dial 911, but I quickly realized I didn't know Cole's address. Moving away from the door, I was about to head down the drive to look for a house number when I heard movement behind me.

I screamed and jumped around to face the criminal, but it was just Cole on the back step, looking pale and completely rattled.

"Are they in there?" I asked him, holding my phone close in case I needed to dial quickly.

He shook his head. "No."

And then I thought of his sweet dog. "Ohmigod! Bailey!"

Cole came off the step and over to me. "She's fine," he said. "She was in her crate."

I blinked. "She was in her crate?"

"Yeah," he said. "And we didn't do that. So, somehow somebody got her into her crate and locked her up."

"Okay, so what'd they take?"

"The file," he said.

"The what?"

"The murder file, Lily. It's gone. That's the only thing missing."

"But...but..." I tried to make sense of that. "What the hell would a robber want with an old murder file?"

"I don't think a robber would want it," he said. "But the murderer would."

The air left my lungs so quickly that my knees buckled. Cole got an arm around me just in time or I would've scraped them on the pavement.

"You okay?" he said, holding on to me until I was steady enough to stand on my own.

"Yeah," I lied. "We talked to the murderer today?" I said weakly.

Cole looked back toward the house. "Maybe."

I put a hand over my mouth. "Oh my God, Cole."

He nodded. The bravado from a few moments before was gone.

"Okay...okay..." I said, trying to think this thing through. "What if there's a logical explanation? What if your mom took it and the broken window is just a coincidence or something?"

"She's been at work all day," he reminded me. "And if she came home and found that on the kitchen table, Lily, she'd be calling me two seconds later to tell me to get my butt home. She never would've waited till later to say something to me. The window and the dog can't be a coincidence."

I was shaking all over now, and Cole led me to a set of lawn chairs. "We have to call the police," I said.

Cole looked back toward the house. "And tell them what? That I had a murder file that'd been illegally obtained by one of their own guys, and it got stolen?"

"Well, at least you can report the break-in!" I insisted. "Cole, if he left any prints behind, the police might be able to catch him and then we can tell them about the file. We just won't tell them where it came from."

Cole considered that for a minute, then nodded. "Okay. But let me take you home first."

I bit my lip. It felt like he was dismissing me. "I can stay," I told him.

But Cole reached for my hand and said, "I think I'd feel better if you were locked safely behind that big gate on your grandmother's estate."

What neither of us said out loud was *Unless she is the murderer.*

"What about you?" I asked him. "Cole, if the murderer really did come here and steal the file, then you and your mom are in more danger than I am."

Cole rubbed his temples. I could tell he was trying to keep it together even though the break-in had unnerved him.

"The guys are gonna be here at eight," he said. "Which means we'll be safe for the night at least. Tomorrow Mom's headed to Newport News to stay with her boyfriend. He lives there."

"Maybe you should go with her," I said. "Or call that guy you know from the FBI and tell him everything that we've found out so far, and that your house was broken into. Maybe he can do something."

Cole smiled. "I'm not gonna crash my mom's night off with her boyfriend," he said. "And Special Agent Presco isn't going to do anything other than tell me there's not much he can do. We need more, Lily."

I looked to the window. "But this just got really serious, Cole. Dangerous even."

"Only if we go back and try to interview the same people we did today," he reasoned. "It's gotta be someone we already talked to."

"Unless Bishop figured out who we were," I said.

Cole tapped his thigh with his keys and looked toward his black vintage Mustang. "He could've followed us back to the car and run my plates somehow."

"But we didn't even talk to him," I said. "Why would he get suspicious?"

"We talked to Grady Weaver and Sara Radcliff. But no way did she have time to get over here and break in before us."

"She could've called someone," I said, looking around the yard. Dusk was already starting to settle, and the wind had picked up a little. Swaying trees were throwing long, creepy shadows, and I gave in to an involuntary shudder.

Cole swept a hand through his hair. "None of this makes any sense," he said. "The more people we talk to, the more people we find out could've been the killer."

I sat down again and held on to Cole's hand, as much to lend him support as to get some support in return.

"Maybe you're right," I said. "Maybe we do need a little more. Maybe Britta will be able to tell us why Sara was acting so weird, or why Grady Weaver was so guarded, or why my grandmother gave a fired schoolteacher a million-dollar lake house."

"Okay," Cole said. "Let's make a deal that we talk to Britta and whatever she tells us we take to Special Agent Presco."

"I think that's a good plan," I said. "But, Cole, I'm gonna talk to my mom about all this."

He looked like he wanted to protest, but then stopped himself.

"Yeah," he said. "That might be a good idea. And if she doesn't let you come with me tomorrow, don't sweat it. I'll talk to Britta alone."

"Oh, you're not going alone," I told him firmly. "Even if I have to sneak out of the house, I'm coming with you."

He softened and swung my hand back and forth. "You make an awesome sidekick, you know that, Lily Bennett?"

That made me smile, too. "I've got mad skills, baby," I mimicked. "Mad skills."

Amber

"DON'T BE MAD," SPENCE SAID AS HE SAT ON THE swing on our back porch.

It was late. I was tired from studying for finals all day, and worrying about what Sara had said all weekend. Spence had been conveniently out of touch most of the day until after dinner when he'd finally returned my call.

"You need to come over here so we can talk," I'd said evenly the minute I'd heard his voice. By that time, I was seriously angry.

Now here he was, and he seemed to think I was ticked off because we hadn't hung out together over the weekend.

"Hey," he said, reaching for me. "Ambi, come here. Sit with me, okay?"

I was standing at the railing, arms crossed, and caught between feeling heartbroken and so angry I could scream. I avoided his touch and continued to glare hard at him.

"Is it true?" I finally managed to say, my voice quavering.

He frowned at me. "Is what true?"

There was an edge to his voice. The same edge that'd been present in so many of our conversations the past few of weeks. I thought it was time to put everything on the table. "Are you breaking up with me?"

He sat there for a long moment and just stared. "No," he said at last. "But you should probably break up with me."

I stared at him, dumbstruck. "What the hell does that mean, Spence?"

He hung his head and, to my utter shock, his shoulders started to shake. He was crying. All of my pent-up anger evaporated, and I went to him to wrap my arms around him.

"Spence," I whispered. "Spence! What's the matter? What's wrong?"

He grabbed me and pulled me to him, crushing me against his chest like he was holding on for dear life. "I'm so sorry," he cried. "Ambi, I'm so sorry!"

I stroked his hair and held on to him for a long, long time until he calmed down. Finally, he loosened his hold on me and sat back on the seat to gather up my hands, but he wouldn't look at me.

"Tell me," I said gently. "Spence, please tell me what's going on?"

"I didn't get the scholarship," he said.

His words were slow to sink in. "Okay," I said. "What about the financial aid package?"

"The deadline for that was last week, Amber. Mom told me she sent it in, but when I called, they said they never got it. I went through the house and found it. She never filled it out. When I confronted her about it, she broke down. She said she couldn't make it without my help. I can't go," he said, his voice choked with emotion. "She needs me. Stacey needs me. I want to go with you so bad, but I can't."

He started crying again and buried his head in his hands, then leaned himself forward and just cried in my lap. I hugged him while my mind whirred.

"Okay," I said at last. "Spence, I understand. We just have to figure out what to do now. That's all. Either way, we'll figure it out and it'll be okay. I promise."

But it wasn't going to be okay. I could feel my dreams slipping away. Dreams of a life together with Spence in California. Me, as a psychiatrist, and Spence working his way up the corporate ladder. I'd imagined us living a little farther south in San Diego. We'd find a cute bungalow together. We'd raise our children there. I wanted three: two boys and a girl. Spence would make an amazing father. We'd be happy.

I realized then that I'd held that dream for so long I'd made it my reality. What I'd forgotten was Spence and the crushing weight of responsibility that he carried.

Of course he couldn't leave his mom and his sister. I wondered if he ever would have, even with the money for school. Would he have left them?

"Hey," I said, lifting him up to face me. "Please don't cry. We'll figure it out, honey. We will."

"How am I gonna let you go?" he asked me. "You're the only good thing in my life, Amber. The *only* good thing."

"Spence," I said, stroking the side of his cheek. In that moment I loved him more than anything or anyone in the world. A future in California was nothing without Spence.

He was my future. "If you have to stay here, then I'll stay with you."

His breath caught. "What?"

I kissed away the tears on his cheek. "I can go to UVA, Spence. They have a good program, too."

He shook his head. "Amber, going to California is your dream."

I nodded. "It's not a real dream without you in it, Spence." He stared at me in shock or relief or gratitude, I couldn't tell which. Maybe all three. "We'll stay here together and figure it all out. Momma's gonna love that I'll be staying home."

At last he shook his head. "I can't let you," he said. "I can't let you give up your dreams just because I can't go with you."

I placed my hands on the sides of his head and forced him to look me in the eyes.

"I'm staying," I said firmly, and I almost said it without giving away the heartbreak in my voice. I could give up moving to California, but not without a few tears of my own.

"Amber—" he began.

"It's settled, Spence," I said, shaking my head to clear away the tears blurring my vision. "I'm staying. I'll get in touch with UVA tomorrow. They've already accepted me; I just have to let them know that I've changed my mind and I'm going to attend classes there in the fall."

"But—"

"No buts," I said, cutting him off. "It's you and me. Together. Forever."

Lily

IT SEEMED TO TAKE ME FOREVER TO GET READY THE next day. I'd changed six times before finally deciding on an outfit and what to do with my hair on the muggy end-of-summer morning.

At least I'd slept a little better the night before. I'd had the usual nightmare, but it'd only been the portion of discovering Ben in the field. When I'd woken up, I'd even been a little less devastated. Maybe I was becoming desensitized to it. But I knew that Amber was still very much with me. It was almost as though I could feel her hovering close by.

Mom was still asleep when I snuck out to meet Cole by the front gate.

"How'd it go this morning with your mom?" he asked me right after I'd gotten into his car.

I sighed. "It didn't."

"You guys got in a fight?"

I shook my head. "I was gonna talk to her, but when she

got home she was asleep on her feet. I've never seen her so tired, so I didn't want to get into a long discussion with her. I'll tell her this afternoon when we're done talking to Britta."

"We can wait," Cole said. "I mean, if you want me to go back inside with you and help you explain, I will."

I put my hand over his, which was resting on the gear-shift. I liked the easiness of our relationship, as though he were someone I'd known far longer than a week.

"She's still asleep, Cole. I left her a note, and she prob-ably won't get up until after noon. We'll be back by then."

"Okay," he said, then added, "Let's do this." And we pulled away from the estate.

"How'd it go at your house last night?" I asked. "Did you tell your mom about the break-in?"

Cole blanched. "No."

"Did the police come and take a report?" I pressed. Something about the way he seemed to be working hard to avoid my gaze bothered me.

"They did," he said. When I eyed him skeptically, he crossed his heart with his fingers. "I swear, Lily, they did."

"And your mom didn't see the police?"

"She got home after they were already done. I told her that I'd broken the window playing fetch with Bailey."

"Why'd you lie?"

"Because the cop who responded to the call said they weren't gonna waste their time dusting for fingerprints if nothing was stolen. He said it was probably just some kids in the neighborhood. He told me that there've been a few cases where back windows had been pried open and small stuff—a couple of iPads, some headphones, and about a hundred bucks—had been taken. In one case, a neighbor saw the kids coming out through the window, but they haven't been able to identify any of them yet. Anyway, he thinks it's the same group of kids that hit my house."

My jaw dropped. "You don't think it was the killer," I said. "You think it was a kid."

"That window wasn't opened very wide," he reasoned. "That's what the cop pointed out to me. That the window into the laundry room wasn't opened far enough to let in a full-grown man. And I could see a little shit vandal coming across a murder file and thinking it was cool enough to steal. I'll bet it ends up online in the next day or two."

I crossed my arms. I wasn't buying it. "You really think it was kids?"

Cole sighed. "I don't know," he said. "Nobody we talked to yesterday seems like they'd track down where I live and break in to steal a file they never could've known I had."

I sat with that for a minute. He was right. But it nagged at me. The whole thing really nagged at me. "Are we still going to talk to your FBI dude after we talk to Britta?"

"Definitely," Cole said. "And I'll let him know about the break-in, just in case."

"Okay, good," I said, thankful that Cole hadn't lost all his good sense.

We stopped for a breakfast sandwich at McDonald's on the way to Britta's. Cole had gotten her address off the Internet. It was freaky how easily he could look up anybody and get their address. It made me think that anybody else could do it, too.

We got to Britta's by eleven A.M. I was a little worried

she might be at church, but when we pulled up alongside her house, it was obvious by the two kids playing soccer in the side yard and the minivan with its hatch open to reveal bags and bags of groceries that she was home.

The house was a big white structure with gables that held steep peaks and perfectly maintained landscaping. There were large flowerpots on the front porch overflowing with flowers. Cole and I parked at the curb and headed up the drive.

The kids—maybe between twelve and fourteen—spotted us first and stopped chasing each other. I waved to show them that we were friendly. They stood there motionless.

"Hello?" I heard to my left.

Cole and I turned to see a very thin woman coming out of an open door. Dressed in a sleeveless shirt and short shorts, her limbs, while toned, were painfully thin. Her skin was tan and a bit weathered, and her shoulder-length brown hair looked dry and brittle, as if it was unhealthy. But she had a very pretty face, even if it was a little gaunt.

She moved over to the minivan and set her hands on two of the bags. "Can I help you?" she asked.

Cole stepped forward. "Hi, Mrs. Schroder?"

She nodded.

"I'm Cole, and this is Lily. We're juniors at Chamberlain High. We're on the school newspaper and we're researching an article for our first column of the year. It's an exposé on Amber Greeley and Ben Spencer. We're trying to come at it from the angle that Amber didn't really murder Ben, and we heard you were close to Amber in high school. We'd like to hear what you think might've happened that night."

She squinted at him, as if trying to take in all that he'd said and make sense of it enough to be able to comment. "You said your name was Cole?"

"Yes, ma'am," he said, without offering his last name, which is what I thought she was fishing for.

"Cole Drepeau?" she said.

Cole and I exchanged a surprised look.

"Uh . . . yes, ma'am. How'd you know?"

"I have a brother who used to work for your dad before he moved back to Canada. He's met your mom, and he even met you when you were a baby. Plus, you look like Spence." Mrs. Schroder then grabbed one of the bags and handed it to him. "Come on, you two. Help me with the groceries, and we'll have a chat."

We emptied the minivan and followed Britta inside. She held herself with a bit of an air, especially when she looked me up and down. It was weird because it was a sort of quietly aggressive move that I'd expect from other girls my age, not someone old enough to be my mom.

We entered the back door into the kitchen, and I'd never seen a space so sparkling white. The cabinets were white. The countertops were white marble. White bar stools. White floors. The appliances at least were silver and offered a small amount of contrast.

Still . . . the interior of her kitchen reminded me of an operating room, and then I remembered that her husband was a plastic surgeon. I wondered, suddenly, if she might have heard of my dad.

"So!" she said as she began to put the groceries away. "You two think Amber was innocent, huh?"

"Yes, ma'am," I said, standing close to Cole. Britta gave off a weird vibe, and for whatever reason, I didn't think I liked or trusted her.

She paused at the open fridge to smirk at me. "Well, that's cute," she said. "But I know that Amber did it. Spence dumped her and she snapped and shot him, then acted like she had nothing to do with it until the guilt caught up with her."

Cole rubbed the back of his neck and said, "Yeah, I hear you, but we've learned some stuff that might be pointing us in another direction."

"Oh?" she asked, pausing again with her hand halfway inside the grocery bag.

"We heard that there was something going on between Spence and a teacher. Mr. Bishop."

Britta's brow rose up. "That twerp? Oh, please. He didn't have the backbone to kill Spence."

"Then you heard about the issue between them?" Cole said carefully.

Britta rolled her eyes. "Honey, I heard about everything. At that school, I was dialed in! Spence and Bishop brought it on themselves. I mean, you don't get a below-average score on your SATs two times running, and then suddenly score in the ninetieth percentile without somebody noticing. Spence's scholarship to play football at UCLA was taken away and Bishop got suspended, but I heard he moved to Bumpass and did okay for himself, so where's the harm? He hated teaching. It was probably the best thing that ever happened to him."

"Why are you so sure that Spence broke up with Amber

at prom?" I asked. What she'd said earlier bothered me. It felt untrue.

"Because that night, Spence gave a note to his best friend to give to Amber, telling her that they were breaking up."

I was stunned. "What note?" Cole asked. "We didn't hear anything about a breakup note."

Britta shook her head. "I never saw it, but my boyfriend, who was Spence's best friend, told me all about it. He said he gave the note to Amber out in the hallway, and she read it in front of him, then ran off, probably to find Spence. I'll bet he still feels responsible for setting things in motion. Anyway, he made me promise not to tell anybody about it, not even the police. I had misgivings about that, but then Amber killed herself and that sort of settled things. Plus I didn't want to get my boyfriend in trouble. He and Spence cheated on those SATs together, only Spence was the one who got caught."

"Spence's best friend told you this?" I said. "You mean, Grady Weaver?"

Britta stiffened and curled her lip at me. "Grady was a little douchebag and definitely not Spence's best friend."

"Bill Metcalf?" Cole tried.

Again, Britta rolled her eyes. She was good at that. "I'm talking about Jamie."

Cole and I exchanged glances. That was the first time we'd heard the name. "Jamie?" Cole said. "Jamie who?"

Britta turned with her hands full of produce back to the fridge. "For investigative reporters, you two sure miss a lot. I'm talking about the high and mighty Jamie Bennett." At the mention of my father's name, I sucked in a breath and held it. "There's another douchebag for you," Britta went on. "He dumped me the day after Amber killed herself. What a jerk. I hear he's some big cardiac surgeon in Richmond now. My husband said that Bennett just dumped his wife and got his receptionist pregnant. Tells you what sort of a guy he is, huh?"

There was a loud clack on the floor as my cell phone fell out of my hands and hit the tile. Cole put an arm around my middle to steady me and reached for the phone.

I watched in a heart-pounding daze as Britta turned around to look at me. "You okay?" she asked.

I'd gone from holding my breath to taking in short, panicked pants, and I could feel the throbbing of blood in my ears as my heart raced.

"We should go," Cole said, taking me by the hand and easing me toward the door.

"What's wrong with her?" Britta asked.

"Nothing," Cole said. "Thank you, Mrs. Schroder."

I sensed my legs moving more than I felt them, and even though my body was starting to rebel against me, my thoughts were crystal clear and terrifying.

We made it to Cole's car, and he gently eased me inside. My eyes were barely open because I was trying so hard to focus on breathing. Sweat trickled down my back and matted my hair to my head. My arms and legs were trembling, and if Cole hadn't been there, talking soothingly to me, I'm positive I would've blacked out.

He got in next to me and started up the car, blasting the AC and turning all the vents toward me. It actually helped.

At last, my breathing slowed down and the panic attack subsided. "Talk to me," he said.

"She was talking about my father, Cole. *My father!*"

"Your dad?" he said. "Are you sure?"

I began to check off the facts on my fingers. "My father's name is James. It's possible he went by the name Jamie when he was younger. He also grew up in Fredericksburg, and he probably attended Chamberlain High. He's never talked to me about his childhood, not even high school, and now I think it's because he's had something to hide. Plus he would've been eighteen in nineteen eighty-seven. He also just dumped his wife—my mom—because he got his receptionist pregnant!"

Cole sat there, looking at me with such sympathy. I could tell he was also putting a few things together. It was all making sense now. The discordant pieces. The betrayal. The lies. The cover-up.

"He and Spence cheated on their SATs. Spence got caught and got into that fistfight with my dad over it. Maybe he threatened to rat out my dad. Maybe my dad killed him, and convinced his parents to help him cover it up. Maybe they bribed the schoolteacher who helped him cheat with the beach house."

"We don't know that your dad had anything to do with Spence's murder," Cole said.

I laughed mirthlessly. "Oh, come on," I said. "You heard Britta. My dad's an asshole. He's cold, calculating, ruthless. He threw my mom and me away like litter. He's a bastard. He could've totally killed them, Cole. He could've."

After confessing that, I dissolved into a puddle of tears.

Amber

BRITTA WAS CRYING IN THE LADIES' ROOM, AND I was so mad at her that I couldn't really drum up much sympathy, but for the sake of ten years of friendship, I tried.

"Britt? Are you going to come out of that stall so we can talk?" I asked, raising my voice above her sobs.

"Leave me alone, Amber!"

I leaned my head against the stall door and closed my eyes. "Did you really expect it'd be okay, Britt?" I asked her. "I mean, you came to prom with Jamie on your arm and acted like you didn't even know us, and then you wanted us to care that he ignored you all night and left you at the punch bowl?"

"You should've let us come to dinner with you!" she screeched.

"Britt," I said, trying to keep my voice level. "Come on, honey, you know Spence was never going to go to dinner with Jamie. I wanted nothing more than to have you at our table, but you made it impossible for us to include you when you said yes to him."

The door suddenly opened and I had a good look at Britta's tearstained face. "It wasn't like anybody else was asking me, Amber," she choked out.

And that's when I knew what this was really about. "Oh, Britt," I said, taking her in my arms. She sobbed on my shoulder and I winced at how skinny she was. "You're a beautiful girl, and I know that you know that. You could've just come with us and had a good time."

Britt whimpered and wiped her cheeks with hands. "It's not the same as having a gorgeous guy as your date," she said. "I just wanted someone to like me enough to ask me to the dance, Amber. I know Jamie and Spence aren't friends anymore, but it was so nice to have someone like him ask *me*, you know?"

I bit my lip. "You never thought that Jamie had an ulterior motive, Britt?"

She backed away from me in an instant. "What're you saying?" she demanded.

"Isn't it obvious? If Jamie got you to come tonight, he knew it'd make Spence mad."

Britt's jaw dropped. "You take that back, Amber," she said.

There was such hurt in her eyes. Dammit! I thought. I never should've told her.

"I take it back," I said. "I'm sorry. I think it's that I just don't trust him. Not where my best friend is concerned."

Britta eyed me suspiciously. "He asked me because he likes me," she insisted.

"Of course he did," I said. Then I offered: "Jamie has always said he thought you were pretty."

Britta wiped her cheeks again, appearing at least a little mollified. "He has?"

"He has. And I'm so sorry that it worked out like this, Britt. I love you, and I don't want us to be angry at each other."

She looked at me then and wrapped her thin arms around my neck. "I'm sorry," she whispered. "I'm so sorry, Amber. I should've turned him down, but I was so flattered, you know?"

"I do," I said. "And it's okay." I patted her back until she calmed down, and when she let go of me I smiled to reassure her. "Why don't you take a minute to fix your makeup, and I'll meet you back out on the dance floor? You, me, and Sara can all dance together. Screw the boys and their stupid fight, right?"

She laughed wetly and nodded. "Okay. But give me a few minutes. I must look a mess!"

I gave her arm a gentle squeeze, then headed out of the ladies' room to find Jamie and give him a piece of my mind. It was one thing to be mad at Spence. It was a completely different thing to use one of my best friends like a pawn in his game of war with my boyfriend. But first, I wanted to find Spence and make sure he was okay.

Despite our talk a week ago, he'd continued to be withdrawn and distant with me, but tonight he'd shown up with a radiant smile, and he looked so beautiful I could hardly take my eyes off of him. He'd treated me like a queen, and it was just like it was before all this UCLA and SAT business started.

And then, a half hour ago, we'd been dancing to a slow song and he'd said, "You know I'll always love you, right, Ambi? Forever. And if forever ever ends, then I'll love you all over again."

It was such a funny thing to say—"if forever ever ends"— but it was so sweet, too. Approaching Bill, I said, "Have you seen Spence?"

Bill motioned to the exit. "He left about ten minutes ago. Said he was gonna go cool off."

Spence and Jamie had gotten into it again right after our slow dance. No fists this time, but plenty of words. Britta had tried to defend Jamie, and he'd told her to shut up, which was why she'd run off to the ladies' room.

"Where's Jamie?" I asked Bill, thinking it would be the perfect time to yell at him myself.

"He walked out, too," he said. "About five minutes before Spence."

"Oh, boy," I muttered, and hurried toward the exit.

Out in the hallway I tried to decide where either of them might be. I started with the parking lot—no sign of them—then I moved through the halls searching each section. When I got toward the back of the school I heard a car backfire, and wondered at it sounding loud enough from the road to echo into the school.

Then I finally found Jamie, wandering the halls of the science wing. He saw me and froze, and there was something in his expression—something so sad that my anger faded away. I walked quickly to him.

"Hey," I said. "We need to talk about Britta—"

Unexpectedly, he reached down and picked up my hand. "I talked to Spence," he said, interrupting me.

"I saw," I said, pulling back on my hand, but Jamie held tight.

"No," he said. "Amber, we talked it all out. Spence and I are cool. He..." Jamie paused, and I was surprised to see his lip quivering. "He wanted me to give you this." Jamie placed a note in my hand.

I looked down at the tightly folded piece of paper with my name on it. "He told me that he's breaking it off with you, and he couldn't do it in person. I'm really, really sorry."

Lily

"I'M SORRY," I SAID, WIPING MY CHEEKS. I HADN'T been able to stop crying for the past five minutes.

"Hey," Cole said, putting a hand on the side of my face to get me to look at him. "You're good, Lily. Don't worry about it. The question is, what do you want to do?"

I swallowed hard and wiped another tear away. "What do I want to do?"

"Yeah," Cole said. "We can drop all of this, you know. All of it."

A small, mirthless laugh escaped me. "My father could've killed your uncle and you'd be willing to just...drop it?"

Cole's lips pressed together. "Yeah," he said. "If your dad was involved, Lily, what good would come of it? It'd ruin his life, your life, and probably my mom's life, too. Plus, if your grandmother was involved in the cover-up, she'd probably get carted off to jail as well."

I shook my head. My evil grandmother. Everybody

feared her. Well, except for my dad. And suddenly, I wondered why. Why hadn't he ever been afraid of her?

"We need to confront him," I said. If my dad had never been afraid of his mother, maybe I didn't need to be afraid of *him*.

Cole looked at me admirably. "You're sure?"

"Yes," I said. "Positive."

"When?"

I pointed to the road in front of us. "Now's good."

We were in Richmond twenty minutes later, and I directed Cole to my old address. When he pulled up to the locked gate, I gave him the code and we drove through while I sweated about who would greet us at the door.

I knew someone inside would be alerted to the gate opening, because any time the code was punched in, there was a small ping from the alarm panel.

Sure enough, as Cole parked next to my dad's Jag, the front door opened and his pregnant girlfriend stepped out onto the top step to put her hands on her hips and glare down at us.

"You can't just enter the gate without calling the house," she snapped as we got out of the car.

I walked purposefully up the steps, narrowing my eyes at her and silently daring her to try to stop me. Pregnant or not, she wasn't gonna prevent me from confronting my father.

"Where do you think you're going?" she demanded when I started to push past her.

"Inside *my* house," I told her.

She stepped in front of me, blocking the entrance.

"Don't you have another place to call home now?" she sang meanly.

I looked her in the eyes and said, "No, Jenny, I have *two* places to call home now. As much as you'd like it to be different, *this* is still *my* home."

"Not as long as I have anything to say about it," she insisted, putting her large belly in my path to block me from entering. I squared my shoulders and stepped forward. I was taller than Jenny, and I stared her down as I began to press in against her and move her backward.

"Hey!" she yelled, raising her hands to shove at me. Before she could actually manage that, though, Dad appeared out of nowhere and barked, "Jennifer!"

Her hands fell instantly to her sides and her face flushed red before she backed all the way up and allowed both Cole and me to enter.

Cole shut the door behind us, and there was a very lengthy pause before Dad said to Jenny, "You look tired. Maybe you should go upstairs and rest."

It wasn't even a question. Dad spoke the words as if they were a command. Jenny jumped on the chance to save some face.

"Yes," she said, putting a hand on her stomach. "The baby kept me up all night. I think a nap would be perfect." She went very slowly up the stairs in an obvious effort to eavesdrop in on our conversation.

"What're you doing here, Lily?" Dad asked.

I felt a small pang in my heart. Not even a greeting. I hadn't seen him in weeks and he didn't even start the conversation with a "Hey there, sweetheart. What brings you by?"

But then, my dad never was the sentimental type. I squared my shoulders and lifted my chin. "You and I need to talk," I said. "Now."

In all of my sixteen years I'd never disobeyed him or talked back or challenged him in any way, so this was a first. And he noticed.

"I see," he said, his eyes flickering to Cole. "And who's this?"

"His name is Cole Drepeau."

"Sir," Cole said. He tipped his chin politely, but his posture was guarded.

Dad turned back to me. "Are you in trouble, Lily?" he asked, his eyes dripping with disappointment.

I laughed at the irony of the fact that his pregnant girlfriend was mere feet away and he had the gall to ask me if *I* was in trouble. "No, Dad. But I think you are."

"What's that supposed to mean?" he asked, and I could tell his patience was waning.

I took a step toward him and pointed back to Cole. "Like I said, this is Cole Drepeau. He's the nephew of a friend of yours. Ben Spencer. You remember Ben, don't you, Dad? The guy you cheated on your SATs with, then probably murdered to keep him from telling anyone else? Or maybe you know David Bishop? We met him the other day. He's got a nice house out by the lake. I think you might even remember it."

All color drained from my father's face and his mouth fell slightly open. He stared at me like he didn't even know me, and maybe he didn't. Maybe all the time he'd spent ignoring me in favor of building his career as this big-time surgeon had caused him not to know me at all.

"James?" Jenny asked from midway up the stairs as my father continued to stand there in stunned silence.

"Go to the bedroom," he finally said to her.

"But—"

"I said go upstairs, Jenny!" my father roared as color flooded back into his face.

She gasped and rushed up the steps, clawing at the railing to help her along the way. Dad then turned back to me and said, "Why don't you come in, Lily?"

Cole stepped closer to me. It was a protective move, and it let my dad know that he was watching my back. My father's flinty glare settled on him.

"This is a family matter," he said to Cole.

"Yes, Dad," I said. "It is, but it's not just our family matter, is it? Or did you miss the part where I explained that Cole is Ben's nephew? You either talk to both of us, or we go to the FBI this afternoon."

Dad paused to work his jaw a little. "FBI, Lily? Kind of dramatic, don't you think?"

"There's no drama about it," I told him. "Not after your mother worked to shut down the investigation into Ben Spencer's murder." Dad seemed taken aback again. "Oh, yeah," I said, anger continuing to fuel my words. "We know about that, too."

"Fine," he said. "Then both of you come in, and we'll talk."

We followed as my father led us to his study at the back of the large house. I couldn't help but notice that Jenny had already started redecorating. She was so obvious, too—any room that had a feminine touch to it, she was having the color and furnishings redone, as if that alone could wipe the memory of my mother from my father's mind.

Finally, we were seated in front of his large, elegantly carved wooden desk, but instead of sitting, my dad moved over to the bar and poured himself a scotch.

"I didn't kill Ben Spencer, Lily," he said with his back turned to me. "His girlfriend did."

"We don't believe that's true," I said. "We think it was either you or David Bishop."

Dad took a sip of his scotch and turned to face me. "It wasn't either of us. David Bishop was already settled in at the lake house by the time Ben was murdered."

"And what about you, Dad? Where were you at the time that Ben was murdered?"

"I was back at the dance," he said. "I'd just let Amber know that Ben was breaking up with her."

I shook my head. I didn't think I could ever believe anything he told me again. "Ben told you he was breaking up with her?"

Dad came over and sank down into the chair at his desk. "He did."

I sat there staring at him moodily, bouncing my knee. "I'm not buying it," I told him.

Dad sighed and something about his expression softened. "Spence was my best friend," he said. Looking at Cole he repeated, "My *best* friend. We came from completely separate worlds—my family had money, his had nothing—but we each had parents who were abusive, both verbally and physically, and that was enough to bond us like brothers.

"Spence never cared about my money, and I appreciated

that I was able to just be me around him. I didn't have to put on airs with him, or pay his way. He never even let me buy him a meal. He always had to pay his fair share. He was a great guy.

"So when he told me that he wanted to get into UCLA, but didn't have the SAT scores to do it, I confessed to him that I'd found a way to ace the test. One of the freshman math teachers—Bishop—had connections to the SAT organization. He approached me when he overheard me complaining to some girl about how badly I needed a good score: I was under an immense amount of pressure to follow the family line into Yale, and the temptation to cheat was too much for me to resist. When I relayed to Spence that Bishop could get me an answer key for two grand, and that I'd get the corresponding test to that key on test day, Spence was in, too, but only if I let him split the fee with me. The money was no easy thing for Spence to raise, but he did it.

"I've always wondered how Bishop obtained the answers—they're normally kept under lock and key—but he assured us that he was very well connected and could provide it to us and, on the day of the exam, Spence and I knew that our two thousand dollars had secured us each an entry into our respective schools. The key was a perfect match to the test. It was actually easy.

"Everything was perfect until the day Spence's house was broken into and some money and his answer key was stolen. He never told me why he kept the key—I destroyed my copy—but the same person who broke into his house must've made the anonymous call that got his scholarship revoked.

"At the time, Spence was also up for a scholarship funded in large part by my mother. She had been willing to pay for part of his tuition and room and board once he got to UCLA, but then she heard about the inflated test scores and withdrew that scholarship, too.

"Ben was so desperate to go with Amber out to California that he confronted Mother and threatened to let everybody know that I'd cheated, too. I think he thought it was the only way to stay with Amber, because he was convinced he'd eventually lose her if he didn't go to California with her.

"But you don't threaten Maureen Bennett and get away with it. First, she strung Spence along, telling him that she'd give him the money, but it was just a ploy to keep him quiet long enough to investigate it on her own. She called Bishop and demanded an audience with him. He had a feeling what it was about and went to Spence's house to threaten him, but Bishop met with Mother anyway. They worked out a deal to secure Bishop's silence. Living in a lake house year-round, rent free, will keep a man's mouth shut like not much else. After all, Mother wasn't about to let me get kicked out of Yale. The scandal alone would've discredited our entire family, and my father's name and reputation meant *everything* to both my parents.

"Mother then quietly made a few phone calls and found out who Spence's mom was cleaning houses for before she began spreading rumors that Trudy Spencer was stealing from her clients. Mrs. Spencer was fired from three jobs within a week, and, as this terrible shock was hitting the Spencer household, Mother called Spence up and said that she had no intention of funding his education. She told him that if he even whispered my name in connection to the cheating scandal, she'd break him and his family with a snap of her fingers. He backed off fast.

"Once she was sure he wouldn't talk, Mother turned her sights on me, forcing me to confess and then threatening to disinherit me once I did. Only my father's intervention saved me from getting tossed out on the street. Still, after that I was on a very short leash with my parents, something I still resent, I suppose.

"At the time, however, I was most furious at Spence for betraying our friendship, and we got into it a couple of times and beat each other black-and-blue. We didn't speak for weeks. Then, at prom, we fought again—just words that time, but after I went to cool off, Spence found me and we talked. I forgave him, and he forgave me. He told me that he'd never speak a word to anybody about me having also cheated, if I'd do him a favor."

"What?" Cole asked when my father paused.

Dad let out a sad sigh. "He wanted me to find Amber and tell her that he was breaking up with her. He said that he was tired of pretending that their relationship could survive her moving to LA. He wanted her to go to college a free woman. He gave me a note to give to her and I found her a little later, wandering the halls, looking for Spence. I gave her the note, and said what he wanted me to say to her. She read the letter, fell apart, and ran off to find him. Twenty minutes later, we all heard he'd been murdered."

I shook my head. "But that doesn't mean she killed him! I mean, Dad! Where'd she even get the gun?" I realized suddenly that Cole and I had never even discussed that, because I'd been so convinced of Amber's innocence.

Dad looked down into the bottom of his drinking glass. "She got it from Ben's car, Lily. And I know that because I'd seen for myself that Ben carried his dad's gun with him in the glove box. He rode around with it because once a week he mowed this big industrial field next to a sketchy neighborhood. He'd been mugged there his junior year, and after the break-in at his house he made sure the gun was close by at all times.

"When I heard that Spence had been shot, the memory of the gun sparked in my mind, and I ran to his car to check the glove box. The gun was gone, but there was an open box of ammo there, and one of the bullets had even fallen on the floor mat. I knew immediately that Amber had gone to Spence's car and gotten the gun. I felt so guilty for my role in her coming unhinged, so I scooped up the ammo and the bullet and got rid of them.

"Anyway, it didn't matter in the end because she killed herself and confessed to the crime."

I shook my head again. It was impossible. Amber couldn't have killed Ben. She just couldn't have, and I *knew* that because I could feel it in my bones. "But how do you know that Amber was the one that took Ben's gun? Maybe she didn't even know about it!"

Dad shook his head sadly. "Lily," he said. "She knew about it. She knew about it because she once told me she was glad he carried a gun with him when he went to mow that field."

My eyes watered, and I blinked furiously to keep the tears

from leaking out and down my cheeks. "I don't believe she did it," I said.

Dad sighed. "I know, honey. It sounds like you've been looking into this thing a lot, and you probably think you know Amber, but you don't. I did. I saw how upset she was when she read that note. She was desperate. Crazed. She was quite capable of murdering Spence that night."

I got up and stood in front of him with balled fists. Cole got to his feet, too. "I need to go," I told him before I said anything more that I might regret.

"Lily," Dad called as I fled the room. I didn't look back. I just ran.

Cole caught up to me at the car. "Hey," he said, wrapping me in his arms. "What can I do?"

I shook my head into his shoulder, and squeezed tightly against him. I felt like everything that I'd ever counted on was slowly being ripped away from me.

"I just . . . I just thought she was innocent," I said. "I mean, I *really* thought she was innocent, Cole!"

"I know," he said while I cried. "Me, too."

We drove back to Fredericksburg, and I was still pretty teary. I just couldn't believe that Amber had done it. And if she had, then why the hell was she hanging around me?

"Are you gonna be okay?" Cole asked, and I turned to see him looking sideways at me.

"It was almost easier to think that my dad was guilty than it was to think that Amber did it," I admitted. God, I felt shitty saying that out loud.

"Hey," he said, reaching to squeeze my hand. "Don't take it so hard, Lil. At least we know your dad isn't a murderer."

I blinked at more unbidden tears. "Yeah, but it feels like that means that *I* am."

"But you're not, Lily. I can't see you ever doing something like that. That was all Amber."

I swallowed hard. "Then why all this?" I asked, making an expansive motion. "Why is she in my head, hovering around, pushing me to solve the mystery, if she's the one who did it?"

Cole shrugged and shook his head. "Maybe she just wanted you to know the truth."

And that struck me, because that's what I felt in my own heart. I felt that Amber really did want me to know the truth, even if the truth was that she was guilty. I guess I just hadn't been prepared for how tragically sad that ending was.

We rode the rest of the way mostly in silence but when we got off on the exit toward home, Cole said, "Is it okay if we stop at my gram's house to put the yearbooks back? I want to get them into Ben's room while she's at work."

I sat up a little from my slouched position. "Uh, sure," I said. "Whatever you need to do."

We got to his grandmother's house, and Cole drove past to make sure her car wasn't there. It wasn't.

"I'm gonna park the next block over," he said. "I can sneak in through the backyard." He circled to the other side of the block and stopped the car under a low-hanging oak tree. "Be back in a minute."

He reached for the yearbooks, and I suddenly felt like I didn't want to be alone.

"Hang on," I said, knowing I was being a little bit clingy, but not really caring. "I'm coming with you."

He paused halfway out of his door. "You're sure?"

"Yeah," I said. "If she comes home, though, you'd better not run faster than me."

He smiled. "Deal."

We crossed the empty lot behind Mrs. Spencer's backyard and around to the gate, letting ourselves in. Cole hustled to the flowerpot and lifted it, but the key was gone.

"Shit," he said.

"Where'd it go?" I asked, peering over his shoulder.

"She might've needed to use it and forgot to put it back," he said. "Hang on . . ." Cole moved over to the kitchen window and took out a pocketknife to ease the screen up, then he pushed up on the window and it opened easily. "She always forgets to lock it," he said with a triumphant smile. "I'll be out in a sec."

Using some pretty good athleticism, Cole let himself into the kitchen and came around to the back door to let me in. I followed him inside all the way past the kitchen, through the living room, and down the hallway to a closed door at the end of the hall.

"You coming with me in here?" he asked.

"I'd like to see Ben's room," I told him. I was very curious about it, and maybe it was standing up to my father earlier that had emboldened me to trespass on his grandmother's property, but maybe there was something more, too. I couldn't put my finger on it, but I had such an urge to see Ben's room for myself. It felt a little weird.

Cole worked the latch with his pocketknife and opened the door, letting me go in first. I handed off the yearbooks to him and walked inside to take it all in.

Amber

I COULD HARDLY TAKE IN WHAT JAMIE HAD JUST said. But there was the note in my hand, with my name written across it in Ben's blocky lettering. I tore at the note to unfold it, and scanned it in the dim light.

Reading what he said to me, how he tried to justify it all . . . my heart felt like it was exploding in agony. My world shattered apart like a thousand shards of glass.

"No!" I cried. "No, Spence, noooooooooooo!"

A moment later, I was running away from Jamie as fast as I could. I had to get to Spence. I had to convince him not to leave me. I had to convince him that we belonged together. And if I couldn't convince him, then I'd make sure we died together.

Lily

COLE CAME UP NEXT TO ME AND, TOGETHER, WE looked around. The room was a surprise. It was sparse, but also soothing and so familiar in that same way that other things had been familiar. The same way Cole had seemed familiar the first time I met him. And Fredericksburg itself had seemed familiar. As well as Gina. And Bailey.

A light-headed feeling was slowly taking over, and an odd pressure formed inside my skull. In an instant I knew that Amber was exerting herself, sharing the space in my mind, overpowering my own memories with hers.

"Cole," I whispered, feeling my conscious thoughts being pushed backward to make room for Amber.

"Hey," he said, looking at me with concern. "Are you having another panic attack?"

I shook my head vigorously, as much to clear it as to let him know this was something else entirely. I'd been in this room before. I'd been naked in that bed, wrapped in strong arms and making love to my soul mate. I'd loved him so much. He'd been my whole world.

I pushed away the thought and tried to focus on Cole. On me. On Lily Greeley. No, wait, that was wrong. Amber Bennett.

I put my hands up to the sides of my head. Why couldn't I get my name right?

"Lily?" Cole said again, and I felt his hand on my arm. I closed my eyes, trying to get a grip.

Why, Amber? I asked. *Why are you doing this?*

"Hey," Cole said. "Come on over here and sit down before you pass out."

I felt him guide me to the bed and sit me down, but my eyes were closed and I tripped a little on the rug. I plopped down indelicately and that helped to jar me back into myself.

"Can I have some water?" I asked.

"Sure," he said. I heard his footsteps hurry away. Taking a few deep breaths I focused on my name. Lily Bennett. Lily Bennett. Lily Greeley.

"Dammit!" I muttered, and opened my eyes to glare at the floor. "Get out of my head, Amber!" I whispered.

But she wasn't letting up. And then, I noticed something odd on the floor. The rug was now askew and there was something weird about the floorboards underneath. Amber bulleted into my thoughts again like a battering ram, and I sank off the bed to my knees with the force of it. Her attack on my psyche was so forceful that it stole my breath, but then it receded and I hovered there on all fours panting. I stared at the floor again and saw that I'd slid even more of the rug aside.

Next to my hand was a very small latch. "Here," I heard from above me. Cole had come back with the water.

I ignored him and instead pushed the rug farther out of the way, then sat back on my knees, pointing to the latch. "Look," I whispered.

"Whoa," he said, squatting down next to me. "What the hell?"

Again Amber battered at my thoughts and my mind flashed with a memory of a window open in this very room, the rug pulled to the side, the trapdoor open and Spence frantically digging into the well, searching for something he'd never get back.

"Lily?" Cole said. I was breathing hard again trying to fight Amber off.

I didn't answer him. Instead, I reached for the trapdoor and pulled it up. And there, in the light of the room, I could see something familiar. Lifting it up, I handed it to Cole.

"Holy shit!" he said. "It's the murder file!"

I looked back inside the well. There were three pieces of paper there. One of them was splattered with small droplets of dried blood. I took that one out first and opened it carefully.

I read the words out loud to Cole.

Spence

Dear Amber,

I know what I'm about to do won't make sense to you, and you might hate me and never forgive me for it, but it's the only way I can make sure you follow your dreams while I keep my promise to take care of Mom and Stacey.

You'll never leave me to become the awesome woman you were meant to be. You'll never reach your full potential as long as I'm there to hold you back, and I know I've been holding you back, Ambi. All these years we've been together you've been burdened by me, my family, my stuff. It's time I cut you free of all that.

I want you to go to LA. I want you to become someone even more amazing than you already are. I want you to help poor, dumb bastards like me who can't seem to ever get it together, because they'll need your help even more than I did. I want you to soar, not stay here with your wings clipped.

By the time you read this, I'll be gone. It's better this way, but I know you might not understand that right now. You didn't make me do this. No one did but me. It was my choice. Mom and Stacey will have the life insurance money to get them through the next couple of years, you'll get to go off to UCLA, and I won't wreck anyone's life ever again. Mom is going to help me make it not look like a suicide, but you can't tell anybody that or she won't get the insurance money. I left her a note, too, so she'll know what to do.

Please know that I love you forever. And if forever ever ends, Amber, then I'll love you from the beginning, all over again.

Spence

Amber

I FOUND MRS. SPENCER SITTING IN A CHAIR IN THE backyard. My mom had told me that Stacey was being looked after by her best friend's parents. Bailey and I stood next to the gate, watching Mrs. Spencer sit in her chair, staring into space, and for a moment I felt such tremendous loathing for her—such seething anger—because I'd figured it out. I'd put it together the morning after Spence died. She'd been the one to stage the break-in in his room. She'd stolen the money from his hiding place and the SAT test key. She'd made the anonymous call to UCLA to tell them that Spence had cheated. She'd done it all to ruin his chances of coming with me, and having a life free from her clutches.

And now he was dead because of her.

After working it out, I'd snuck out of the house without anyone knowing, and to keep Bailey from barking as I left, I'd taken her with me.

Her leash slipped through my hand as she approached

Mrs. Spencer and laid her head on the woman's lap. She could sense the heartache and the pain. But I hardly cared what Spence's mother was feeling.

I approached and stood in front of her. At last she lifted her head like she'd just become aware of me. We stared in silent antipathy at each other for a long time, each blaming the other for the light in our lives winking out.

"What'd you do with the gun?" I finally asked her.

She didn't answer, but I saw her eyes flicker to the shed behind me. She must've hidden it there. I turned my head toward it to let her know that I'd caught the subtle tell from her eyes.

"You helped him," I said, unfolding the note I'd carried clutched in my hand. "You'll need to help me."

She considered me for a long time in silence, but there was interest now in her eyes to go with all that hate. She was eager to comply, but also wary. She'd be taking another risk.

I didn't care. About anything. Nothing meant anything to me without Spence, and no matter what he'd said in his suicide note, I was to blame. I'd pushed so hard for him to come with me, and clung so hard to him, helping him with everything, that he'd never gained the confidence to know he could survive without me. And I couldn't live with myself knowing that his death was partially my fault. I'd loved him too much, and let him love me too much. Neither of us could survive now without the other.

I realized that the car backfiring that I'd heard in the school wasn't a car at all, but Spence shooting himself in the heart. That devastated me most of all, I think. He'd shot himself in the space he'd reserved to love me. I hadn't heard the second shot. I'd probably been with Jamie when Mrs. Spencer arrived in the field to find her son dead or dying, and she'd taken the gun from his hand, held it over his chest, and pulled the trigger again.

The coroner could've suspected one bullet wound as having been a suicide, but two? That was murder. And Cole's life insurance policy would be swiftly paid out to the grieving mother and sister. He'd keep his promise to take care of them.

"When?" she asked me, eyeing the note in my hand. I knew she was curious about it. I knew she wanted to take it from me and keep it. I'd let her have it if she did the deed.

"Tomorrow," I said. "Jamie's going to arrange a dinner for Spence's friends. My parents will go. You should decline. I'll decline. The back door will be unlocked."

The sun was starting to come up then, those first rays streaking across the backyard to touch the branches of the tallest trees and bathe them in pink embers of light.

"And if I say no?" she said glaring at me with such hate that I knew she only said it to toy with me. I could clearly see she blamed me entirely for Spence's death. The same way I blamed her, and I knew in that moment that she wanted me to die as badly as I did.

Still, I played along. "Then I'll show everyone the note that Spence left for me. I'll let them all know that he killed himself so you could get your hands on that insurance money."

"Tomorrow, then," she said, stroking Bailey's head.

I picked up the leash and gave it a slight tug. Bailey followed after me, and I never once looked back as I left the yard.

Lily

I HEARD A SOUND COMING FROM THE YARD, BUT I was too focused on the letter I'd just read to Cole to pay it much attention. For his part, Cole had slid to the floor and was propping himself against Ben's chest of drawers, looking like he might pass out himself.

"How did it get here?" he asked me, pointing to the letter.

I reached into the well again and pulled out another letter. I unfolded it, saw that it was the letter Spence had written to his mother, telling her that he'd taken his life, and he was out in the field by the high school, waiting for her to come and make it look like a murder so that she could collect the insurance money.

I read it silently, my lower lip trembling before I handed it to him. He took it with shaking fingers and read it, too.

Cole let his hand holding the letter fall to his lap. "Why?" he said, as if he couldn't really fathom any of it.

I reached into the well again and pulled up another piece of paper. Unfolding it, I saw that it was a series of letters, next to a sequence of numbers. The letters ranged from A to F, and I understood almost immediately what it was.

I showed it to Cole. "The test key," I said.

He closed his eyes and shook his head. Then he opened them again and picked up the first letter from his lap. "Whose blood?" he asked.

Everything depended on the answer. We both knew that.

"Amber's," I told him. I knew it as certainly as I knew my own name. Lily Bennett.

I smiled sadly, and whispered, "Lily Bennett."

The moment the words left my lips, the pressure that'd been constant in my mind for these many long weeks lifted, and that overlap of consciousness that I'd had with Amber vanished. In an instant, I was once again Lily Bennett, and only Lily Bennett.

"What are you doing here?" a voice behind us demanded.

Cole and I both jumped and turned to find Mrs. Spencer standing threateningly in the hallway.

Cole got immediately to his feet, holding tight to the letter from Spence with Amber's blood on it. His grandmother's gaze went to the note, then to him, then to me, then back to the letter again.

"That's mine," she said evenly.

"No," I said to her, once again fueled by a burning anger for the injustice done to Amber. "It's not. It belonged to Amber Greeley. And you killed her."

Mrs. Spencer's eyes narrowed. They were murderous, and very quickly I realized just how dangerous she actually was.

"I took care of Amber," she said softly. "And I can take care of you, too, Little Miss Nosy."

Cole stepped in front of me. His grandmother was tall, but she was no match for Cole. "No, Gram," he said. "No, you won't."

"Cole, honey," she said, wide-eyed and reaching for his hand, but he pulled it away. "This can all be fixed. No one has to know. We can make it look like an accident. She's been having those anxiety attacks, right? We can make it look like she had another one of those while she was driving."

I sucked in a breath and backed away a step. Was she serious?

"Lily," Cole said firmly, keeping his gaze focused on his grandmother, "stay behind me. I'm not going to let her hurt you."

"Think of your mother," his grandmother said. "She benefitted from that money, too, Cole. If this comes out, we'll both have to pay it back!"

"She won't care," Cole said. "And I'm really surprised you don't know that about her, Gram."

And then the pathetic, whimpering old woman vanished, and Mrs. Spencer stood tall as she reached behind her and pulled out a gun.

I squealed and shuffled back to the bed, but she trained the muzzle right on Cole.

"Do you know what it's like to shoot your own flesh and blood, Cole? Because I do." She spoke in a voice so cold, so deadly, that it frightened me more than I could say.

"I shot Ben while he was taking his last breath." I gasped and her gaze flickered to me. "Oh, yeah," she said, turning her attention back to Cole. "He was still alive when I got to him. And I wasn't gonna do it, I swear I wasn't, but then he said that whore's name. Not mine. Hers. I didn't even flinch when I pulled the trigger, and I loved that boy a whole hell of a lot more than I love you."

I cringed away up the bed until my back hit the headboard. It was hard to fathom someone so clearly psychotic.

"I've also staged a robbery or two in my time," she continued, "and no lawman has ever suspected that it was me. I'm just a lonely old woman who's had a series of tragic things happen to her, and this'll be just one more. The police will come, they'll look around, and they'll tell me as I cry on their shoulders that it was probably some drugged-up junkie who broke in here, started rummaging around my murdered son's stuff when my only grandchild and his girlfriend walked in, and he shot them both. Tragic stuff happens to good people all the time. Maybe they'll even set up a fund to help me while I grieve."

Cole hadn't moved a muscle since his grandmother pulled out the gun, and while I trembled on the bed, he stood rigid and still. I didn't know what was about to happen, but I prayed for Cole in that moment. With every ounce of me, I prayed that he could do or say something that would make her lower the gun.

What he said next came out slowly in an almost gentle tone. "Gram, do you remember last summer when I went to DC and took that future-agents-in-training seminar at Quantico?"

She didn't answer him. Instead, she glared hard and raised the gun a little higher while her gaze focused on his chest. I thought she might've been aiming for his heart, which made me almost physically sick. She was considering shooting her grandson in the same place she'd shot her own son.

"Anyway," Cole said, and I saw that his stance had suddenly relaxed, "the agents took us through some weapons training on the last day we were there. And the funny thing about that gun in your hand, Gram, is that it's not going to hurt anybody."

Her eyes narrowed and her lips thinned.

"Don't believe me?" he said, widening his stance and crossing his arms. "Go ahead. Shoot me."

Something awful glinted in Mrs. Spencer's eyes and before I could even shout, "No!" she extended her arm slightly and pulled the trigger.

The gun clicked harmlessly.

She pulled the trigger again and caused it to click harmlessly a second time. Then again. And again, until Cole reached out and grabbed the barrel, twisting the muzzle up and away. With his other hand he pried it out of her fingertips and tossed it to the floor. Then he grabbed his grandmother and held her by both wrists.

Pulling her close to him he said, "You left the safety on, Gram. I'll be sure to mention that to Detective Hasslett when he shows up." Looking over his shoulder at me, he added, "Lily, could you get all the evidence together and the gun—use a sheet to pick it up so you don't get your fingerprints on it—and head to the kitchen to call Detective Hasslett? Don't tell anybody else but him what's going on."

With my heart still pounding hard in my chest, I hurried to do just that.

Several hours later, I sat in front of my own grandmother, my mother at my side, feeling nervous but determined.

"Well, Lily," my grandmother said tersely. "What is this little *meeting* that you insisted we have together?"

I decided to go for the blunt truth. "I know about the lake house in Bumpass," I said.

My grandmother's eyes narrowed a bit. "What about it?"

"I know that David Bishop has been living there rent-free for the past thirty years, and that you've held that over my dad's head as leverage as much as he's held it over yours. It'd probably wreck your world to have it leak out that Dr. James Bennett cheated on his SAT scores and committed fraud to get into Yale. It could even lead to his medical license being revoked, right? And I bet it'd be even worse for you if it also leaked out that you knew about it, covered it up, and persuaded the police to blame Amber Greeley for the murder of Ben Spencer."

Grandmother sat up and leaned forward angrily. "Such a petulant young lady," she snarled. "What do you want, Lily?"

"I want you to make up with Dad," I said. "I want you to stop trying to control all of us. I want you to talk him into settling the divorce with Mom so that we can move out of the guesthouse, and then I never, ever, ever want you to get involved in our business again.

"I don't want to take over the Bennett enterprises," I

continued. "And I don't want this estate or anything to do with it, except for one thing, which, to you, will probably be pretty small, but, to me, will mean everything."

Grandmother studied me for a long moment, at the end of which I could've sworn there was a hint of amusement and perhaps even pride in her eyes. "And that is?"

"When I graduate from college, I want you to fund an animal rescue. A sanctuary for lost, abandoned, and abused animals. Mom and I will take care of building it, and I'll run it, but I want you to fund it, and I want your name on it, too. I want people to know how generous and kind you are, Grandmother, because under all of that attempting to control the truth about what happened to Ben and Amber, I know that you have a real heart. Because of what you did for Gina Greeley when the grief of losing her only child nearly killed her, I know. And, I also know that you could've paid off David Bishop, but you knew he'd never get another teaching job, and he was probably a pretty lost soul, too, so you took care of him, as well. So it's in keeping with that same charitable spirit of yours, Grandmother, that I want you to help a lot more souls. And I want you to get the credit, because it'll be deserved."

My grandmother studied me for a long moment before she suddenly laughed lightly and brushed her nose delicately with one finger. Eyeing my mother, she said, "She gets that confidence from me, you know."

"I do," Mom said, smiling, too.

"Very well, Lily," my grandmother said. "I agree to your terms, but I have one of my own."

"Yes?" I asked.

"You must spend one Sunday a month with me for tea. I will not let you out of my life that easily."

I grinned. "I can live with that."

Epilogue

IN MID-OCTOBER, THE HEAT WAVE WE'D HAD ALL summer finally broke, making the outdoor temps absolutely perfect for sitting outside on a Saturday, soaking up the sun and enjoying the outdoors.

Cole and I were relaxing in the new lounge chairs that Mom had bought. It was the perfect way to spend my birthday, chilling out on the deck, which extended from the new house we'd moved into the week before. It was so nice to be able to hang out in our very own place again.

Mom and Dad had come to an agreement about their divorce shortly after he and Grandmother made up. Well, made up the best that those two could. Dad and I were on speaking terms again, but only because he'd been making a huge effort to apologize to me. Hell, he'd even apologized to Mom, and for a man who almost never admitted when he was wrong, that was pretty big.

So we were all getting along much better, and Jenny had even been invited over for tea with Grandmother. I bet Jenny was loving that.

Still, Dad had asked me to be involved in my baby brother's life when he finally arrived sometime in December. I'd agreed, although this whole big-sister thing was going to take some getting used to.

Cole's grandmother had been indicted and was awaiting trial. I think Cole and I were both surprised that, once she got to the station, she'd made a full confession. Her lawyer, however, had talked her into pleading not guilty, and I couldn't imagine what kind of a defense he'd put on in the face of all the evidence Cole and I had uncovered as well as her confession. The trial would be months away, so we'd see.

Cole's mom had been really upset by the whole thing, and I felt so sorry for her. She truly hadn't known any of it, and I suspected she felt guilty for not having guessed it. In the week that followed the arrest of her mother, Mrs. Drepeau had shed a lot of tears, and Cole had been really worried about her. Who would've thought that my own grandmother would've stepped up without my asking her to do something really amazing to help Mrs. Drepeau move forward?

Grandmother had used her powerful position on the board of the hospital to get the administration to offer Stacey Drepeau the head RN job on the floor of the ICU. She'd be making a lot more money, and wouldn't have to work any more weekends, and I thought that was probably a pretty good restitution on the part of my grandmother.

Another amazing thing had happened once the story

hit the local news. A package had arrived and inside was a photo of Sara Radcliff and Amber, taken sometime during their senior year, or so the accompanying card said. Sara had written me a note that read,

Lily,

From the bottom of my heart, I thank you. The best friend I ever had in the world is now finally at peace. And even though we only met briefly, I sense that you must be every bit a good soul, and a good friend as Amber was. Your best friend must be so lucky to have you in her life. May this photo rest next to the photo of the two of you to remind you that true friendships never die.

With love,

Sara

I'd cried after reading the card, but I'd taken the framed photo of Amber and Sara up to my room and set it on my desk. Then I'd rummaged through a special box I'd kept hidden under my bed, and I'd brought out a framed photo of Sophie and me, in our fishtail braids, hugging each other and looking forward to a future where we'd be best friends forever. The gift from Sara had felt so magical, and I'd had the strongest feeling that Amber had somehow influenced Sara's decision to send me the image and the note.

"Message, received," I'd said to her photo, and I'd known in that moment that I could find a way to forgive Sophie simply because having her in my life meant more to me than almost anything else.

In the meantime, Cole and I had continued to hang out, and we'd officially changed our statuses to "In a relationship" on both our Facebook profile pages. I found myself falling in love with him with each passing day.

And today, on my birthday, he and I had gone with Mom to pick up our newest addition—a little eight-year-old, twelve-pound mixed breed named Scamp, whom we'd rescued from the shelter. Mom was currently walking around with him, rocking him in her arms.

"He's so adorable!" she kept saying. I think she already loved him more than I did.

Cole leaned over when Mom went in to get the pup some water and kissed me sweetly. When he lifted his face away, he set something in my hand.

"What's this?" I asked, looking down at the rectangular box covered in pink wrapping paper that he'd given me.

"Open it," he replied, without even a hint of what it was.

I pulled at the wrapping paper and got the lid off to reveal a gorgeous bracelet made of perfectly spaced beads of amber. "Ohmigod," I whispered. "Cole!"

"You like it?"

"I love it!" I said.

"I made it," he added proudly.

I laughed. "I can tell!" He helped me put it on and I admired it on my wrist. He still wore the amber bead at his neck, and I loved that he continued to silently honor Amber that way.

Cole had been the one to visit Mrs. Greeley and tell her what'd happened. He'd apologized to her on behalf of his family and he told me she'd cried for a long time, but she'd thanked him in the end. She'd told him he'd brought her peace and she knew her daughter could finally rest.

I knew it, too.

The doorbell rang and I sprang to my feet, almost too excited for words. "I'll get it!" I yelled as I raced past the screen door, through the living room, down the hallway, and to the front door. Taking just a moment to pause in front of the mirror hanging in the front foyer, I smoothed out my hair and tried to compose myself. When I opened the door I saw a beautiful girl there with long black hair, big brown eyes, and a smile as wide as Georgia.

"Lily!" she cried, flinging her arms around me.

I hugged her back so tight and felt the tears slide out from tightly closed lids. For a long time, we were too overcome to speak, and we just stood there hugging each other. At last we pulled away and I reached down and took her hand, silently thanking Amber for inspiring me to make this moment happen.

"Come to the back," I said. "I can't wait for you to meet my boyfriend!"

Taking charge of her, I marched us through the house to the deck again, and when Cole turned to look up at us I said, "Cole, meet my best friend, Sophie. Sophie, *this* is Cole."

Acknowledgments

I'D VERY MUCH LIKE TO EXPRESS MY SINCEREST gratitude to my dear friend and agent, Jim McCarthy, my wonderful editor, Kieran Viola, and everyone else at Hyperion who has worked so hard to bring this novel together.

I'd also like to thank all those in my personal life who consistently support (i.e. don't seem to mind) the long hours I work; the missed weddings, parties, weekends, and evenings out I fail to attend; the emails, cards, gifts, and letters I either flat-out ignore or am horribly late to acknowledge; and my general appearance on those mornings when I'm *waaaaay* behind deadline. You all have the patience of saints, and I'm very happy you're all still in my corner!

Last, one very special shout-out to my amazing sister, Sandy, and her beautiful beau, Steve. This book is for the two of you. Love you. In this life and the next.